The
Witching
Hours

Kensington Books by Heather Graham

Alliance Vampires
Beneath a Blood Red Moon
When Darkness Falls
Deep Midnight
Realm of Shadows
The Awakening
Dead by Dusk

The Graham Clan Novels
Come the Morning
Conquer the Night
Seize the Dawn
Knight Triumphant
The Lion in Glory
When We Touch

The Fire Series
Princess of Fire

Anthologies
In Need of a Cowboy
Must Love Christmas Cowboys

Standalones
Tempestuous Eden
Night, Sea and Stars
Queen of Hearts
Tomorrow the Glory
Blue Heaven, Black Night
Lie Down in Roses
Ondine
The King's Pleasure
Down in New Orleans
An Angel's Touch
Up in Flames
Witness to Death

The
Witching
Hours

HEATHER GRAHAM

KENSINGTON
PUBLISHING CORP.
kensingtonbooks.com

KENSINGTON BOOKS are published by

Kensington Publishing Corp.
900 Third Ave.
New York, NY 10022

All Kensington titles, imprints, and distributed lines are available at special quantity discounts for bulk purchases for sales promotion, premiums, fundraising, educational, or institutional use. Special book excerpts or customized printings can also be created to fit specific needs. For details, write or phone the office of the Kensington Special Sales Manager: Attn. Special Sales Department, Kensington Publishing Corp., 900 Third Ave., New York, NY 10022. Phone: 1-800-221-2647.

Library of Congress Control Number: 2025945760

ISBN: 978-1-4967-5844-6
First Kensington Hardcover Edition: February 2026

ISBN: 978-1-4967-5848-4 (ebook)

10 9 8 7 6 5 4 3 2 1

Printed in the United States of America

The authorized representative in the EU for product safety and compliance
is eucomply OU, Parnu mnt 139b-14, Apt 123
Tallinn, Berlin 11317, hello@eucompliancepartner.com

The Witching Hours

CHAPTER 1

Usually, Skye McMahon just *saw* things.

And in those images that appeared before her eyes or within her mind, it was as if history itself had been captured on a video hard drive and could appear before her clearly as if events had been caught for the viewer to enjoy exactly as they had taken place, over and over, in Technicolor on a life-sized screen.

Good things!

And bad things. Very bad things.

That was history.

And that was life. And she had learned long ago as a child, that it was possible to maintain her sanity by knowing that what she was seeing wasn't real—not at the time, at any rate— just like seeing events on a movie screen wasn't real.

But something was different that day. And it was strange, because she had been to Salem, Massachusetts, many times when growing up. And while she had seen and sensed the past before, there was something new . . .

And this wasn't why she was here! The real world, the one they were living in *now*.

She wasn't just *seeing* what had taken place. She wasn't just *hearing* everything that was being said.

She was *feeling* it.

It was a bizarrely beautiful day and a breeze was stirring. She could smell the grass and the trees, *see* buildings in the far background, small wooden homes and farms that were far spread. In the distance, she could see a town center, and yet they were away from that center because . . .

People were gathered on the outskirts of town. And she quickly saw why. There were prisoners there.

Prisoners lined up to die.

She could *feel* such a mix of emotions. Fear. Horrible fear. Faltering faith . . . indignation, and a mix of anger and terror and a determination from one of the condemned that they would die well. Because soon, bodies would fall from the ropes strung high on the hanging tree.

She heard a sniffle of fear, a young woman, surely still stunned and confused, because of course . . .

None of them were really witches! No one was in league with the devil.

If the condemned had really had any kind of the power it was suggested they possessed, they'd have broken their bonds; if they'd been in league with a devil, surely that devil would have jumped out of his fiery pit to save them.

More . . .

Those who watched.

Many with relief to see what they'd been told was evil get its due! Shouting out that justice was being served . . .

Some were looking on with confusion clear on their faces. Puritan life was hard, and everyone knew the devil could walk on earth with man, that evil was real in the darkness of the forests, but these were their neighbors! People they lived among.

The accusers were there, of course. Any little wrong could be avenged. A cow had died. It had been cursed! By a witch!

Some indeed thought that justice was being done.

But others, no matter how pious, good people at heart in any age, had not expected the horror of hearing whimpers or sobs and seeing the way the feet of those hanged began to twitch so horribly . . .

Along with the strange and agonizing sense of the past, Skye felt a taunt from her childhood enter the stream of words that surrounded her.

Ding-dong! The witch is dead. Which old witch? The wicked witch!

In her mind, she also loathed herself for thinking of the song from the 1939 film *The Wizard of Oz.*

But it went with the flow of consciousness from those around her, a tangle of arguments in her head that became pure torture. A cacophony in her mind.

There were so many thoughts from those watching!

And the thoughts of those watching were torn.

This is all such a horrid lie! She's not a witch! They just want her property confiscated. I need to protest to stand up . . . and if I do, I'll die as a witch, too.

I thank Thee, great Lord in Heaven, for taking her; that witch might have cursed my family! Look at the children! Tituba started this, and she told the girls stories about things done in her land. And she *said herself that others were involved.*

But if she hadn't, if she hadn't confessed . . . she'd be ripe for the gallows, too!

No, no, no . . . this can't be happening. People are just afraid of the dark, falling for the ridiculous pranks of spoiled children!

Good riddance!

"Skye!"

She blinked, startled back to reality.

The voice that said her name was real. Yes. Current. In the real world, where she was living at the current date.

Her vision ended as if blacked out.

And she was jolted back to the reality of the here and now.

The visions of the past were gone and were replaced by a pleasant day, and beautiful foliage surrounded them; the majesty of the earth was rich here with greenery.

They were still in a field. Jackson Crow had stopped for a minute so that she could get a good concept of the area where the old Bolton house stood. They were a small distance from the center of the city, not that far from the main streets and the tourist and historical attractions that had come into being from the past. They were near a rocky tor that was known as Proctor's Ledge and an area known in the past as "the crevice"— where bodies had once been tossed and discarded, more than buried—now a memorial to those executed there on three different occasions.

Skye had seen the past.

And it had been painful. Different times, different beliefs—and still, human beings were always as conflicted as ever, and where it seemed there was always the suffering of the innocent . . .

There were things that were horrific and tragic, no matter the time and place in the history of the earth and humanity.

She gave herself a firm mental shake.

Thankfully, she was back to the present!

Well, hopefully, she would be able to help now—there was nothing she could do to change the past, she could only hope this strange sense she possessed could help her make something better in the now!

Salem today, of course, was so very, very different!

Today they could take a short drive—or walk—and reach the modern commercial area, places like the Peabody Essex Museum; the Old Burying Point, or Charter Street Cemetery, the memorial there to those who had died; the Salem Witch Museum and so much more. There were many, many shops that now featured "potions" and other such paraphernalia that were needed by a practitioner of the modern-day wiccan belief.

"Skye!" Jackson repeated.

"Yeah!" She smiled at Jackson, who was the SAC, or special agent in charge, of the Special Circumstances Unit of the FBI, called the "Krewe of Hunters" by some, since their first case was in the city of New Orleans, or . . . well, the "Ghostbuster Unit" by a few as well.

On paper, they dealt with cults, with unusual circumstances, and those killers who thought they had legendary or mystic powers—or just wanted to pretend they did.

"Are you all right?" Jackson asked softly.

His hand was resting gently on her shoulder. Near him, Angela, Jackson's wife, and also a special agent with the Bureau's Krewe of Hunters, was watching her with concern.

They knew. They understood she could see the past replay before her in all its Technicolor glory.

Not many people did, of course. They would be convinced she was—partially at least—crazy, and it was all in her mind. Well, in a way, it was in her mind, but . . .

Angela was looking at Jackson, and while Skye *didn't* read minds, she knew what Angela was thinking.

Angela is worried that it had been a mistake. A mistake to bring me here. It was cruel to make someone witness that much tragedy and pain.

But it wasn't a mistake, Skye thought. She'd learned her weird ability to see the past could be helpful.

Painful, but helpful. Sometimes she just brought justice to victims. Sometimes she was able to save them. And that made whatever discomfort she experienced worth every minute.

It had been incredibly difficult, of course, because she couldn't tell her co-workers just what helped her see the truth so often.

Which was what was so amazing about today. Jackson and Angela knew! Unbeknownst to her . . . they'd been watching her.

She had known about the Krewe, and she'd considered trying to transfer; but it was almost a hands-off operation, even when it came to the highest circles with the Bureau. They were an "elite" unit, both here and in Europe.

And now that she had been interviewed and knew what the Krewe of Hunters was about, she understood why they accepted the weirdness that was her.

Skye gave herself a serious mental shake. She forced a smile to her lips.

"I'm fine—I mean, as fine as anyone can be here, wondering how on earth we—as human beings—ever believed that pacts could be made with the devil, and witches could curse their neighbors!"

"Sadly, this wasn't the only occasion in the colonies," Jackson said, looking toward the ridge. "In 1636, the Plymouth Colony made it illegal to 'form a solemn covenant with the devil by way of witchcraft.'" He shook his head, looking back at Skye. "The first so-called witch executed in the colonies was in 1647, in Hartford, Connecticut, Alse Young. In Massachusetts, the first recorded event was in 1648, when Margaret Jones was executed in Boston. Cotton Mather, a truly respected theologian, believed in the power of the devil and that people could make a pact with him—he was influential in all that happened."

"Wow, you're, um . . . up on all this!" Skye murmured.

"Well, we've been around," Jackson said. "In Cotton Mather's book *On Witchcraft,* which was published in 1692, and another of his books, *The Wonders of the Invisible World,* published in 1693, he defended his role in the trials. People believed in the devil, and the darkness scared them. Native Americans were different . . . Still, they estimate that anywhere between sixty and a hundred thousand people were executed in Europe during the craze, so it seems that someone here got a grip of things a little faster."

"Governor Phips, of the Province of Massachusetts Bay, dissolved the Court of Oyer and Terminer in October of 1692, and when his wife was accused, he really stepped in! By May of 1693, all of the accused had been pardoned," Angela put in dryly. "He thought that 'spectral evidence' was . . ."

"Bull?" Jackson offered.

"Yeah, that kind of describes it!" Skye said. "But being pardoned didn't help everyone. You had to pay for prison, for chains if you were bound; some people couldn't pay, and they rotted and died in prison."

"So sad," Angela murmured. "But again, the whole thing was horrible; so many people around the world were accused and—oh!"

She stopped speaking, looking dismayed.

Skye looked at her curiously. They were friends; they'd become so when Jackson had called her in for an interview with himself and Adam Harrison—and naturally, the master of research, fieldwork, and more, Angela.

At that time, Jackson had asked her point-blank about her strange ability to find the truth on many cases, admitting he and Angela and the Krewe had their own strange truths. He was a striking man, a mix of Native American and Northern European heritage, with strong cheekbones, dark hair, and light eyes, a man whose strength was often in his compassion.

And Angela . . .

Well, she was a beautiful, tall, shapely blonde—and didn't look like a law enforcement official, one who could take down the worst of the worst.

Which she had often done.

And now . . .

Now, after the interview, and knowing her, they had called on her because of her "special talent," her strange ability to see the past. A talent Skye, of course, never usually shared with others, since she knew too well what they might think about what she tried to explain or describe, and she wasn't fond of the idea of being sent to a mental institution.

"You had a . . . vision, I imagine," Jackson said. "Anything—"

"I know," Skye said. She smiled at him. "I saw one of the days when executions took place. And I could hear people's thoughts, and it was a lot like it's been throughout history—people know something is wrong, but they're afraid to speak up, lest they be persecuted, too."

"Time passes, but we're still human beings," Angela said quietly. "And we can still be very cruel."

"Nazi Germany," Jackson murmured. "Many, many people knew that extermination of their neighbors was wrong—but they were terrified of winding up in a concentration camp themselves."

"Exactly," Skye murmured. She knew now that Jackson, Angela, and the Krewe of Hunters were capable of seeing—and talking to—the spirits of the dead who, for one reason or another, didn't move on.

"Were you, um, able to talk to anyone who might have been useful in the current situation?" she asked.

Jackson shook his head. "I wonder . . . if those who are wrongfully persecuted aren't . . . Well, we do believe there is a heaven; and I think maybe those who suffer so much, who have their lives so wrongfully taken, might get . . . I don't know." He glanced at Angela. "We have met those who were killed in wars and who have remained, but in this case . . . I think they may get to have peace immediately. And anyway . . ."

He looked at Angela.

"And," Angela said, "while we're always aware that history is important—seriously, the poet, essayist, novelist and philosopher George Santayana said it best, 'Those who cannot remember the past are condemned to repeat it.' We can't live in the past—but we can learn from it. When we let ourselves!

"But history—well, history over which we have no control—is not why we're here!" Angela continued. "Skye, I'm so sorry. Maybe this was really wrong of us. We don't mean to be torturing you—"

"No, no! Seriously, no. Sure, thinking about what happened here creates a heavy heart in anyone. But—" Skye began.

"We can't let ourselves be weighed down in the many, many cruelties of history!" Angela murmured. "Not when we brought you here specifically today for history that occurred yesterday!"

"Right. New history is the reason we're here," Jackson said. "Skye, if you're sure you're all right with this—"

"Hey! Okay, I've never admitted the truth to any of my co-workers or agents or bosses, but I've been working in the NYC office for almost three years. I'm good with what I do!" Skye protested.

"And you can be even better, working with people with whom you can be honest," Jackson assured her. "Let's head on over to the Bolton house and see . . . what you can see there."

The Bolton house wasn't one of Salem's eighteen "first period houses," but the base for the house itself *had* been there since the late 1600s—but that was just the foundation and a few walls. The house, as it stood today, did date back to the latter part of the eighteenth century; it was a beautiful and historic home. It had been lovingly tended by the Bolton family through the centuries. Mike Bolton had turned the house over to his grandson, Justin Bolton, just the year before, since they had lost Justin's parents years ago when he'd been a teenager. Mike's son died from cancer, and his daughter-in-law died from a heart condition. A widower, Mike Bolton had helped his grandson make his way through college. When Justin's second child had been born, Mike had convinced his grandson it was time for something bigger than the apartment they lived in downtown. Mike reminded him that the house was historic, and the family had cared for it for years and years, and now it was Justin's turn.

Justin had accepted the responsibility, but he hadn't wanted his grandfather to move out. So they'd arranged for a family apartment to be created out of the old garage or old carriage house. Justin, his wife, Alicia, and their children could reside in the main house, but Mike never needed to be far away—or worse, alone.

They had been a happy family because with Mike there, neither Justin nor Alicia had to worry if they ran late at work and the nanny needed to get going because she was taking classes. Mike was more than capable of watching the kids for an hour or so.

But Alicia had returned from work one day to find her grandfather-in-law dead in the carriage house—and their nanny, along with their oldest child, Jeremy, age five, were gone. No note, no possible explanation. They were just . . .

Gone.

She found their baby, Lily Marie, just eleven months old, alone and terrified, crying in the playpen.

Alicia had naturally been terrified and in a panic herself, but smart enough to call 911 first, and then her husband before she had, by all accounts, broken down completely. It had been her husband, Justin, who had forced down his emotions to give them all the information they did have—the nanny was Patricia Yale, just twenty, a student at the local college. She was a young woman who had grown up in foster care, but had done exceptionally well with her studies while working at the same time. She loved children, especially both the baby and Jeremy, and they loved her. She had worked for another family in the area who had used Patricia frequently for date nights, and they had recommended her to Alicia and Justin Bolton with glowing praise.

Jeremy was a smart little five-year-old. He knew his parents' phone numbers and his home address. He was a loving child who was always eager to meet people, but they had tried to teach him a little about stranger danger.

But nothing was heard from little Jeremy, and Patricia had not returned to the apartment where she lived with three other college-aged friends.

Because there had been no explanation and no clues to be discovered in the hours that came after what the ME had classified as a murder—not a death—in the house, Lieutenant Gavin Bruns, a friend of Jackson's from a situation years before, had called on the Krewe of Hunters.

Skye had looked Bruns up online, since he had been the one to call on Jackson and allow for the Krewe, or "Feds," to come in. He was a man in his midthirties and had risen swiftly within the department, mainly because of his expertise in weighing a situation, using logic, and never attempting to micromanage those with him.

Jackson Crow was a keen observer of people.

And Skye knew now Jackson had been watching her and her investigations, interviewed her, and knew that while she wasn't "different" in the way that he and the Krewe were, she was "different" in her own way, and so . . .

Here she was.

For this case, Jackson had arranged for Skye to be "on loan" from the NYC field office. But she also knew Jackson had other plans for her. He was creating yet another special unit within the Bureau with the help of Adam Harrison, a man who had lost a beloved son with special abilities and thus had begun to put the true but unimaginable together and . . . get things done!

"Onward! To the Bolton house. In truth, I'm happy to be here," Skye assured them. "I came often while I was growing up—back then, I had lots of family in the area. I met several true wiccans. Laurie Cabot brought the first Witch Shoppe to Salem in the early 1970s, my mom said, and there were a lot of people who were practicing wiccans at the time—not people who did any harm. Wiccans wouldn't. Kind of like voodoo— doing anything evil would come back by a factor of three on the person who did."

"Crow Haven Corner is still here, but with different owners, I think. If I'm not mistaken, Laurie may still be involved,"

Jackson told her. "Anyway, it is a fascinating town. There's more history, too—"

"Seafarers!" Skye said. "Pirates and more!"

They'd reached the car, and continued chatting on the way, but it wasn't much of a drive to the Bolton house.

Crime scene tape remained on the door, but it had been broken. Someone was already in the house.

"Zach must have beat us here," Jackson said. "That's his car on the street." He pushed open the door and shouted. "Zach— it's us, Jackson, Angela, and Skye!"

Skye had yet to meet the man she was being partnered with for the case. She knew his name was Zachary Erickson, and that he had been with the Bureau for several years, based in Boston.

She also knew Jackson had watched him—just as Jackson had watched her—and determined they'd be right for federal investigation, one that they'd been asked in on by the local police.

"In here!" a male voice called.

They entered the house. It was a truly handsome historical residence, with a large parlor decked out with Victorian furniture, a staircase that curved to a balcony and hallway and rooms above, and arched doorways that led to side rooms.

Zachary Erickson made his entrance.

Her first impression of the man was . . .

Interesting.

He came into the parlor carrying a baby's rattle, shaking it as he walked. He was a tall man, with dark hair and blue eyes so dark they almost appeared black. She knew that he was thirty-three, that he was originally from Harpers Ferry, and later moved to Boston and had been with the Boston Police Department before joining the FBI. Like most field agents, he appeared to be fit and professional.

Which made it appear a bit more ridiculous that a tall man in a pristine dark blue business suit was waving a baby's rattle.

But he was looking at her, too, maybe wondering what kind of a weird being he was being set up with, she assumed. According to Jackson, Zach's ability was a little more common than hers, one that had been utilized by police many times— even if it wasn't the accepted norm or a "talent" believed in by skeptics.

According to Jackson, Zach had psychic abilities. He could touch objects and see things through them . . . sometimes, people or places.

Where they had been.

And possibly, where they were as he held the object.

He was staring at her, of course.

She wasn't tall, but she wasn't tiny, standing about five-five. And on a good day, she weighed almost 120 pounds. She had long light-auburn hair, and she was thinking she should have put it back that day, maybe add a little leverage to a look of professionalism . . .

She had, at least, worn a pantsuit and hoped she would appear to be professional in dress, if nothing else.

"Hi," he said, looking at Skye.

"Um, good to meet you," she said. Of course, she didn't know yet if it was or wasn't.

"Enjoying yourself with that?" Jackson asked him, referring to the rattle.

"They never touched the baby," Zach told him. "Small favors. As far as Mike Bolton, I just got the ME's report in on my phone; you must have it, too."

They all pulled out their phones.

"Cause of death, heart attack. Method . . . cocaine?" Jackson said, looking up at them.

"Ingested," Zach said. "The man had no history whatsoever of drug use. So whoever was here kidnapped the nanny and the kid, and forced or tricked it into the old man somehow."

"He would have done it if someone threatened the children," Skye said.

"Do you want to go to the outbuilding and see what you can get?" Angela asked Skye. "I mean, if—"

"Yes, of course, and I'm fine!" Skye assured them, making a point at not looking at the man who was supposed to be her partner for the enterprise.

Angela and Jackson had to be back in DC for a case involving a lobbyist; and while they had other agents there in their stead, the powers that be wanted them.

Everyone here is weird in one way or another! she reminded herself.

So she looked straight at Zach Erickson and said flatly, "Lead the way. Let's see if there is something that I can . . . see."

He nodded. She tried to determine if he was skeptical or not. Well, he shouldn't be.

And she shouldn't be acquiring such a chip on her shoulder already. The man hadn't acted in any way that suggested he thought she was a fake.

"Out the back door is easiest," he said. "Of course, here's where the forensic crew that the police sent out were stymied—there was no break-in. There were no fingerprints found anywhere that didn't belong to the nanny or to family members or friends we've already seen and questioned and who all have alibis. And kids, of course. A five-year-old has playdates, so . . . Anyway, the grandfather was found in his little apartment, out here."

Zach led the way through the house.

An archway led from the parlor straight back into a kitchen that had been modernized, Skye thought, within the last ten years. There was a breakfast table with a booster seat and a high chair drawn to it at the one side, with a large work island toward the middle of the room. A large refrigerator-freezer, double sink, oven, microwave, and more of the usual made up the rest of the kitchen.

The door to the rear of the house was right behind the breakfast table. It was probably new as well, with a window that looked to the back and could be covered by a pretty, flow-ered drapery.

Zach opened the door and headed out.

The rest of them followed.

The distance between the main house and the outbuilding was about twenty feet; it sat a little to the left of it, from their perspective.

The yard itself was charming. Trees surrounded the back, and flowering bushes had been planted close to the house.

A little trail of stones led to the quarters where Mike Bolton had died.

"The man was eighty," Zach murmured as they walked. "A healthy eighty, from all accounts; a man who taught high school until mandatory retirement age; was loyal to his wife, who died after a stroke about six years ago; and a good father. From all accounts and records, he was a model citizen, a man who never even accrued so much as a parking ticket."

"No suggestion that his lifestyle might have caused him to, um, imbibe a bit?" Skye asked.

Zach looked at her and shook his head.

"From everything we've learned, he didn't *imbibe* so much as a sip of champagne at family weddings. And in an age when the world smoked cigarettes or pipes or cigars—nope. Never smoked, never drank, never did drugs," Zach told her.

"Zach was up here yesterday," Jackson informed Skye. "I know we just dragged you in this morning—"

Skye laughed. "You didn't drag me in. If I can help find a child and help solve a cruel murder, I'm happy to be here."

Jackson nodded.

Zach studied her while opening the door to the outbuilding.

It, too, had been sealed with crime scene tape, but the tape had been broken—by Zach Erickson, Skye thought.

He'd been here. He'd been studying the case. And as of now, he had nothing.

She entered the small building. She knew it had once been a

carriage house, and she hoped desperately her vision wouldn't take her further back than she needed to go. She had to concentrate on very recent history.

It appeared to be a typical grandparent or in-law dwelling. There was a small room that was furnished with a sofa and an armchair and a large-screen TV. The area stretched into a small kitchen area, which held a small refrigerator, a microwave, and a sink. There was a doorway that led to the bedroom.

Skye knew she needed to head into the bedroom.

She brushed past Zach to reach the doorway that led to it. It was like brushing by concrete.

He didn't seem to notice.

Like Jackson and Angela, he followed her into the small bedroom.

It offered a bed, a dresser, a closet, and a single chair. She looked at the bed, knowing that it was where the deceased man had been found.

She sat in the chair by the bed and closed her eyes.

And waited.

And then, the movie in her mind began.

And . . .

The door opened; Skye saw the person . . . the being . . . slip in.

Mike Bolton had been sleeping. He didn't open his eyes with alarm; he was expecting his grandson, perhaps, or his little great-grandchild.

But then he saw the being . . .

It appeared extremely tall, but that was because of the witch's hat, broad at the brim and pointed at the top. The person was clad in an encompassing cloak over a ruffled black shirt with a high neckline.

The face was . . .

Green.

Like that of a witch in a movie.

Mike Bolton stared in disbelief for a moment. Then he opened his mouth to scream.

As he did so, the thing rushed toward him, snatching his pillow from beneath his head, shoving it over his face. And when the green being lifted the pillow from the man's face, Mike Bolton opened his mouth, desperate for air.

As he did so, the being shoved something down his throat. The man gagged, twisted, turned . . . fought . . .

And the being put the pillow over his face again. Not enough to kill him . . .

Just enough to cause him to pass out.

Satisfied, the green being headed for the door, looking back to make sure the man wasn't going to regain consciousness.

Then the being was gone.

Skye heard the bedroom door slide shut in its wake.

Then the door to the outbuilding.

And then . . .

She heard the scream. Startled. Quickly cut off . . .

And . . .

Nothing.

Skye opened her eyes and blinked away the past. They were all staring at her. Jackson, Angela, and Zach Erickson.

She swallowed hard.

"Well? You saw something!" Jackson said.

She nodded.

"What?" Angela prodded softly.

Skye winced, looking at them all.

"Mike Bolton was killed by . . ."

"By?" Zach pressed.

"By a witch," she said. "A green witch, like one might see in the movies. With the black pointy hat as well. Or I am assuming, someone dressed up as a witch with pointed black hat, green flesh, and all."

She expected the looks she received from them.

But Jackson shook his head. "Great. So we're in Salem, Massachusetts, and someone is dressing up in a movie-version witch costume—and attacking people." He paused, grimacing as he looked from Zach to Skye and said quietly, "Looks like you've got your work cut out for you."

Zach stared at Skye, arching a brow. "A witch . . . a modern concept of a witch, someone painted green and running around in black clothing and wide-brimmed and pointed hat?"

Is he skeptical, or just assuring himself that he'd heard correctly?

She grimaced. "That's right, I'm afraid. We're looking for the Wicked Witch of the West."

CHAPTER 2

"Can you do this? Now that it's just us—and the local detectives?" Zach managed to ask softly. He'd pretended he needed Skye to put something in his car, to give them just a few seconds alone as Jackson and Angela departed—and their local counterparts remained waiting in front of them.

"It's harder, now that the detectives are here," Skye murmured carefully in reply.

They were on their own with the local law enforcement because Angela had glanced at her watch and then she and Jackson had apologized when the detectives had arrived, and introductions had been made. They had to leave, to get to the airport, because they needed to be back to the DC area as quickly as possible.

So far, the pair had been polite enough, accepting of the additional help from the federal side of things.

Zach nodded and said quietly, "Naturally, knowing we were here, they're going to be here. They're local; even if the federal government has been asked in, but we weren't asked—and we're not authorized—to take control, just to provide assistance."

"I wish Angela and Jackson could have stayed a little longer," Skye murmured. "I do understand, but . . ."

"All right," Zach said. "I can give you a few minutes in here.

I can keep our police detectives outside, talk about the road, the surrounding area. That will give you time inside." He sighed softly, shaking his head. "I had the place for about thirty minutes alone before you three arrived this morning. But there was nothing in particular the criminals touched that took on a glow. And the police had already been in here, of course, so what I was getting was images of them being here." He winced. "Whatever the thing is that I have, it's best when something is pristine, when I can be there first. This thing with you . . . it's really cool. It works no matter what has happened when, right?"

She glanced at the two detectives—they were engrossed in conversation, studying the main door to the residence.

Detective Constance Berkley appeared to be in her early thirties, an attractive woman, with dark brown hair and a lean face. She was about five-three—small next to Detective Vincent Cason, a man who stood at about six-two, broad and fit, blond-haired and strong-jawed, perhaps a decade older than his partner.

"Well, not so simple, I'm afraid. I've seen horrible things, but I came here to see what happened in this house and I still don't really have any kind of a full and complete picture. So far, my best image has been of a hanging during the Salem Witch Trials," she told him ruefully.

But he shook his head. "I'm sorry, but you also saw something here that is really going to help guide this investigation. We know we're looking for someone who wants to play dress-up while they're committing crimes. Of course, the *why* is going to be important. Was the costume someone's idea of the typical black hoodie that's so favored by criminals—along with half the population when the weather is chilly. Or is there some symbolism behind it?"

"What could that be? The innocents accused of witchcraft back in the day were just ordinary citizens." She grimaced.

"Frank Baum's *The Wizard of Oz* wasn't written for another few hundred years."

He laughed softly. "*The Wonderful Wizard of Oz,* to be precise. And it was published in 1900. So, yeah, you're right there; it was a long way off. Thankfully, long past the day when the world believed in spectral evidence and screaming kids—most probably influenced by words their parents had said. Hey, if you're mad at someone or you feel that person slighted you in some way, why not accept they made you miserable because they were a witch, dancing with the devil, consumed with darkness. Oh, and our friends are on the way over here," he added, indicating the doorway.

He turned and offered a grim smile to Detectives Cason and Berkley as they walked back over toward the house, Vincent Cason shaking his head and telling them, "Of course, we've kept the family out of the house since Alicia returned home yesterday—we've got them in a hotel in town. But at this point, we've had our crime scene unit through the place and . . . well, you know. Whoever was in here wore gloves and left nothing. We're going to let them come home, although . . . that's not going to be easy for them. Mike dead and the kid missing. Have you gotten anything?"

"I'll take another look, if you don't mind," Skye said, stopping to add, "Oh, Zach—"

"It's okay; I'm right behind you. The detectives can give me a better idea of the immediate surrounding area," he said.

She disappeared inside.

"So," Zach said, shaking his head, "I think you're right; whoever did this also did a lot of studying on our easily accessible social media sites, or they've practiced what they're doing, being criminals. Someone had to know, however, that Mike Bolton was older, and he had the usual 'older body' problems. Not a stretch to think that breaking and entering, and threatening the children, was enough to get him to imbibe the drug that could bring on a heart attack in just about anyone."

"Yes, that's what I was thinking," Constance Berkley told them earnestly. "And it's frightening to believe whoever did this is from the area. You can't imagine how dense the forests around here can be, and just how many derelict buildings haven't been discovered yet by the parks department." She sighed softly. "We're a tourist town. Go figure, tragic history makes us commercially viable. But we do get our share of . . ."

"Weirdos, wackos, and kooks," Cason offered. "Trust me, you don't want to be here around Halloween!"

Zach laughed softly. "Hey, I've been here for Halloween. My parents loved the place. I grew up in Harpers Ferry and then Boston, but had a great-aunt who lived here when I was growing up and we met here fairly frequently, Detective Cason. But, of course, at that time, all I had to do was watch with awe all the incredible costumes and things going on—didn't have to deal with any of the things that could go on when it all got a bit crazy."

Cason grinned. "First, looks like we're in this together for the long haul—please, just call me Vince."

"And I go by Connie!" Detective Berkley told him.

"Well, then, of course," Zach said. "I'm Zach and my partner is Skye."

They all nodded, looking at one another with small smiles. Working together was always easiest when everyone was on the same page.

"Hey, as I was saying, I'd love to get a better idea of the outside of the house—there's a forest to the rear, right? But neighbors to the left and the right—" Zach began.

"Come on, we'll show you," Connie said. "Should we wait for your partner?"

"Right, sorry!" Vince Cason said, pausing.

"No, no, we're fine. She just wanted to go back in there for a second; get a good sense of the flow of the house. Right now, it appears Patricia must have opened the door to whoever did this—which suggests, as we discussed before, that it was someone she knew, or someone who claimed to be part of the electric company or some such thing. I'll be right out," Zach assured them.

How the hell could I ever explain to anyone just what it was that my partner did? Of course, that's the whole point of the "special" units within their law enforcement community; they didn't have to explain.

Because, of course, they were all gifted, cursed, or just plain crazy.

But what Skye McMahon had . . .

He could barely put *his* mind around it. To *see,* to *literally* see things as they had happened . . .

Damn. Well, he was good and useful, too. And Jackson Crow seemed to think that their talents would complement one another.

That remained to be seen.

More importantly, a missing child and a young woman needed to be found.

Alive.

And right now, that mattered more than anything.

Skye stood still, closing her eyes for a minute, willing herself to see the past—and hoping it would be the past that she needed. And she was lucky; time unfolded exactly as she'd hoped.

The bell rang. Young Jeremy was sitting on the sofa in the parlor, reading from one of his schoolbooks. The baby was in her playpen, lying down, laughing up at a cloth doll. Patricia Yale, a young ponytailed brunette in a T-shirt and jeans, had been answering Jeremy on how to spell the word "believe."

Patricia heard the bell; she'd come out of the kitchen to answer Jeremy. She had, perhaps, been getting a snack for one of them.

She opened the door.

She stepped back, laughing, not alarmed.

"Hey, it's not Halloween! Funny, funny, who the hell—" she began.

But that was when the green witch, with the pointed black hat, produced a gun. "You, the boy, out here with me, now!"

It was the same witch who had killed Mike Bolton.

But the voice . . .

Male? Female? Distorted mechanically?

"I can't just leave the baby—" Patricia said, trying to get out a sentence again.

"Well, I can shoot her if you like," the green being said.

"No, no, no! Of course not! Uh, Jeremy . . . wait, please! You're not going to hurt the boy, please—"

"Obey every word I say and neither of you gets hurt. But you don't want the kid dead? Then don't give me any grief! Out here, now!"

Jeremy sat on the sofa, staring in pure terror at the creature. But Patricia didn't intend to give the witch any excuse to hurt the boy. She ran to the sofa, sweeping the boy up and into her arms and pausing just a second by the playpen to whisper desperately, "Your mommy will be home soon!"

She ran out, pausing at the door as she stared at the bizarre witch.

"Now! We go," the witch said.

Patricia stepped out, Jeremy still in her arms.

The door closed in their wake.

It closed with a slam—the witch's way of leaving, so it appeared.

* * *

It was the noise of the door falling shut in the past that brought Skye back to the present.

One person? Dressed up as a witch? Or . . .

Were there a few people running around dressed up as green creatures? Or was it just one person in makeup who was running around with green skin, a pointed hat . . . making a mockery of the tragedy that had long ago plagued Salem?

Skye quickly strode through the room, joining the others in front of the house.

Cason was pointing to the street and talking to Zach about Salem.

"Way back when, the entire area was 'bewitched,' one might say. Danvers was Salem Village back then; people were also arrested in Ipswich and Andover . . . It was a different world. A lot of people speculate that the 'afflicted girls' were prey to a fungus on the wheat or some such other physical cause. But I'll tell you one thing—look at some of the forests around here at night. The darkness is unbelievable. And, remember, at the time, there was a fear of the Native American tribes. The tribes were so very different in their way of living, their beliefs, and their forms of worship. Maybe it wasn't so hard that in the darkness of time and place to believe bad things might have been caused by witchcraft or another form of evil, something that awakened or partnered with Satan himself."

Skye frowned, wondering if Zach had mentioned she'd "seen" the kidnapper—a person with green skin and a witch's pointed black hat.

But he shook his head almost imperceptibly, and she knew that he had not. They had just fallen into a conversation that might be normal in the community.

Standing nearby, Constance smiled encouragingly at Skye and reiterated their request to be known as Connie and Vince. Then she grimly asked, "Anything?"

"Well, we're late to the party, but I agree with the theory there was no break-in regarding the main house, and Patricia Yale simply opened the door. It doesn't appear that the house was torn apart in any way. Of course, we're a little later than you and the local police are to the situation, but it does seem what you've surmised so far must be the truth. Except, I don't believe Patricia was involved with her own disappearance and the little boy's kidnapping. I believe she was threatened, just as I believe Mike Bolton was forced to swallow the cocaine that brought about his heart attack," Skye told them.

"These guys have just been showing me the area," Zach said. "Directly in back are woods; but to the right and left are homes, and they are a few acres apart. A little more country out here, although we're still walking distance to town and the tourist areas—if you really like walking, of course. But"—he paused and pointed—"look past the semicircle of the drive right before the house; there's a place where you can pull a car in, far to the right, where it's all but hidden from the street by the trees and foliage in the yard."

"So, then, you think someone kidnapped Patricia and little Jeremy and simply drove away with them?" Skye asked Zach.

"I agree with him," Connie said. "What else? Slide in back and into the forest? What then? Hey, you can wind up in a dense twist of trees, forever and ever, back there. I mean, don't get me wrong! Salem is no Boston, but it's a huge tourist area and still—lots and lots of deep dark woods, just like back in the day, as Vince was describing it. I don't think the park rangers know everything around here, to be honest. To me, it makes far more sense for them to have been whisked far away—and easily—via a car."

"What about traffic cams?" Zach asked.

Vince let out a sigh of frustration. "Not until you're more into the populated area; and by then, a car could have come from anywhere, and just about everywhere, in the area. Yes, of course, we looked at what we could. No sign of the boy or Patricia Yale in any vehicle."

"'Fin' Yarborough," Connie said, looking at Vince.

"Of course, we've read the files. Fin—Phineas Yarborough—is Patricia's boyfriend, right?" Zach said, looking at the two detectives. "From what I understand, he's an amazing student himself at the college—"

"Okay, it bothers me that there was no break-in," Vince said. "Patricia would have just opened the door to Fin. And who else might she have done that for?"

"I don't know," Skye said, smiling. She didn't want to start off by offending the local detectives. "I've been a babysitter in my day. When you're looking after two children, you can get so busy and torn that you might just open a door. Groceries are delivered fairly often these days, fast food . . . maybe she thought that even Mike Bolton might ring the bell, knowing she was watching the kids."

"True," Connie murmured. "But it's true that . . . well, for one, Fin is a history major, completely taken with the area. He's been published in a few magazines, though, and wants to teach himself. Maybe the two of you should interview him, see what kind of a vibe you get from him."

"We should do that," Zach agreed. "Does he have an alibi?"

"Oh, yeah, sure. He was home studying," Connie said.

"Any witnesses?" Skye asked.

"Of course not, that would be too easy!" Connie told her. "I just . . ."

"You're just so tired, you're about to keel over," Vince said, turning to Skye and Zach. "We've been on this since Alicia Bolton came home from work last night and found Patricia and her son gone, and her grandfather-in-law dead, and—"

"We'll take over for the next few hours," Zach promised.

"And we won't stop; and anything that happens major, we'll get to you immediately!" Skye assured the two detectives.

Vince nodded and looked at Connie. "Go home. That's what I'm going to do. We have the Feds on our case now." He looked back at the two of them. "Thank you!"

He pointed to his unmarked car in the drive, looking at his partner.

Connie smiled at him, nodding. She quietly added, "Thank you" to Skye and Zach before heading to the car.

With a wave, Vince joined her.

When they were gone, Zach looked at Skye.

"Well? Do you think it was the boyfriend?"

"I'm not sure."

Skye wondered if he sounded skeptical. But . . .

A man who touches objects and can see something about the person who had touched it last should hardly be mocking any strange perception.

She was probably just being touchy or defensive.

She lowered her head for a minute. Her sight or vision or whatever it was had come down to her through her grandmother, a woman who had been born just outside of Dublin and who had also told a few fantastic stories in her day.

But she had seen something in Skye when Skye had been a child, and she'd been quick to warn her that people wouldn't believe her. She needed to make sure she kept her ability silent, because others didn't have it—and others wouldn't understand. Not even her own parents. And until she'd been interviewed by Adam, Jackson, and Angela, she'd kept the secret to herself and found other ways to explain to co-workers before now why she had come to certain conclusions, why she had been able to discover the truth when they hadn't seen it.

"Skye, are you all right?" Zach asked. He seemed really concerned. Maybe he didn't doubt her, or . . .

Maybe he thought she saw what she wanted to see or thought that she should see?

Anyway, his behavior was respectful.

And Jackson believed in her—that was what mattered. Her new partner was going to have to accept her words.

As she would have to accept his.

"Yes, yes, of course, I'm sorry. Yes, I saw the exact moment she opened the door. I guess it's pretty natural it was the same person who arrived at Mike Bolton's little apartment, entered with a gun, and forced the drug into him. Whoever it was—I can't even tell if it's a man or a woman—had a gun, threatened to use it . . . and I saw Patricia. She is in no way or shape involved. She was almost crying as she told the baby her mom would be home in a minute and swept little Jeremy up. Of course, the witch threatened the child; and I believe with my whole heart, Patricia was worried about her own life, of course, but Jeremy's life even more."

He let out a soft sigh, looking out at the day.

"Well," he said. "She should have known if it was Fin—even if he was painted green and in a costume. But we need to start somewhere. Let's interview the man."

"We don't really have a place where we can bring someone in—except, of course, the local station," Skye reminded him.

"And in this case, at least, I think we're better off if we just talk to him. I have notes in my phone, and I'm assuming that you have the same notes. Yes, right," he said, looking at his phone. "I have an address for him—it's an apartment right off Essex Street. I have a car, so we'll head on over."

She nodded.

Zach reattached the crime scene tape to the door, glancing back as they walked away.

"I was just wondering if they should have a patrol officer looking over the house," Skye murmured.

"Well, if not for you . . ."

"What does that mean?" she asked him.

She'd slid into the passenger seat. He slid into the driver's seat and grinned at her.

"I don't believe anyone is after anything in the house—they wanted Jeremy or Patricia or both of them. I'm going to say they wanted the kid, too—or else they could have left him the same as they left the baby. You're seeing someone dressing up as, what I guess we should call, a movie-style witch. After all, the historic so-called witches were just ordinary-looking people. No, whoever did this wanted Patricia and the boy. That's why I don't feel like making waves over having an officer watch the place."

She shrugged. "Seems like . . . Well, I was told that Connie and Vince were two of the best, so . . ."

"Let's take this in the direction we can," Zach said. "We'll interview Fin; then I'm going to suggest, if you're willing, we get some research done on movies being made in the area or just on local costume or monster shops. I think there are a few."

"All right. It's a plan," Skye agreed. "In fact, I'll start looking . . ."

She pulled out her phone, keying in costume shops for the area.

"And?" he asked.

She winced, glancing his way. "Here and in the surrounding areas? Dozens of costume shops, makeup shops, and even more wiccan shops and monster shops! Museums with movie monsters . . . tons and tons of shops."

"Okay, from what I'm seeing through what you've said, this is a very particular costume or look. We can try to see who might carry that costume."

"True. If we can combine that with green body makeup . . ."

"We might have a shot."

Zach was watching the road as they headed toward Essex Street.

"And," he said, glancing her way quickly, "I still say that we take a look at those traffic cams. Whoever took Patricia and Jeremy could have forced them down in the back or maybe even forced one of them into the trunk. At least we'll see who might have traveled from the outskirts to the center—"

He frowned, his speech just stopping.

"What is it?" she asked.

"Why—why would you kidnap two people and bring them back—dressed as a green witch—to an area where you might have a dozen witnesses?" he asked.

She shook her head. "Good point."

"Okay, and it seems . . . We're here. Well, where I can park legally, and we can walk."

They were a block off Essex. He'd found street parking right by Salem Common, and near the Salem Witch Museum.

She looked up at the museum.

"Something?" Zach asked.

She shook her head smiling. "I came here often as a child. I always liked that museum, the history, the displays. I mean, I've seen the trial records, and you could read forever. But if you want a great synopsis of what happened here, that's a great place to go."

He laughed softly. "Yeah, I've been here, too. And I do love this museum. And others—the Peabody Essex, the New England Pirate Museum . . . and the homesteads, the Rebecca Nurse Homestead—"

"I got it! You've been here, too!"

He shrugged.

"Count Orlok's Nightmare Gallery, Crow Haven Corner, and more—great shops," he said.

She grinned at that. "Maybe we can go shopping when it's all over."

His smile faded slightly. "Yeah."

"What? That took you a minute," she said.

He gave himself a shake. "I'm just afraid that . . ."

"That it's not over?" she asked.

"Not by a long shot. There's our apartment building ahead. Let's do this."

"He may not even answer," Skye warned.

But he did.

Phineas Yarborough, or Fin, opened his door when they knocked. He looked at them with a frown of confusion.

Of course.

He'd already been interviewed by the detectives assigned to the case.

"Yes? May I help you?"

"We think you can," Zach said, producing his credentials. "We're—"

"Did you find her? Did you find Patricia and the little boy? Oh, God! Oh, no, you're not here because you found them . . ."

He looked as if he was going to burst into tears.

"No, no, we haven't found them! There's no reason to suspect that they're dead!" Skye said quickly. "But we're determined we will find them. That's why, I'm sorry, we need to speak with you again, to see if there is anything at all you can say that might help us!"

He was a good-looking kid, blond, blue-eyed, medium in height and build. He stepped back, indicating that they should come in.

"Anything, anything—I'll answer any question that I can; I'll do anything!" he swore. He looked as if he was about to shed tears.

Maybe he was a great actor.

But . . .

"Sorry, I'm in college, financial help from my folks, but it's still not much of an apartment. A studio, but there are a few chairs," Fin said.

He indicated the apartment: His bed and a TV were in the

center, but there was a small kitchenette with a table and chairs near the door.

"That's great," Zach told him as the three of them took chairs at the table. "We're grateful you're willing to be helpful. So, when is the last time you talked to Patricia?"

"That afternoon. She had gotten Jeremy started on his homework. He kept asking her if he was spelling words right. Simple words, of course, he's not that old. He's a great kid, just a kid, loves to play baseball . . . This is so horrible! I think it was about three o'clock. I was home, here alone. As you can see . . . well, it wouldn't be a great place to share with anyone else. Of course, I know I'm a suspect, and this place doesn't have a doorman, so . . . no one saw me here. But you need to understand, I love Patricia! I would never, never, in a thousand years, hurt her in any way, shape, or form! Please!"

He did start crying. Burying his face in his hands, he cried softly, whispering, "I'm sorry, I'm so sorry!"

"We believe you," Zach told him.

"But it might have been my fault!" Fin said.

"Your fault? How would that be?" Skye asked gently.

He shook his head. "I don't know . . . Maybe I angered someone out there who was on the verge!"

"How?" Zach pressed.

"I just published an article about the witch trials," he told them, rubbing his face and trying to regain his composure.

"There are a gazillion articles about the witch trials," Skye said. "So—"

"I compared what happened then to the way that people are easily deceived today, you know. If it's on the Internet, it must be true. We're just as susceptible to lies now as we were then. And I couldn't help but think that . . ."

"Wouldn't someone come after you then? Why would they go to the Bolton house—and take Jeremy and Patricia?" Zach asked.

He shook his head. "I—I don't know. Maybe . . . do you think they meant to kill Mike Bolton?"

Skye glanced at Zach. "You heard he was murdered?"

They had just gotten the emails that the elderly man's heart attack had been purposely orchestrated.

"They just put it out there in the news," Fin told them. "I guess people thought at first that whatever had happened caused his heart attack. I guess that's true in a way, but the news is saying he was fed a substance that caused his heart attack. Which, of course, just keeps making this all worse and worse. Whoever did it has already committed one murder, so . . . if you've committed one, what's to stop that someone from committing more murders?"

"First, Fin, let's work on faith. Whoever killed Mike Bolton kidnapped Patricia and Jeremy. If they were just out there to kill people, they would have killed them, too. So we're going to be optimistic; we won't stop until we find the truth," Skye promised.

Zach glanced at her. They weren't supposed to promise they would solve a case.

There were too many cases in history that had never been solved.

But she hadn't promised to solve the case; she had promised not to stop until she did find the truth.

Still, wrong, but . . .

She believed Fin.

"Okay, so you went to your classes, you came back here, and you were studying when all this happened. And when you talked to Patricia, everything was fine?"

He nodded. "Patricia didn't have a great childhood. When her parents died, she went from foster home to foster home until she aged out. She's in college with a great scholarship because she's so smart, and she makes extra money babysitting because she really, really loves kids! She's just an amazing person. And I promise you, she's not in on it. Don't waste your time thinking she's in on it, and that she's going to demand a ransom for Jeremy—"

"We don't think that at all," Zach assured him. He glanced at Skye, almost smiling. "Trust me, we believe you. Patricia is not involved; we know that she's a victim. And we will do everything in our power to get her back."

They stayed a little longer as Fin told them about his day. Zach wanted to know if he drove, and Fin assured them that he did; that's why he kept busy writing articles. Besides school, room, and board, he had a car payment; but he'd gotten a great deal on a new dealer's demo car.

He was happy when Zach told him the car's GPS could be obtained, and they could prove he had gone to school and come home.

Finally, Skye and Zach glanced at one another. They'd gotten all that they could get, and it was time to go.

"All right," Skye said as they headed back to the car. "Costume and makeup shops. I'll find a place to start—"

"After food. During food, we can make a list," Zach said.

She looked at him and he laughed.

"Maybe you can go forever; I need something to eat."

"Gotcha. Okay, well, we're right by the Hawthorne, and they have a great restaurant—" Skye began.

"Sold!"

They were just a block or so away; they left the car where it was parked, and headed into the restaurant. Skye never read the menu; she was already looking up shops and trying to determine where they should start.

"I'm not sure how we're going to explain my obsession with costume shops," she stated. "I mean . . ."

"Not to worry. We can say it's a theory that someone dressed up as something else. How else could someone con a man like Mike Bolton into taking something that he knew would kill him?"

"They can say he reacted to his great-grandchildren being threatened."

"Except," Zach reminded her, "there was nothing out of order. It doesn't appear the person was in his little in-law apartment with Justin or Patricia. There were two separate entries."

"Aha!" Skye murmured. "Thank you, good thinking."

He ordered the Fisherman's Platter.

She did the same, engrossed in studying the different shops online and seeing just what they sold.

"I'm not seeing any major movies being filmed at the moment," Zach said, studying his phone as well. "Of course, that doesn't mean, these days, that someone isn't doing something shorter or smaller for one of the social media outlets—reels and shorts are becoming more and more popular on just about every site out there. Our lives are all on social media these days."

Skye laughed. "Not mine. Well, okay, a little. But I'm only on one site and that's to see family and friends."

"Wave of today and tomorrow," Zach said dryly.

She shrugged, thanking the waitress when their food came, her attention still on her phone as they began to eat.

"Okay, I do play around on certain social media. I like the dog sites," she admitted. "I really should say, I like animal sites. Cute creatures doing cute things . . . Oh, here! I found a place—" Skye broke off.

Her phone was buzzing; Zach's was, too.

An urgent message popped up on her screen.

Another woman and child were missing.

"I've got the bill; we both have expense accounts," Zach said, rising to pay their waitress. "Damn, and dinner was delicious!"

"Zach!"

"What?"

"A woman and child . . . they just disappeared from the Prince of Darkness Costume Shop and Monster Gallery!" Skye said.

"Right. I read about that, and yes, it's concerning, but—"

"No, no, Zach! They sell a witch costume like the one I saw on the person at the Bolton house—and a full line of face and body makeup there."

CHAPTER 3

The Prince of Darkness Costume Shop and Monster Gallery was quite fantastic—even from the outside.

If the situation hadn't been so deadly on this particular trip to the area, Zach thought, he'd have enjoyed a trip to the store.

Movie monsters could be fun and entertaining. When they stayed in the movies.

The store was located just over the border in the town of Swampscott, Salem's neighbor to the southwest.

The store was the sole occupant of a large standalone building with giant, sculpted creatures at the entrance—a fanged vampire to the right of the front doors and a werewolf to the left. Entering the shop, where local police were talking to a distraught man, they could see that monster mannequins were set up all around the store, some fronting rows of costumes, others with arms—or paws—out to indicate makeup displays.

Of course, as Zach had driven, Skye had read to him about the store from their website and from reviews online.

It sounded like an incredible place.

And more.

Of course, it had been too bizarre that she had been reading about it just as they had received their messages on the alert from the local police—and that they were now on their way, rushing to the place.

Zach quickly identified himself to one of the local officers who was outside. Inside the shop, he and Skye hurried forward to do the same with the uniformed officer speaking with a man who was apparently Keith Howell, the very distraught owner of the place.

And though he was anxious and tense, Howell appeared to have a stern grip on himself; he was a man who stood about Zach's own height, a solid six-three, fortyish, and—despite the dramatic appeal of the store—quite down-to-earth himself, with dark blond hair neatly kept in something almost like a crew cut, and a mode of dress that was simple. He wore a long-sleeved cotton shirt, jeans, and a tailored denim jacket.

The officer, a weary-looking, middle-aged man, glanced over at Zach and Skye as they arrived and quickly said, "You're the Feds, right? I've been trying to tell Mr. Howell just because he got here and found the place locked and his wife and son gone, they're not really missing. He just got here forty-five minutes ago—"

"Unlocked!" Howell interrupted, shaking his head.

"She might have stepped out quickly, decided to close early, and perhaps your daughter was . . . anxious about something, and your wife needed to get her home quickly or to the doc-tor—"

"I've checked every local hospital! I did so immediately after calling 911!" Howell said with aggravation. "And we never lock up this early!" Mr. Howell added adamantly, seri-ously agitated and wincing, trying to keep calm while getting law enforcement to take him seriously. "My wife would have called me if something was wrong—if she'd been able to do so!"

"Still—" the officer began.

"It's all right, sir. We've got this!" Skye quickly and politely told the officer. "We can take it from here," she added pleas-antly.

"Mr. Howell doesn't seem to understand that things do happen, and people do forget their phones. And it's most likely Mrs. Howell probably took the kid and went home and left her phone somewhere," the officer grumbled. "You are the Feds investigating the Salem case, right? Good, whatever, this is all yours!"

With a nod that offered gratitude, frustration, and bewilderment, he left them.

Zach looked over at Skye. At least local law enforcement didn't seem resentful; in fact, they seemed relieved, here at least, to have them around.

Howell appeared to be confused for a minute and then his eyes opened wide. "Feds! Right. Oh, my God, yes! Yes. Because that elderly Bolton man had been killed, and his great-grandson and the nanny have disappeared!"

That Bolton was dead, and that it was an accepted fact that something bad had happened to his great-grandson and the nanny, appeared to strike a hard chord within the man. "Oh, no, no, no . . ." he said with dismay.

Howell's voice trailed and he looked at them with sheer misery.

"Sir, if you can explain to us—" Zach began.

"Right. I'll start over. I'm Keith Howell. My wife and I own and manage this place. We cater to moviemakers, bloggers, you name it—people are always doing something here, paranormal shows, history shows, their social media sites . . . you name it. And, of course, Halloween is huge, and we cater to every kook and kid out there who likes dressing up. But we close at eight—every night, we close at eight. Our assistant manager is on alone for about an hour at three when my wife gets Sophie from school. At this time of the year—for just a few more days since we bring more people in as Halloween approaches—we are our only employees, except for Debbie Dailey—our assistant manager. We are a true mom-and-pop place, except for one employee—Debbie. She leaves at five, and I'm back here by five from my day job, so no other employee is here when we close. And honestly, we're still good parents. We have a little room in back with a bed, desk, and TV, all things for Sophie to rest, play, and do schoolwork between the time she gets off school and the time we go home. When I got back here today, no one was here. That was at just about six o'clock. The door was open, as it should be during business hours, but I searched through the entire place. No sign of anyone. Naturally, I called my wife, no answer, so I called Debbie, and she told me everything had been simply fine at five o'clock when she left, that Sophie had been doing her homework in the room; and before she'd left, she and Jane—my wife—had been talking about the fact we were happy, we've been doing great, and we were going to hire another salesperson full-time! That would mean more time off— we close on Mondays and Tuesdays now, except at Halloween, and we wouldn't need to close any day anymore with another employee and . . . and . . . what the hell does any of this matter! They're gone. My wife and child are gone! And I don't care what that idiot cop told me, my wife would never, never just leave the store with no one here, everything wide open! And my little girl . . . my beautiful, precious, smart little girl! Something awful has happened and I know it! He said that something could be done because Sophie is just six, but that Jane is an adult and can disappear when she chooses. She's not missing when it's only been a matter of hours since I've heard from her. They also said that I'm panicking unnecessarily— that my wife just lost her phone and that she's off somewhere with my little girl!"

"Security cameras?" Zach asked.

Keith Howell winced and shook his head. "This is not a high-crime area in any way, shape, or form. And we've been doing well, but getting a security company in here seemed like an expense we couldn't afford—we've only been open a couple of years—and we haven't gotten to it. Oh, my God, if I'd only . . ."

"We'll get a trace on your wife's phone and check the security cameras in the area," Skye assured him quickly and compassionately. "We need your help, and we believe if you help us, we can help you a great deal more. Now, this may sound strange, but do you sell wicked-witch costumes and green makeup?"

"We do. You'd be surprised. A wicked-witch costume is huge around here, though it doesn't really make much sense, but a lot of people don't know history. They just know that Salem is famous for historic witches and local wiccans. They think that it's funny or great to dress up as a wicked witch. Go figure."

"We need to see your sales receipts," Skye told him.

He frowned. "You think someone bought—or stole—a costume before they kidnapped my wife and child?" he asked.

"Possibly. Or stole something in the past. At the least, we'll see who was in the shop last," Zach told him. He wanted to be reassuring.

Maybe they could be—although it would have been one hell of a help if they'd had security cameras.

He wasn't so sure his "talent" would be helpful here; dozens of people had probably touched most of the things in the shop.

However, Skye . . .

Her abilities were amazing, so amazing . . .

He almost wondered at the wisdom utilized when he had been partnered with her. Then again, maybe her strengths could make up for . . .

His weaknesses? He hadn't seen himself as weak in a long time—not since he'd learned at a young age that he needed to be careful. And if he ever wanted to use the strange things he was able to know, he needed to be what people called "the strong, silent type." Like most of any of the people he'd met with their different abilities, they weren't often shared. People were quick to ridicule others or worse—accuse them of needing serious therapy.

But . . .

Right now? Being partnered with her was proving to be incredibly helpful on this case. He had to admit, he had been doubtful, but . . .

She was entirely credible. He was surprised to discover that he did believe what she said, what she saw . . .

And beyond that, she was simply bright and he had already found himself liking her far more than he had imagined he might.

They needed to see the register receipts.

And we need a way for her to try her unique sense of vision.

They could get going on the receipts, and he could distract Keith Howell and give Skye the opportunity to do her thing.

"Anything, anything!" Howell muttered, leading them toward the register. Zach could see that while the place might not have security cameras, the register was set to the left when facing the door.

Someone standing at it and staffing the register could easily see if someone was trying to walk out with merchandise without paying for it.

"They don't believe me. The police don't believe me," Howell told them. "I don't get what they don't understand. I know my wife! She would never leave the shop open and disappear. Something happened. Something bad! And . . . okay, we don't have cameras, but there is an alarm by the register. If Jane had been at the register when something happened, she could have hit the alarm. The police are close by; they can be here fast. Of course, a smart thief would be gone, but it's not like this is a major bank or anything. Someone just trying to pilfer a costume is unlikely to be a hardened criminal."

"We're going to find out what happened, Mr. Howell. We believe you, but I'm afraid this is going to take time," Skye said.

"I'll make a call and see to it that we have an alert out on your daughter," Zach told Howell as the proprietor went behind the counter and keyed in numbers on his computer that brought up the store's receipts. "I'll need a picture of your daughter—"

"I have one of Sophie with my wife—a good picture," Howell said.

"I'll take that, perfect," Zach murmured. He'd get it to the right people; they'd make sure it was sent out everywhere.

As he managed notifications for alerts to go out with the news and on signs on nearby highways and wherever else possible, Skye started on the receipts.

They had a chance to glance at one another. He gave her a slight nod; she returned it. A minute later, he found an excuse to get Keith Howell to show him to the back so he could see the little room where Sophie went after school, did her homework, played until it was time to close the store, and head home for the night.

"We're alone up here on a day-to-day basis," Howell explained, as if he needed an excuse for the fact that his child came to work with them so often. "Jane's folks are gone. My mom is still with us, but she's in Boston. She'll come on out for a few weeks here and there—especially at Halloween. This is a great place; we have plenty of friends, good friends, but we rely on one another and—"

"Mr. Howell, this is a great little place; and I can see that you really take a lot of care that Sophie is with you and has everything she needs," he said. He wasn't lying. Sophie had her television, a desk, shelves filled with books, crayons, paints, coloring books, and more, along with a giant dollhouse and a trunk filled with toys.

Zach could only imagine what her room in her home looked like.

"I guess it's weird, too, that a kid spends so much time with . . . monster mannequins and so on. But we've been big on telling her the difference between imagination and pretend monsters—and real monsters, animals that can hurt her—including people. She meets people all the time. She's cheerful and loving; but, of course, even in Swampscott, we've given her lessons that she knows to be really important when it comes to stranger danger."

"Honestly, as I said, I'm sure you and your wife are great parents," Zach told him. "This is an incredible hideaway for your little girl. But you said when you talked to your assistant manager, Debbie, she said that Sophie had been back here when she left?"

"Yes. But there was an hour between her leaving and my arriving," Howell told him. "Do we need to get back out there—"

"Everything that can be done is being done," Zach said calmly. "I've got someone checking the closest cameras. Pictures of Sophie will be going up all over, and someone will have seen something."

He believed he had given Skye the time she needed. He paused just a minute longer, looking around Sophie's little "work" room.

He needed something. In his current state, he didn't think Howell would be willing to hand over something his daughter loved, a toy of some kind. But maybe . . .

In a pretense of walking around the room, he paused looking at a picture over her little desk. There was a little stuffed zebra on her desk.

He slid it into his pocket, glad that Howell was too distraught to notice.

Then turned back to Keith Howell. "I want to get back to the register to help my partner go through the receipts. If we have names on purchases for those costumes, for green paint . . ."

"You may have a place to start?" Howell asked, bewildered. "What makes you think they might have dressed up with wicked-witch paraphernalia?" Howell asked anxiously. "And green . . ."

No way to answer with the truth.

"There was something online that suggested such a thing—disappeared right away, but it gave us an idea of *which* way to look," Zach lied.

They headed out to the register. Skye appeared to be carefully studying the computer and the sales records. She glanced up.

Strange. She didn't even need to nod anymore; he could read her eyes.

Yes, she had seen something. Enough? Probably not, but they were grasping at straws; women and children were missing.

"Find anything?" he asked.

"Seven bottles of Evergreen Green in the last four weeks," Skye said. "Only one corresponds to a purchase of the Which Witch Is Which costume, and that was three weeks ago. And the purchases were made with cash."

"Of course," Zach mumbled. Well, they'd lied to Howell. Maybe it was time to lie to backup law enforcement as well.

He turned to Keith Howell. "Sir, I know that this is going to be impossible for you, but you need to go home and try to get some rest."

"Rest!" the man said incredulously. "My wife and kid—"

"Someone may try to reach you at your house. We'll see that an officer is sent out there, too. But again, someone may contact you wanting a ransom, trying to get you to exchange something for your family. And while—"

"I need to be looking for them!" Howell protested.

"Sir, you want to help. Being at your home will be the biggest help. Getting dozens of officers out looking for them will be the best way to possibly bring them home." Zach had his phone out.

He could call the detectives on the Bolton case, but he decided he wanted to call Jackson first and let him know what was going on—that another woman and another child had been kidnapped.

He didn't reach Jackson; he did reach Angela. He learned Jackson was already being briefed on the situation in the DC area, but Angela assured Zach she'd get people out as quickly as possible from the Boston area, and she'd smooth the way through with the local police as well.

When he finished the call, he saw Skye had been speaking quietly with Keith Howell; and she'd gotten him to understand he'd be the best possible help by going home. As he listened, Zach felt his phone vibrate in his pocket; he pulled it out. An officer would be there momentarily to escort Howell home.

He and Skye needed to come into headquarters. Detectives Cason and Berkley had been ordered to get sleep, but the police needed a task force meeting *now* so that they'd be brought up to speed on developments in the morning.

Howell locked up the shop, and an officer arrived to follow him home and stay with him through the night.

When they were finally in the car alone together, Zach could ask Skye just what she had seen.

"A cape," she began.

"So, not a wicked-witch costume—"

She turned to him, shaking her head. "A single person arrived wearing a long brown hooded cape. But they were green and wearing the witch costume beneath the cape. Again they had a gun. Jane Howell was forced to get her daughter, then forced to wear the cape. Zach, the poor woman was terrified. The person dressed as the witch beneath the cape told her in no uncertain terms her child would be shot through the eyes if she didn't obey everything said. The mother was great with her little girl; she made her think they were just going off on an adventure. The witch took another cape from a costume rack so even if there are cameras somewhere near the shop, all they'll have picked up are two figures in capes and a little girl hugging a teddy bear—holding hands with the one figure and smiling."

"Okay, but we know that, again, someone has decided that dressing up as a wicked witch is the way to go. And we know that person is wielding a gun, choosing victims who are good people with no knowledge of how to defend themselves. Whoever it is, they're from here. They knew the Bolton family's schedule—and they knew when Jane Howell and her daughter would be here alone, when the shop was the least busy, and that there were no guns hidden by the cash register."

"Great. We're looking for a local," she said wearily, leaning back. "Definitely."

He didn't answer at first.

"Does it . . ." he began.

"What?" Skye demanded.

"Does it wear you out when you try to see the past, especially when . . . well, there are hundreds of years to go through. I imagine that . . ."

She smiled, her head back on the seat, her eyes closed.

"I don't know, of course. So far, there's been no way to study this phenomenon. Still, I can't help but wonder if sometimes it's a matter of residual energy—usually the last surge of energy, and sometimes, maybe, the strongest surge of energy. There are many articles regarding people—and paranormal groups—being at Gettysburg and there are certain places there where people may not see the past, but they feel it or claim to feel it—or it's really there."

He glanced at her. "That must be painful for you."

"I've been there; now, I avoid Gettysburg!" she said.

"So it is painful."

She grimaced. "So much agony, anguish, and death," she

said. "And yes, it can be painful. When something is needed, I'm . . . It sounds weird, but the pain is worth it when it can give me something that helps someone. Then the good feeling is incredible, too. But . . . I can't change the past. I can only use what I learn from it to help in the present or the future."

"Of course," he murmured.

She turned to look at him. "What about you? When you hold something and see what you see? Does it hurt? Is it exhausting?"

"Nothing like what you go through," he told her. He tried to smile lightly. "As you said, I don't run around trying to touch things that have a horrible past—unless it can do something to help in the present, or as you said in the future."

"You didn't get anything from the shop?"

He shook his head. "That wasn't the kind of place where . . . Okay, too many people handled too many things, if that makes sense."

"Of course!"

"But . . ."

"But?"

He produced the zebra.

"Cute. And?"

"I couldn't do anything with Howell there and"—he paused, wincing—"I didn't ask Howell if I could take it. Of course, I'll return it! But . . ."

"So, did you get anything yet?"

"I may get more when I have time to keep holding it. Right now, I know she wasn't afraid; her mother kept her from being afraid."

"I guess every little mercy needs to be appreciated!" Skye said.

It wasn't much of a drive to reach the headquarters. When they were there, they discovered that a crew of officers, state and local police, and extra agents from the Boston area had been gathered by the man who had seen to it that Jackson brought people in; they were all to be part of a task force and/ or at least aware of what they were looking for.

They met with Lieutenant Gavin Bruns first.

He was, as she had expected, a serious man with cleanly cut dark hair and a professional demeanor that was tempered by a warmth beneath as he greeted them. She was certain as they spoke that he had a deep empathy for victims. He didn't dig when Skye said they'd seen something online that had almost instantly disappeared, someone claiming they'd witnessed a green witch with a pointed hat head toward the Bolton house.

He was a friend of Jackson's. Maybe he had learned he just needed to let Jackson and his people go—accept the good without question.

Zach didn't know what had happened in Salem before; but whatever had gone down, Bruns had been impressed. He didn't appear to want to pry or feel any need to pursue the why behind their explanation of what they believed had happened.

He just wanted them to talk to the assembly of law enforcement officers they had gathered.

They needed to warn the force that was being sent out to find the victims. And they wanted to make sure that those who would be working their regular beats needed to be aware of what they should be looking for.

Bruns, recently given a promotion, was managing a few cases; he had sent Detectives Cason and Berkley home. No one could work efficiently when they'd gone too many hours without sleep. The next morning, as soon as they reported in, the two partners would learn what they needed to be doing, and looking for.

"And you two! After this meeting, you're going to let other officers and agents work through the night. I promise you, we will be looking for these women and children. But you also need to get to your rooms and get some sleep. *No one* works well when they are so exhausted that they are about to keel over. Not even Feds," he said, offering a smile and a dry shot at humor.

They were ready for the meeting.

After having met with Bruns, they both were disappointed he wasn't going to be working with them, but he was, of course, just a phone call away at any time they might need him. He brought them out to introduce them to the squad, to many of those who would be handling any tech on the case.

"I must admit, I haven't had much time with them or any time. They've been in the field, and I've been stuck behind a desk," Bruns told the pair. "But you're introduced, take it away with these folks."

Skye gave Zach a nod, and he knew she wanted him to do the talking.

It was going to be easier for him to lie, he figured.

Because there was no choice. They had to make use of lies. Easier was his only choice.

Zach did his best, first telling the assembled law enforcement what was simple fact, then telling them that the rather ridiculous possibility of someone dressing up as a witch to carry off the crimes appeared to be what was happening. The second place hit had been the costume shop, where there was evidence that someone, paying cash, had purchased both the makeup and the costume.

Some of the team apparently thought the idea of such a thing was still theory; others believed if they could find a suspect who was holding on to the costume paraphernalia, they might well have a case against them.

The meeting was over, and officers in Salem and surrounding areas would be on the search through the night for the kidnapping victims.

While neither Skye nor Zach believed Fin was involved, a search warrant would be issued so his tiny studio and his car could be searched.

Then . . .

Then there was no choice. They were being asked to get sleep.

They'd been set up at a small nineteenth-century home near Salem Common. It was close to the station; but as they settled into the car, Skye closed her eyes again, and it appeared she was almost wincing.

"Are you all right?" he asked her. "Sorry—I do keep asking that. It's just that I was pretty worthless today, and I guess it took a greater toll on you."

"I am fine, just tired, and historic witch trials—and a green witch. Human beings . . . we're capable of being so ridiculous!"

"Beyond a doubt. Beyond a doubt. Human—and then inhumane. But . . . while things were bad here, did you know that werewolf trials took place in Europe in the fifteenth, sixteenth, and seventeenth centuries?" Zach asked her.

"Trials—for someone being a *werewolf*?" Skye asked. "I must admit, that never came up in any of my history classes."

He nodded grimly. "I know of one that was . . . horrific. In Germany, 1589, Peter Stumpp. He was tied to the large wheel of a cart, his skin was removed with hot pinchers, and his head was cut off before his body was burned on a pyre and then the head was put on a wooden pole designed to look like the body of a wolf—you know, warning to other werewolves. Of course, after some pretty extreme torture, he admitted to being a werewolf, eating sheep, goats, and, naturally, women and children. Was he a killer? Who knows—but his mistress and daughter were killed alongside him, a bit more mercifully strangled before they were burned on the pyre."

Skye winced. "I knew, of course, about the witchcraft trials in Europe—and Asia, and all over the world just about. It's estimated that somewhere between sixty thousand and maybe even two hundred thousand people were persecuted and executed. When you're looking back at something like the Peter Stumpp situation, maybe he was a criminal, if not a werewolf, or maybe his neighbors just wanted revenge for some wrong or slight."

"The world never really changes," Zach said. "People will always believe what they want to believe. Indoctrinated and brainwashed sometimes, perhaps by a community in which they live or grow up, maybe forced into belief sometimes, but . . ." Zach paused, shrugging. "But these days? Someone believing in a green witch with a black pointy hat—I'm not seeing it. The gun this person is wielding is doing all the talking."

"But what then?" Skye wondered. "What is the end game? There haven't been any ransom calls. And thankfully, I mean, the bodies of the kidnapped women and children have not been found, which—very hopefully—means the missing women and children are still alive. So, are we going on the concept they are alive? Then where are they being kept and why?"

"That's why a task force is going to be so important. And every officer out there knowing that they're looking for a green person in a witch costume . . . everything that you saw today is really going to help, Skye!"

She smiled at that, leaning back again.

"I have a feeling," she said.

"A paranormal feeling?" he asked lightly.

That drew a smile. "No, just that gut law enforcement feeling thing," she told him. "Tomorrow . . . tomorrow we're going to find something—and you're going to be the most helpful!"

He smiled. And as they did so, he saw the little house that had been rented for them just down the street. "Ah, parking!" he murmured. "Magic! There's a space almost right in front of the place."

They headed on in. Zach had arrived first that morning; he'd set his computer up on the dining-room table.

He saw she had done the same thing when she'd arrived.

When Jackson Crow sent agents out, it appeared that he did so carefully. The house was small; it offered just two bedrooms upstairs, the kitchen, dining room, and parlor downstairs.

Of course, the dining room as a work area made sense— there was really nothing else.

"Scotland," Skye said suddenly.

He turned and arched a brow to her. "Scotland?"

"James VI of Scotland, who also became James I of England," Skye murmured.

"I think he's been dead awhile," Zach noted.

"Right. But he was one of those people—one with great power—who became obsessed with the idea that witches and witchcraft were real and evil. He wrote a dissertation called *Daemonologie,* which was published in 1597—ironically, several years before the King James version of the Bible. The man had been married by proxy to Anne of Denmark, and a fierce storm almost killed her when she was on her way to Scotland via ship. James went to Norway—part of the Danish empire at the time—to retrieve her himself. They spent a bit of time in Copenhagen and then Oslo and boarded a ship to head back to Scotland.

"Once again, a storm swept up. James had always been paranoid about people wanting to kill him—possibly since his mother, Mary, Queen of Scots, had been beheaded. Who knows? But people—mainly women—were accused of causing the storms in the Danish empire. And, of course, it's always amazing what people will admit to under torture. Someone confessed, others confessed . . . and it all started up all over again in Scotland. Not that witch trials hadn't existed there before, but beneath James's kingship . . . it all went a little crazy, and thousands were burned at the stake."

"We've been aware that history is—" Zach began.

"Tragic!" Skye finished, shaking her head. She looked at

him. "It makes it all the more perplexing! What the heck is going on? Who would dress up as a wicked witch in Salem to commit a murder and kidnap women and children?"

Zach grimly studied her. "The *who* is what we must find out. And the *why* . . . well, that's probably going to be really crazy, but—"

"*But! Again!* Maybe finding out the *why* will give us the *who,*" Skye cut in.

"And I have the strangest feeling . . ."

"Feeling?" she queried.

"Just a feeling," he said, grinning. "A feeling that it's just not going to be what we're expecting at all. Anyway, the little zebra and I are going to bed. Maybe holding it in the darkness, I'll get a few visions of my own."

CHAPTER 4

It had felt later than it was the night before.

But it had been one hell of a long day. An odd one, being picked up in the airport to fly to Boston on the Krewe's dedicated private jet—nice, of course, as far as flying went, but a little nerve-wracking, starting what Jackson was seeing as a new unit and not having any idea of how everything would go.

No different. It was still a human being doing horrible things to others and needing to be apprehended. And scary—but exciting, too. Working with someone with whom she could speak honestly!

And . . .

He wasn't bad! Zach Erickson was proving to be an excellent partner. Of course, they had only been partnered for a day, but it had been one long day. Easy enough when they'd arrived at their little rental; he'd taken the toy zebra and gone to bed, and she'd headed in.

She awoke at six and immediately checked her messages.

No new developments had occurred during the night. Patricia Yale, Jeremy Bolton, and Jane and Sophie Howell remained among the missing. Traffic cams had been studied anew by sharp eyes back at Krewe headquarters. Anything near the Bolton house or the costume house had been studied, and while there had been nothing that stood out, the results were now readily available on their computers. Since they were on the site, they might notice something that others—no matter how good— might not.

Even though it was early in the morning, Skye dressed and explored the kitchen; she was sure it had been stocked for their usage.

And it had been.

First, she discovered that when she'd departed to her bedroom last night, Zach had apparently come back out and prepared the coffeemaker. All she had to do was push the button.

She found eggs, bread for toast, cheese, vegetables, all kinds of things for an omelet.

She wondered about her partner. They parted for their separate rooms almost immediately upon their arrival. But it would only be polite if she was making an omelet for herself, to make one for him, too, and, well . . .

She could just hope he didn't hate eggs. There were so many things that partners learned about one another, but it took time.

If she was making omelets, yes, of course, she'd make one for him, too.

Why not? She'd been taught as a child not to waste, but she'd seen a few stray cats roaming the area. Surely, if Zach didn't want an omelet, a cat would be thrilled to have one!

Ah, but did he have any allergies?

Whatever!

She decided to add cheese, tomatoes, bell peppers, and a few onion bits to her mix. As she was working, he made an appearance, dressed and ready to go for the day, she assumed. Except he wasn't wearing a pristine business suit, but rather appeared to be dressed for hiking.

"Food!" he said appreciatively as he saw her working at the stove. "I know that brunch is when you mix breakfast and lunch, but yesterday we had to mix lunch and dinner. Not sure what you call that, and we had to leave before dessert."

"Well, I hope you like omelets," she said.

"I'm grateful that you concocted food for us both. Oh, and I promise, I can cook, too. I'm best with a grill, but not horrible when it comes to a few other things," he assured her.

She smiled. "Hey, they even left us paper plates. I'm honestly not into being wasteful, but let's go that route this morning so that we don't spend too much time picking up! Oh, and thanks. Button pushed on the coffee—should be brewed!"

"It all works for me. I'll get the plates—and how do you take your coffee?" he asked.

"Depends on when and where. In a pinch, black. When it's easy enough, a little cream, milk, or white stuff."

Zach opened the refrigerator and laughed. "You have a choice again—milk, cream, vanilla cream."

"Vanilla cream."

He poured cups of coffee, while she spooned out the omelets, and they were quickly seated, eating.

She was glad she'd gone pretty big on the omelet; he was hungry. But then, of course, he was a tall man with broad shoulders and, she assumed, made mainly of muscle.

"Delicious, and thank you, thank you so much," he assured her.

She smiled, taking a sip of coffee and saying, "Nothing new overnight?"

"And that's why I'm wearing jeans."

She arched a brow to him.

He let out a sigh. "Okay, it's possible that our wicked witch had a hideout somewhere in town, on the outskirts . . . or even in a neighboring town. The costume-slash-monster shop is geographically in the town of Swampscott. But there was something about the Bolton house."

"You mean that the rear of the house joins up with the forest?"

He nodded.

She pondered his words. "The only thing is . . . well, okay. Let's think about the area. There are incredible tours to go on here that are given by historians. Then people go to see places like the Rebecca Nurse Homestead, and, of course, the Witch House, the one building still standing that is directly associated with the trials, the old home of Judge Corwin, a man directly responsible for the first executions. But—"

"Don't *judge* him too harshly," Zach said sarcastically. "He was a product of his time."

She nodded and said, "The point I'm making is that along with all the historical things you can do, people love the area for hiking! Salem Woods has dozens of trails for people of all levels of ability and—"

"You're thinking that it would be difficult for someone to really disappear into a forest."

"I am."

He was thoughtful for a minute. "Difficult, maybe. But not impossible—again, especially, for someone from this area—someone who knows the landscape and surrounding areas very well."

"So, do you want to go running around in the forest?" she asked. "Do you know these forests?" She smiled. "Of course, I read the company info on you. You were born in Harpers Ferry, West Virginia, moved to Boston, brilliant kid, but you chose the military, and then you got a degree in criminology from the University of Miami—"

He laughed. "Hey, the military paid for the degree!"

"Well, since you survived it all, good planning. I just didn't see anything in your general bio that suggests that you're great at running around in forests."

"You didn't notice that Harpers Ferry kind of borders the Blue Ridge Mountains?" he asked lightly.

She arched a brow. "Harpers Ferry. Another place where

history, epic events, and certainly tragedies have taken place. You follow it around—or it follows you around. And the Blue Ridge, true! Lots of forests there! Places to trek. I'm sorry! I didn't mean—"

He laughed, interrupting her. "To be honest, I didn't trek the Blue Ridge all that often. Though, of course, I do appreciate the incredible natural beauty to be found there—and Massachusetts, too. But I did all my trekking in a slightly different way." He paused, looking at her, then shrugged and told her. "I had a great professor at the university. He taught forensics techniques, and he was fascinated with the psychology of criminals, which wasn't really part of his classroom agenda, just something he liked to ponder. He had worked for the Bureau for several years before retiring to teach, so he was able to rely on dozens of friends to come in and talk to us. Professor Adams was great! He never thought he knew everything and always invited in whoever he could when he believed that person to be way more experienced than himself in aspects of law enforcement. I 'trekked' through school. Adams taught us all so much."

"And in his teaching . . . did he give you something you can use here?" Skye asked.

"Well, you can never be sure, until you do have the truth—the whole truth and nothing but the truth, if you ever do—but I have a few impressions because of him. Our boyfriend Fin is innocent. And Mr. Howell is right—his wife never would have left willingly without calling him. And someone threatened her daughter. That's why she went with the witch-kidnapper."

"Right," Skye murmured.

"You didn't ask if the zebra and I had a good night," he told her. "I can be kind of useful, you know."

She lowered her head, wincing at that. "I never suggested—"

"It's dark," he told her.

"Dark?"

"Wherever little Sophie is being held now, it's dark. And she wasn't afraid with her mother, but she is afraid now."

"Do you know if there is something or someone specific frightening her?" Skye asked. "Well, other than being held by kidnappers."

"That's why we're going hiking. I think she's being held somewhere that's very dark at night. I'm thinking she's in the woods. We know that there are areas around here where the forests are dense—where rangers never tread. When I held the zebra and concentrated on it last night . . . I saw darkness. And I felt her fear. She wasn't being harmed, and she is alive. That part is good—very, very good." He hesitated. "At some point, I need to get back into the Bolton house. I want to take something that belonged to little Jeremy, put it with the zebra, and see what happens. Maybe we'll see Fin again, too, before tonight and see if he has something that belongs to Patricia or go by and talk to her roommates." He paused, frowning. "That's something we need to do, anyway; find out if someone has been talking to them, if anyone threatened Patricia, or if there's anything they might tell us at all that could help."

"Dark, hm," Sky said, wincing. "Look, I'm not doubting you in any way, but dark could be just about anywhere at night. I mean, people turn lights out."

"Crickets."

"What?"

He grinned. "She hears crickets chirping and other insects, I imagine. She hears the quiet chirp sound of something, anyway. And . . ." Zach paused again, looking reflective.

"What?"

He shrugged. "It seems that we more than 'see' here. It's as if you get a sense of more, of the true darkness, of sounds, of scents . . . She is smelling trees and grass, and sure, there are trees and grass everywhere, but I sincerely doubt they've been abducted to be held on Salem Common," he said acerbically.

"Haha," Skye told him. "Okay, I agree on that. But there is so much forest around here, Zach. Where—"

"By the Bolton house," he said. "Two birds with one stone, as they say. I can pick up something that belongs to little Jeremy, and we can see if we can find anything that suggests they may have just been taken through the woods."

Skye nodded slowly. "I might even add to your theory," she told him.

"Oh?"

"Well, local people, our people—in other words, a ton of people—have studied traffic cams, and they haven't come up with anyone *green* running around. You can doff a hat easily enough, but you probably need some major work to get rid of the green on one's flesh, unless it was a green mask, but I don't think so. To get into the Bolton house without being seen, it might have been possible for someone to just slip from the woods into the house. Then again, what about the costume shop? There aren't any easily accessible woods around that shop, so . . ."

"Sometimes you need to go with the flow. If they didn't need to drive, maybe they didn't. When it was necessary to drive— they drove?" Zach theorized in a question.

"Okay, well, we can get started. Paper in the trash and—"

"Where are the pans, cooking utensils?" he asked.

"I wash as I go—saves having to deal with a mess later," she told him.

"Wow," he said lightly. "You do have some amazingly commendable habits," he told her.

She shrugged. "I'm ever so glad you think so!"

He laughed softly. "Hey, in our line of work . . . Ready?"

"Two seconds! I need boots—I didn't know I was going to go trampling through the woods!" she told him.

He laughed. "Sorry!"

"Not a problem. I like the woods."

"Better in the daylight," he murmured. "I don't know . . . I'm just desperately hoping that we can find something."

"Right! On it."

Skye hurried to her room. She decided to change her whole outfit, no businesslike pantsuit that day. She changed quickly into jeans, a knit top, and threw on a just-in-case lightweight jacket, and then slid her feet into boots. So dressed, she ran back downstairs to meet him.

"Wow!" he told her again. "Commendable time changing, and commendable outfit."

"Wow, yourself!" she told him. "I'll remember to put that on my next résumé. 'Commendable.'"

He laughed, then winced and grimaced at her. "Much better than 'apeshit crazy,' don't you think?"

She just groaned and headed out the door.

He followed her, laughing softly. "Hey!" he called, pausing to lock up with the code they'd been given. "'Commendable' isn't so bad!"

She just grinned and shook her head.

CHAPTER 5

"'Commendable'!" Skye repeated. She glanced at him before opening the door to get into the car.

When they were seated, she told him, "'Brilliant,' 'remarkable'—so much better!"

"Glad you like me," he told her, grinning as he revved the car to life.

She groaned again.

But Zach looked down for a minute, becoming serious and sighing. "We'll need to stop back by police headquarters for a minute. We'll need the keys to get into the Bolton house. And that means I'll need to come up with an explanation—"

"Not with Lieutenant Bruns," she assured him.

"Do you know what happened?" Zach asked, frowning.

"What happened?" Skye repeated. "Oh! You mean why does Bruns have such faith in Jackson? I think they've helped a few times up here. In fact, I heard about one case that occurred about ten years ago now, I believe. Craig Rockwell, aka 'Rocky,' and Devin Lyle were involved. Agents I've worked with. She has a home up here, I believe, inherited from a grandmother. I don't know the particulars." She made a face at him. "Hey, I'm just as new with all this as you are."

"Maybe Jackson should have sent Rocky—"

"He's working something in another city—already on that case," Skye told him.

He laughed softly. "Well, you know more than me."

"Maybe he thought that . . . Well, he calls me a 'mystic.' Maybe he thinks our talents are more useful working on this case, too," she suggested.

He glanced at her quickly and almost smiled. "Well, here's hoping!"

As Skye had expected, they were quickly able to find Lieutenant Bruns and he didn't ask questions. He gave them the keys for the Bolton house, simply reminding them to lock up when they left and see that the crime scene tape, though ripped, remained.

"We haven't kept officers on the house," he told them. "There's no one in it, and we don't believe there's any danger to the house."

"No danger to the house," Zach repeated. "But . . ."

"Go on," Bruns told him.

"A child has been kidnapped. And it seems whoever is doing this is after children—and women. Young women, like Patricia, and Jane Howell is comparatively young as well, in her late twenties. But with a child, well, the kidnapper may need things."

"So you believe they're all still alive!" Bruns said.

"We do," Skye told him with certainty.

"All right. I will see that officers are assigned to keep an eye on the house," Bruns promised solemnly. "And the keys—"

"Will be personally handed back to you this evening," Zach promised.

Then they were out of the headquarters and on their way out to the Bolton house.

"You have the little zebra?" Skye asked him.

He nodded. "Of course. But it isn't going to hurt to have

something that belongs to Jeremy Bolton, too. See if they are together and if he sees the same things that Sophie is seeing."

"As you said. Of course."

Zach drove onto the property and started to exit the car. He looked at Skye and said, "I'll be right out. Stay!" He opened his car door and headed for the door, calling back, "You don't need to go through it all again. I'll be quick!"

"Hey! I'm not a dog. Don't tell me to stay! I'm fine," she assured him.

"Just wait for me!" he pleaded.

He moved like the speed of light. She'd barely gotten out of the car and made it to the front door before he was out.

He was carrying a toy superhero doll.

"It's Jeremy's!" he assured her.

"You don't think an eleven-month-old baby might like a superhero, huh?" she inquired, deadpan, looking at him. "Zach, don't go trying to protect me! We'll never make it as partners if you do that!"

"I'm not protecting you. I understand that when bullets are flying, you're just about a sharpshooter. I just can't see sending you flying back into the past, when you don't need to be there—not when it's a painful past," he told her.

"I . . . I'm all right going in places!" she argued.

"Really? So you had a vision of Salem in the 1600s just by being here, but—"

"Things like this, I sit down, I concentrate!" she told him. "But—"

"But . . . please let's not argue. Sorry. We both have a lot to learn about each other. For now, I think we need to get into the woods."

She winced. "*Into the Woods*—great show on Broadway!" she told him.

He groaned and started toward the back.

"We move quietly and together," he said.

"Of course. But I'm willing to bet that they are deep, deep into the woods. So deep that the average hiker or bird-watcher would never go that far."

"Exactly. And we're back to the *why*," he said.

"Why steal children and young women and go deep into the woods? Zach, sorry, you're really sure that they're still alive, right?" Skye asked. They had passed the in-law building where Mike Bolton had lived—and died. They entered into something that vaguely resembled a trail at the far rear of the property.

"Why?" Zach repeated as they walked. "We need the *why*. More so than ever."

"You've gotten something from the superhero?" she asked.

"Enough to know that he's alive—and Patricia is still with him. He trusts her; she's telling him he'll see his folks soon, and everything will be all right. Sophie is with her mother, and she's scared when it's dark, but in the day . . . she is just confused. But I'm right on one thing—they're in the woods. Neither kid can figure out what they're doing in the woods. I keep hearing the word 'master' go through their minds; someone out there is telling them that they're the master. Or a master, and they're supposed to look at the grass and the trees . . ."

He stopped speaking, stopped moving, and frowned, and looked away as if confused.

"Well, I'm not you, I don't see the past." He frowned.

"Zach! I'm not a mind reader! What's going on?" Skye demanded. She had almost plowed into his back when he had stopped. She stood, watching him. "Zach!" she pressed. "Please! What?"

" 'Beware the devil in the darkness.' "

Skye stared at him; he looked at her. "They're being told the devil may lurk in the forest! To watch out because the devil comes in the darkness!"

"This is crazier and crazier," Skye said. "Someone dressed up in a wicked-witch costume is preaching to kids as if they were back in 1692?"

Zach shook his head. "Infinitely crazy, yes. So . . ."

"Well, I guess we can appreciate the trees and the grass and the bushes that are catching at my clothing and the stones that jab up into my feet," Skye said.

She started to walk again.

There were areas here—as there really were in so many beautiful places around the country—where it seemed that the trees, the forest, stretched on forever and ever. She thought about driving on I-75 through the south of Georgia and into the northern realms of Florida. Sometimes it could seem that the trees and brush were endless.

Even in a car!

But they were on foot.

And already it seemed the back of the Bolton house had disappeared!

This was Salem, Massachusetts. A smaller city surrounded by other smaller cities. The forest could not stretch on forever.

Maybe it was the denseness of it. She didn't think that even she would be particularly happy here at night, especially if there was no moon and the stars had disappeared into the heavens.

Zach, of course, was right behind her. She wondered if she should take the little superhero doll and the stuffed zebra away from him.

He was feeling too much.

Of course, she smiled inwardly, he hadn't wanted her to relive something awful, over and over again.

She didn't want the children's pain filling his heart and soul so much so that it was all he felt!

"Ah, come on!" he said lightly. "The forests are something

that we human beings need to appreciate and preserve. They take the bad stuff we put in the air and more or less recycle it so that we can keep breathing," he reminded her.

"Science 101," she said.

He laughed. "Something like that."

"I do like forests. I think they're beautiful," she said. "I just like them when . . . well, when I know where I am!"

"Salem, Massachusetts," he assured her.

She groaned and kept walking.

"How do you know we're going the right way?" she asked.

"Branches."

"You can read branches now?"

He laughed. "You can see that people have used this trail—"

"Trail!"

"Well, kind of a trail," he told her.

"We look for the broken branches?" she suggested. "And you, of course, know where we're going."

"No, not at all. I just know that someone else has been here recently. And that this almost-trail, if you will, was created by someone walking through here recently," he told her.

"But you know how to get out of here?" Skye asked.

"East, west, north, and south," he told her. "Head back to the west, and we'll wind up in something like civilization again. Warbler!"

"What?" Skye asked. "Warbler—a bird?"

He nodded. "In the trees. They're together—Patricia and Jeremy and Mrs. Howell and little Sophie. They're outside . . . with others. There are some other kids there . . . and someone is talking," Zach said. "They're all listening. Not happily. The kids look . . . uncomfortable. Scared. There's a little girl who apparently had some kind of a fit—and she's been made to stare at a tree, standing right in front of it . . . facing it, of course."

"But who is it that the kids are watching?" Skye asked.

He looked at her, shaking his head. "The wicked witch," he told her.

Skye let out a sound of extreme aggravation. "A green wicked witch is running around—and we can't find him. Or her!"

Zach gave himself a shake, clearing his head of the images he was seeing through the eyes of the children.

"This person is careful, so very careful. He or she doesn't want their identity known by anyone. Oh, there are other children there . . . three of them. And this one will get you—a young man, maybe a teenager, at most about twenty or so."

"Others have been kidnapped, too?" she asked.

"I imagine that's the case. I'm going to call in to Angela and have her find out who might be missing from surrounding areas, maybe down to Boston or beyond," he said.

Skye was silent for a minute. She heard a bird cry, and she looked at Zach. "Warbler," she murmured.

"These woods are full of them. Along with bobcats, moose, and more," Zach said.

"Great. Nothing like running into a bobcat."

He laughed softly. "You leave it alone—and most likely, it will leave you alone."

"Most likely."

"Hey, if a moose charges, hop up a tree as quickly as you can," Zach said. "I hate to kill wildlife, but we are armed if we come upon creature trouble."

"I hate to kill anything, but I'm extremely fond of living!" Skye assured him.

He paused. "Want to take a second and . . . see what you can see?" he asked.

She nodded. "Sure."

And so, they stood very still. She could hear the birds, letting out their chittering, a cry now and then. She could smell

the richness of the earth, feel the breeze, even the gentle movement of the branches of the trees and the brush as they moved
with the soft wind in the air.

And then people!

*Children moving along the trail. A young woman . . . Patricia
Yale . . . sobbing softly.*

And then . . .

*The wicked witch. The green being wielding a gun rather
than any kind of magic!*

"Skye?"

She looked over at Zach, wincing. "You were right," she
told him. "They came this way."

"All right, then. We keep moving," he said.

"Okay, wouldn't it make a lot more sense for us to get more
people out here, searching?" she asked.

"Skye, come on! We need to find something, anything, that
will give us some proof. There's no way the local law enforcement will send an army slushing through the forest if we don't
have something to give them," Zach reminded her.

"Maybe Jackson—"

"Jackson and Angela had to go back themselves. As many
Krewe agents as there are, they're out across the country and
beyond," Zach said. "Give me a minute and I'll put through a
call."

She watched and listened as he did so, somewhat surprised
he could get a connection from where they were. Neither Angela nor Jackson was there, but he spoke to one of their tech
experts who would do a search for them.

"That's done," Zach told her.

"Okay, so we wander in the deep woods a while longer.
We'll find . . . something!" she said. "But what do you think we're
going to find? I'm not sure they'll go for broken branches—or
me telling them I saw the recent past, and they were walking
this way."

"Kids. One of them may have dropped something," Zach said.

"Right. Good call. Let's keep moving."

"Up the hill," Zach said softly. And he paused. "Look!"

It wasn't a clue. It was a moose. Huge and beautiful, standing in a clearing amid a copse of trees and brush.

The animal was beautiful and majestic. And huge.

"Great. We don't want to mess with him, right?" Skye asked.

"No. But he'll move on."

"What's next? An angry bobcat?" Skye muttered.

"Hey, that moose is just standing there. Doing what a moose does. He'll move in a minute, and it will take us longer than that to walk the distance."

Birds kept chirping. The redolent smell of the earth was rich and it was true that the forest could be beautiful, that a walk here . . .

Might have been pleasant.

If it wasn't such an urgent mission they were on.

Something rustled through the bushes ahead of Skye, and she stopped dead.

"It's okay. Just a rabbit," Zach said.

"Right. Okay, so birds, a rabbit, and a moose. Let me think. Black bears, possums, shrews, moles—"

"Don't forget bats," Zach said, grinning.

"At least, it isn't night!" she snapped.

And then she was sorry. His face darkened.

"I'm sorry, I mean, I've been in woods, but I'm more of a city girl," she said.

"No, no, it's all right. I was just thinking about the kids. About them being so frightened when it's night. About . . . about them being told the devil could get them in the night, and the devil could make them do things," he said.

"Coyotes, wolves, and foxes," Skye murmured.

He shook his head. "Whoever is doing this knows North-eastern forests like the back of his—or her—hand. I don't think the captives are in danger from nature or from the forest animals. They are in danger from an animal—man. The only creature I know of that is capable of manipulation, coercion, and pure evil."

"Like the devil in the woods," Skye responded. "Okay, on-ward!"

"Onward."

They kept walking for a while in silence, just listening to the world around them. Skye thought he had to be right about the creatures in the forest—they seemed to be fine unless they were bothered.

Then again, while the bears were probably after wild berries and the fish in the streams, the coyotes, wolves and such were carnivores, hungry . . .

For the cute little rabbits and things hopping about, she hoped. Not that she wished ill upon them.

Just . . .

Better than her!

"Stream," Zach said suddenly.

She had been so focused on the world immediately around her, she almost ran into him again, but managed to stop at his side, instead.

They had, indeed, come upon a stream. It was beautiful. They were just about at noon; and the sun was high overhead, showering down rays of light upon the water, causing it to shimmer beautifully as it danced over pebbles and outcrops along the way.

"Here might be a good place to see what you can see," Zach told her quietly.

She nodded. She willed a vision to come to her eyes.

At first . . .

The growth changed. There was a woman, a Native American woman, crouched down by the stream.

Washing clothing.

She winced, blinked, and gave her head a shake.

And then she saw them.

And she was stunned.

She opened her eyes and looked at Zach.

"You went back too far," he said.

"Just at first. I saw a Native American woman—"

"Naumkeag," Zach told her. "This whole area. Part of the Pawtucket Nation."

"Right, I assume," Skye said. "But then . . . I don't know, I don't know how I change it, by wanting to change it, maybe by *needing* to change it . . ."

"You saw the kids? Or a kid?"

She nodded. "You've been following the right way, Zach. I don't know how. But yes, Patricia and Jeremy crossed the stream here. But, Zach, there's something worse, much worse!"

"What's that? Jeremy is alive; I know it—"

"No, no, it's not that! Zach, there are two of them! Two people who are dressing up, painting themselves green and dressing up like wicked witches."

"So it's not just one criminal. But both responsible for murder."

"Zach, they're kidnapping children and young people and . . . trying to brainwash them from what you've seen. Yet you just made me wonder. If the kids and the young people are the goal, why did they kill Mike Bolton?"

"Interesting question," he said thoughtfully. "I'm wondering . . ."

"What?"

"All right, they left the baby. The baby was too young for

what they wanted. Too young to understand concepts, perhaps. And a baby couldn't identify anyone," Zach said.

"How can anyone identify someone who is that well disguised?" Skye asked.

"Maybe Mike Bolton knew someone who already had the costume. Or maybe, even more seriously, he might have suspected someone of having an agenda—although exactly what that agenda is, we can't begin to fathom."

"It's almost as if someone wants to go back in history—start the Salem Witch Trials all over again."

"Precisely."

"But that's insane!"

"Yes, insane, unless it's behind something else," Zach said. "I have no idea what, but either someone is certifiably insane, or they're planning something else. We cross the stream?"

"Right. But we really need help on this. We need to find something!"

"We will. Ready for a swim?"

"I'm always ready for a swim. But it's not that deep!" Skye said.

"Nope. But we will get wet."

"Lead the way, o great trailblazer!"

He grinned and did so. They could follow a trail of large rocks for the main part, but as he had said, they did get wet.

She felt the water creep into her boots as they hurried along, and it was cold and very uncomfortable. But that was half the job—she'd been uncomfortable before. And she figured, she would be again. Criminals worried about getting away with their deeds, not about being comfortable during a heist, a scam . . .

Or a murder.

They reached the other side.

"Did you see which way they went?" Zach asked her.

She paused, frowning, trying again.

And she was back. Little help. There was nothing but darkness.

She looked at Zach. "I'm sorry. Night fell hard. No moon, no stars. I can't see beyond the stream. It was almost as if the world went black at once. It had been getting dark, but the true darkness fell right here."

"Damn!"

"What?"

"The ground is ridiculously hard by the stream. If there were footprints here at all, I can't see any now."

"All right. So, where?"

"Okay, hang tight for a minute. Let me see where—"

"Branches are broken. I can help! I'll go to the left, you take the right, and we'll meet in the middle!"

He grinned. "West and east," he told her. "Okay. If you're sure—"

"Oh, come on, please! I've got it!"

"Right."

He nodded and headed off in his direction, leaving her to head off in her direction. West. She should know that. Except, of course, that now, the sun was directly overhead, and she was not sure if she could figure out just where it had risen or where it was going to fall. It all seemed natural for him.

But she could tell if branches had been broken, if little feet had traveled through the areas where the dirt seemed to be a little softer, perhaps touched by splashes from the stream.

She couldn't find anything that resembled a footprint.

She studied the branches in the area farthest to the west, before the trees and brush became so thick, only little forest animals might have gotten through.

Nothing at the first break that might resemble a trail.

She moved on.

And again, nothing. And she believed she had learned what the subtle breaks in little branches looked like if someone had passed by recently.

Of course, knowing Zach, if he didn't find anything, he might well be doubtful and start to search here himself.

But I had seen them; they'd had to have gone somewhere.

Then she heard his call to her.

"Here! Skye, I've got something!"

CHAPTER 6

Just exactly what he had . . . Zach didn't know.

But he did know that someone had passed through the extremely narrow path, through rows of oak trees that appeared to dominate in this area. Thick, rich, and lush—winter was not far away.

Then again, he thought, *autumn* is *on the way.*

Soon they would be at the end of September—and even in the next few days, all the major-league prep for Halloween would be underway.

That would be all that they would need!

More and more costumes would be sold. And those who didn't know that a green wicked witch was attacking children might find such a costume amusing for the Salem area, and then law enforcement would be hunting in a bigger field.

They had to move fast—before the fall season was against them.

"Oh, wow!" Skye exclaimed suddenly.

She had hurried over to the area as soon as he'd called her. Now she was hunkered down at the base of a massive old oak.

Holding something.

He walked swiftly to her side, hunkering down as well.

"Look!" she said, staring at him with pleased wonder.

And he looked at what she had found.

It was small, really small. About the size of two quarters, end to end. And it was green and he quickly realized what it was.

A tiny soldier that might go to a kid's army set.

"You were right!" Skye said. "Kids! Kids have toys on them. I have a little niece, Katie, and she loves to stick her little toys into her pockets. Maybe Jeremy is like Katie—he just needs something to have on him, some little toy to have wherever he might wind up!"

"Either that, or . . ."

"Or?"

"Patricia. She knew they were in trouble. These might have been by Jeremy where he was sitting on the sofa, doing his homework."

"Possibly."

"Did you see anything like that when you were in the house—looking back?" he asked Skye.

"I saw her scoop him up. If we go back to the house, I could try to see the particulars of what was going on."

He shook his head. "It doesn't matter now who grabbed it or dropped it—but I think it was done on purpose. And it's what we needed," Zach told her.

"What we needed to get help out here, searching the forest," Skye said.

"Exactly. Except . . ." Zach paused, wincing as he looked at her.

"Except you want to go a little farther before we turn back," Skye said.

"You are a mind reader."

"Nope. I'm just beginning to be able to read you."

He grinned at that. "Well?"

"Sure. What's another hour of walking around in soggy boots!"

He laughed and said, *"I Never Promised You a Rose Gar-*

den," referencing the title of Joanne Greenberg's book. Or the Lynn Anderson lyric from Rose Garden.

She went with the first.

She groaned. "Well, at least you read."

"Cereal boxes when there's nothing else," he assured her.

"Lots of biographies and histories and such?" she asked him.

"Yeah. And you?"

"Sure. Which means that between us, we should know what's going on!" Skye said, obviously frustrated.

"History repeats itself—and creates new foibles within humanity," Zach assured her. "Skye, we will figure it out."

Well, he hoped to hell that they did—and that they did so soon.

"Why do you want to keep going now?" she asked him. "You see something, feel something through the kids?"

He shook his head. "Gut? Just a sense that something is close ahead."

"All right. Let's go."

They did.

"Hey, guess what? I think that my feet are drying out. Hm. But then again to get back, we must go through the stream again!"

"You only have one pair of boots?" Zach asked.

"I travel light."

"So do I," he admitted.

But then he paused so abruptly, she walked into him, quickly drawing back and by his side to see what he was seeing.

Something larger than a single tree, yet . . .

Brown, the color of tree trunks, of wood.

"There's a structure ahead," Skye whispered.

"Right. Let's get close, observe, plan."

"You got it."

They moved in silence until they could stand behind the

closest tree to a tiny clearing that was just a stretch of over-grown grass and brush before a small wooden cabinlike structure. One that was old and dilapidated, falling apart. There were spaces for windows, but there were no windows.

But there was a door.

He looked at her and nodded.

"Front window," he told her.

She nodded. "I'll crawl around the back and see what—if anything—is back there, a back door, anything."

He nodded, wishing they had coms on them, so that they could communicate through whispers once they had parted.

Too late.

They watched for a minute. Nothing. They looked at one another and nodded simultaneously. Then he broke from the trees first. Taking a roundabout path, Skye moved out to head around the back of the old shack.

He kept hunching low, coming to the window, carefully looking in.

There was a bare mattress on the floor. The place was empty. But . . .

He was certain that the derelict cabin had been used recently. Perhaps it had been a halfway stop for the witch bringing Jeremy and who knew how many others through the woods.

Rising, he headed to the door and opened it; it was empty, as he had seen through the window. There was a back door, as aged and crumbling as the rest of the place.

Calling out to Skye, he opened the door.

She came in and looked around.

One old mattress on the floor, no sheets . . . and nothing else much, but . . .

There was a counter to the left of the place with the remnants of cabinets under it. Skye hurried to the cabinets and opened the first.

"Nothing?" Zach asked.

"Nothing. But there was something. Look. There's dust all around, except for right here. It looks as if . . ."

"As if, maybe, there had been a twelve-pack of water, or some such thing stashed here until recently. And that could make sense. If you're stealing children that you intend to keep alive—at least for a while—you might make sure they were hydrated for going on a hike through the woods."

"Perfect sense," Skye said. She was thoughtful.

"What?"

"I'm just wondering . . . what if this is all that there is in the forest? What if they try to take the kids somewhere else, but don't want to be obvious. Bring them here, keep us hunting and hunting through the trees . . ."

"And take off via a road on the other side?"

"Or worse. Make it to the water and disappear on a boat."

He weighed her words for several seconds. "All real possibilities," he agreed. "Except for the whole witch thing and the devil in the darkness."

"You think that whatever is going on is supposed to go on here, right?" Skye asked.

"I do think so. But what the ultimate plan might be, I have no idea. But I do think we have enough to head back in. Even with what we may be able to see, the forest now stretches out forever; and you may be right—we can search the entire thing ourselves, which might take forever, or we can get help," Zach said.

She nodded. "Okay, we hike back. And while there are areas that aren't state or federal forest, I'm betting the rangers are better than even you—or at least as good!" she amended quickly.

He laughed. "Let's head back. Also, I really want to speak with Patricia's college friends. I believe someone knew she looked after the Bolton kids, and that was maybe why they were targeted."

"Patricia might be a crazy fanatic?" she asked.

He shook his head. "No. We have both seen her do her best to keep Jeremy from being terrified. She's as much a captive as he is. And I want to find out what other children may have disappeared from surrounding areas."

"I'm thinking the police might have mentioned it if kids were missing from Peabody, Danvers . . . or any other surrounding areas."

"As I said, as far down as Boston and maybe beyond."

"All right, then! Hiking time again."

They left the derelict structure and started back through the woods. Skye was ahead of him.

This time, she stopped so abruptly, he almost plowed into her.

"Shh!" she whispered.

He came around her and saw what she had seen.

No evil of the human race.

There was a wolf in front of her. A large animal, beautiful with thick black, white, and gray fur. The animal just stared at them.

They just stared back.

Then the wolf ambled on into the trees, leaving them to the trail.

"What a gorgeous animal!"

"Yeah, I could have thought about that all the while that he was eating me," Skye said, wincing.

"Two of us in an area where he has a zillion other things to munch on," Zach told her. "Sure, any animal can attack. But most of the time, they go after what's natural. You don't mess with a nest, little creatures . . . and you're okay as long as you don't present a threat."

"Most of the time."

He grinned. "Yeah. Most of the time. Bad things do happen, but that's life in the wild. And life when you're not in the wild, too."

"Well, I agree on that!" she responded. "Forward!"

It took them less time to get back than it had to reach the strange derelict cabin, or shack, in the woods.

Naturally, Skye had cast him a weary glance as they'd made their way back over the stream.

But it didn't seem quite so bad, and soon enough they were back at the Bolton house and the car.

"Do you think we stink to high heaven?" Skye asked him, once they were on the road and moving.

"You smell okay."

She laughed. "I 'smell okay' and I'm 'commendable.' But if you stink as bad as I do, then you won't know that I stink."

"You want to go shower?"

"No! We need to get this whole thing started while there's still some daylight left!" she said.

"I concur," he assured her. "Hey, if anything, we smell like a forest. It wasn't hot enough in the woods for much sweat. We should be okay. Besides, we just need to return the key and get people out while we can."

"But I want to talk to Patricia's roommates," Skye reminded him.

"Then they'll need to put up with our smell, whatever it may be."

She nodded.

At the police station, Zach was glad to find that Detectives Cason and Berkley were there.

"Anything?" Skye asked anxiously as they approached the group.

"Nothing new, I'm afraid. We've come up to speed. We've assured the Bolton couple we're doing everything in our power to find Jeremy; and, of course, they've heard about what happened at the Howell costume shop, about the kidnapping of Mrs. Howell and Sophie, and . . ." Connie was the one who had spoken, and her voice trailed off as she looked miserably at her partner. "We must find those kids." She spun suddenly on Zach and Skye. "Did you find out anything, anything at all?"

"We did, not the kids—but we know how Jeremy and Patricia were taken from the Bolton house. But we need help," Skye explained.

Vince stared at them skeptically. "How on earth can you know—"

"Zach thought it possible that whoever had taken Patricia and Jeremy might have headed off through the woods. A massive forest starts right behind the house. Anyway," she said, pausing to offer Zach a nod of admiration, "we took a look at the woods, found breakage in the branches that suggested someone had been through recently, and we decided to take a long walk. Along the way, we found this!"

She produced the little army character that she'd found in the brush.

"Uh, what exactly is it, and why exactly do you think it means something important?" Connie asked doubtfully.

"It's a character from a kid's army play set, one you'll discover Jeremy Bolton possesses," Zach explained. "We found that and then a really tumbledown shack in the woods, but it looks as if someone had water or something in there. Whether they're still there or not, Jeremy and Patricia were taken through the woods. But the area is huge, and quite frankly, by the time we covered it all, someone in Jeremy's generation could be president of the United States."

"Right, so . . . a bunch of detectives wasting time in the woods—" Vince began.

"No," Zach told him.

"Then you speak with Bruns and get him to get some people out there," Vince said flatly.

"No problem," Zach assured him. With a nod, he strode toward Bruns's office and knocked on the door.

Skye followed him.

Bruns immediately offered a hand, welcoming them in.

Zach explained the situation again.

"Our detectives don't need to worry. I'll call it in to the big brass, and we'll get off-duty officers and forest rangers on it," Lieutenant Bruns said. "I'll see that we'll get the right people out there. Skye, if you'll give me the army man, I'll make sure that his parents see it and verify that it's something he owns."

Skye handed him the little character, but asked, "Could I hang on to this for now, Lieutenant?"

"Oh? Oh, sure, of course."

"Thanks."

"If it helps," Bruns said, looking at the two of them.

They explained that it did.

"Okay, then, go. Keep in contact with the detectives."

"Will do." Zach glanced at Skye and shrugged. They headed back out to assure the detectives that Lieutenant Bruns would handle the searching through the woods.

"We're heading back to the house to see if we can find something there," Vince said. "We have a forensic expert headed back with us—Jeannette Crane is the best. Maybe she can find something in the house or in the in-law quarters, where Mike Bolton was killed. There has to be a clue somewhere; every crook makes a mistake somewhere."

Zach wasn't sure that he believed that was true.

There were too many unsolved homicides among other crimes across the country.

But it was true that human beings made mistakes. The mistakes needed to be discovered for them to matter.

"All right. We're heading out to find Patricia's roommates," Zach told them. "They just might know something—"

"We already talked to them," Connie said.

"Right. But it never hurts—" Skye began.

"Waste of time. You're the ones big on a forest hideout! You guys should get to crawl through the dirt some more!" Vince said lightly.

"Never hurts to have fresh eyes—or ears—on a problem," Zach reminded them. "Like you said . . ."

"Yep. Something might be said that we didn't hear," Connie agreed. "You two take it in any direction you think will help."

"Right. Fine. Keep us up," Vince said.

"Will do, and we'll ask you to do the same," Zach told him.

"May we have a list of the roommates, please?" Skye asked.

Vince pulled out his phone. "Coming at you, email," he told them.

"Okay, then. Drive-through lunch and onward," Zach said pleasantly. He felt that Vince Cason and Connie Berkley watched them as they left.

And he sensed a little hostility. Maybe his imagination.

It wasn't. In the car, Skye turned to him. "I think they resent the two of us being here," she said.

He nodded. "Strange. I thought they were happy when we first met."

"Well, there are places where the locals aren't happy when the Feds come in."

"What do we know about them?" he asked.

"Hm!" Skye murmured, busily looking at her phone. "Constance Berkley, thirty-two years old, started with the department right after college, worked her way up to detective, just tall enough, and by all accounts, good record, but she has only been with Detective Vincent Cason for about a year. Cason has been with the department fifteen years; he's forty-five years old. But he's still below Lieutenant Bruns on the food chain—Bruns is up for another promotion he'll probably get, according to what I'm reading."

"But it's what we don't read that might matter," Zach said. He shrugged. "The night we met them, I thought they were glad that we were here. Today I wasn't so sure."

"Maybe they just don't like the woods."

"Right. But no one said *they* had to tramp through the woods. Just that someone needed to tramp through the woods. My money is on the rangers, as far as that goes," he said thoughtfully.

"A ranger—or a cop who spent time hiking, hm!" she said.

He groaned. "It's easy. And now you know that it's easy to tell where branches were broken or where people recently walked through foliage."

"Hey. A big bear could have walked through, too."

"Bears don't feel the need to follow or create trails," he assured her. "Okay. So, what about our college roommates?" he asked her.

"University majors on our people," Skye said thoughtfully. "Holly Madsen, Judy McGrath, and Whitney Nottingham. All juniors, just like Patricia. Judy and Holly are in business and administration, and Whitney is majoring in chemistry. No historians among them, far as I can see. But all three are from the area."

"Hey, I did some growing up in Boston, and it was impossible to not hear about the trials in Salem, the Massachusetts Bay Colony, and so on. But I don't see it. I don't see any of these girls being involved in what's going on. You don't need to just know the area—you need to have studied people, timing . . . and forensics."

"All of that information is available through any programming server out there!" she reminded him. "I had a co-worker who learned about all kinds of things by watching documentaries on YouTube."

"True. What I'm hoping is they may know someone that Patricia knew well, maybe someone else who had kids she watched who proved to be a little crazy or a little too focused on . . . something. Or . . . was just plain crazy!" he said. "Let's hope they're in the room, out of class, studying, and not off—"

"We're good. It's almost five and none of them have classes that late. I just got a text from Lieutenant Bruns—he asked them to be there to talk to us."

"Great. And they don't mind—"

"Apparently, they're all friends, and the three of them are sick about Patricia being missing. They've sworn that she'd die before she let anything happen to Jeremy."

"I believe that. From, um, everything that I've seen," Zach said.

"Me too. She sounds like a truly great person. And the way that she grew up was hard, so it sounds."

"It could have made her hard; instead, it seems to have made her more compassionate toward others. None of us gets an excuse."

"You grew up hard?" she asked.

He shook his head. "No. I grew up in Harpers Ferry and in Boston, mom a teacher, dad . . ."

"Dad?"

"A cop," he told her.

"Ah, that explains a lot."

"And you?"

She didn't answer right away. Then she shrugged. "An ordinary life. My mother worked in retail—which meant we did get some great stuff on sale. And my dad was a cop, too, and . . ."

"Go on," he urged quietly.

"My grandmother lived with us after my granddad died. And she would talk to my dad about his cases, and sometimes they would both disappear. When I was older and . . . acted weird, I guess . . . she told me about our talent. And I thought that my dad knew all about hers, because it seemed that she helped him on his cases. But she told him that she'd just taken all kinds of criminology and forensic classes and used a lot of magic. So, to this day, my parents don't know about this weird thing of seeing the past."

"Hey, at least you had your grandmother!"

"Oh, no one in your family knew about you?"

Zach thought about his past and winced. "Kind of, in a way. I'm not sure what he believed, but I talked to my dad. At least, he didn't tell me I was crazy or insist that I have therapy. Sometimes I thought that maybe he had a bit of whatever it is that Jackson and Angela said. I've never seen anyone as convinced that we went on, that human beings had souls. I still don't know if he just sensed those around him, or . . ." He left off with a shrug and looked at her quickly. "My parents were great. So, no, I never knew what it was like to go from foster home to foster home, or even know what it was like to grow up with hardships. But in Boston, I worked with a guy who did get shoved from foster home to foster home—Drake Evans. Never knew his father and he didn't think that his mother knew who the man might be—she died of a drug overdose when he was five. But it didn't make him bitter; instead, it made him a man determined to do good in the world, so . . ."

"Our Patricia is great, and she is going to see that no harm comes to Jeremy."

"It sounds—and feels and looks—that way," he said lightly.

Skye started to smile, but that smile turned to a frown as he made a sudden turn. "Okay, I do know this area, and you are not heading toward the university dorms—"

"Nope. I'm heading to the fast-food joint just down this corner. You're welcome to join me in a hamburger and fries. Or not. Fuel, you know, after a morning tramping around the woods."

"Hey! You're the one who wanted to tramp through the woods!" she reminded him.

"But—"

"Fish sandwich and fries, please," she told him. "And no soda—juice. You know. Fuel."

He laughed softly and continued his way to the drive-through, buying them food they'd be enjoying in the car.

"You're adept at driving with a burger in your hands, I see," she told him once their food had been purchased and they were on the road again.

"And you're not?" he inquired.

"Of course. I was just checking on you—since you're doing the driving."

He grinned and moved on.

They finished eating a minute after he parked and headed toward the dorm room.

"Second floor," Skye said.

He nodded and they headed for the stairs. Evidently, the girls had been waiting for them. The door to room 204 opened before they could get to it.

A young brunette stepped out, a pretty girl with a ponytail, jeans, and a T-shirt that advertised a local band.

"Hey! You're the Feds, right?" she asked anxiously.

"We are," Zach assured her, producing his credentials.

At his side, Skye did the same.

"Please come in! We're so glad you're here. I'm sorry; I'm Holly Madsen! Please, please, we are so anxious to do anything. Patricia . . . oh, my God! We all love her so much; someone has to find her. And that awful woman, oh!"

Skye stopped, glancing at Zach and looking at Holly with a frown. "That awful woman? What awful woman?"

"That detective! Brekley, no, sorry, Berkley. Detective Berkley. She suggested that Patricia had killed the great-grandpa and kidnapped Jeremy! She was horrible! But come in, please, please, if we can help, we want to!"

She opened the door, urging them inside. Zach gave her a nod and held the door, letting Holly reenter first, followed by Skye and then himself.

There was a small living area in the dorm, with an even smaller kitchen that backed it. *Enough for college years,* he thought. A door on either side led to the bedrooms, he imagined.

Two other young women were seated on a sofa; both rose as they entered. A petite girl, with a blond bob, offered her hand, introducing herself as Whitney Nottingham. The second girl, a taller redhead, offered her hand as well, telling them that she was Judy McGrath.

"Sit, please!" Holly said.

There was one sofa and two chairs.

"Scooch!" Holly told the other two, joining them on the couch and indicating that Skye and Zach should take the chairs.

They did so.

Whitney glanced at Holly and she said quietly, "They don't think Patricia was involved in any way."

"We most certainly do not!" Skye assured her. "We believe someone came to the door and maybe called out. What we're wondering is if there might be someone she's met somewhere, and if she recognized the voice and thought that they just needed something, or—"

"She'd have never opened the door to a wicked witch!" Whitney announced. "And in the papers and on the news, they're saying that a wicked witch kidnapped that lady and kid in Swampscott. Could that be . . . I mean . . . it's not even that close to Halloween yet! Well, yeah, wait, especially here—but we're not down to the big festivities yet."

"That's why we're wondering about people Patricia might have known or even just met—if she recognized a voice and just opened the door?" Zach asked. "Or we're thinking that she might have been busy, running between the baby and Jeremy, and opened the door without thinking. But if you can think of anyone who behaved strangely around Patricia or any of you, or if she even mentioned anyone strange."

Judy smiled at them and entered the conversation. "Thank God! You really don't think Patricia might be the bad one, like those horrible cops do! You had to know Patricia. She worked so hard! And she was so nice. We've all tried to help out because our parents pay for our schooling, but Patricia grew up in foster care and doesn't have anyone to help her financially. That's why she works so hard. And it helps that she just loves kids and is a natural with them."

"We know she's innocent," Skye said.

"Of course—I mean, Patricia was gone when the costume shop got held up or whatever," Holly said. "Oh! But I bet you the cops that were here think she kidnapped Jeremy and went back for the mom and the other kid."

"Seriously," Skye said, sitting forward. "We truly believe Patricia is innocent, a victim, and she needs saving. We need all the help we can get. Can you think of anyone who behaves strangely, said something strange, suddenly asked questions or knew her schedule or . . . anything at all?"

Holly looked at Whitney. Whitney looked at Judy.

Judy looked at Holly and gave her a little nod.

Holly spoke for the trio.

"We're afraid to say much of anything because we could be so wrong. But you need to look at Mr. Stanley."

"Who is Mr. Stanley?" Zach asked.

"He teaches history at the university," Judy offered. "He may just be a harmless kook! You know, of course, that you have to take classes that aren't necessarily in your major. Patricia was taking his course on American history. If you read the course description, it takes you from Juan Ponce de Leon,

St. Augustine, Florida, and the Pilgrims, Plymouth, Massachusetts, into the decades that followed, up to the present."

"But Mr. Stanley obsesses!" Judy exclaimed. She looked at the others and continued, "Decades and centuries are glossed over. I know because I take his class, too. And all he ever wants to talk about is Salem—and the trials. But," she added, "he does go on and on about the horror of the trials." She stopped speaking, looking at Whitney.

Whitney took a breath. "I'm in the class, too. And what he's so keen on is the idea that people did see the devil in the woods, or that all that was evil within them came out in the woods, so maybe it was the devil taking hold of the Massachusetts Bay Colony!"

CHAPTER 7

A professor who believed that the devil lurked in the deep woods.

Skye sat back, frowning as she looked at the wide-eyed girls, who were staring from her to Zach, desperate for help.

There were, of course, many ways to think about the devil. Perhaps the devils that had existed in Puritan New England had simply been the devils that lurked in the human psyche, something within humanity that allowed man to create very bad images of another human being because of anger, resentment, jealousy, or a need for revenge.

Many in the past must have felt such things—they were only human. And people were easily made into victims of a culture. And if the culture said the devil was alive and making use of human beings in the deep, dark forests, well . . .

But a professor at a respected university talking about the devil being present at the time of the trials? That was unique.

"We'll definitely speak with this professor," she told them. "But I'm sorry, does he tell you what others thought—or what he thinks himself?"

"He's dramatic!" Whitney offered. "Very dramatic!"

"He likes to act out the things he's telling us about," Holly said, smiling. "In a way, he's a wonderful teacher, fun and informative!"

"But scary, too!" Judy said gravely.

"We'll meet with him. Believe me, we promise we'll investigate any information and any man or woman you suggest might be involved in any way. And you never know," Zach continued, "your professor might lead us to someone else. The main thing is this—we believe with our whole hearts that your friend is innocent, a victim like Jeremy, but a young woman who is still caring with everything in her heart and soul for that boy."

"Oh, thank you!" Holly whispered.

"Thank you, thank you!" Whitney echoed.

Zach nodded and Judy said, "I'm sorry if we're acting . . . badly. It's just that the detectives were horrible!"

"I'm sure they didn't mean to be—" Skye began.

"Oh, what's his name? Detective Cason. He was all right. I mean, we could see his face; and we knew he was suspicious of Patricia, but he didn't come right out and call her a monster. But that woman detective, that Berkley, she was horrible. She wanted us to admit that Patricia was broke, that she'd surely taken Jeremy so that she could demand a ransom."

"There's been no communication regarding a ransom," Skye said softly.

"Of course not! Because . . ." Whitney broke off, shaking her head. "I don't get it! I don't get what's going on at all!"

"At this moment, neither do we," Zach admitted. "But . . ."

He glanced at Skye. They both knew not to make promises that they could solve a case.

But he seemed to feel the same way that she did on the subject.

"I promise you that we will not give up until we do find out what is going on. We won't give up on Patricia, I swear," he said.

Skye lowered her head, smiling.

Well, thanks to Jackson and their new special status, she knew they could make promises in the way that they were doing.

"There's one thing I'd like to ask you for," Zach told the three of them. "And that's something that belongs to Patricia. A hairbrush—"

"Oh, no! You think she's dead and you want to compare DNA!" Holly exclaimed, horrified.

"No, no, not at all. We very much think that she's alive and well," Zach said. "It's just to help us when we're able to find a trail they might have taken, something that Patricia might have touched."

"We found one of Jeremy's little toys in the woods behind the Bolton house—we know they went that way; and rangers and police are searching through the forest now. Having something that belongs to someone in captivity can help in finding out whatever the kidnappers might be planning and what direction they took to where they're holding people now," Skye added quickly, smiling to appear reassuring. "And in this case, knowing a direction can lead us to wherever the kidnapped victims are being held."

"Um, sure, of course!" Holly said. She looked at the other two girls.

Judy hopped up. "She keeps one of her hairbrushes in the bathroom. I'll get it for you!" She quickly returned with the brush; Zach thanked her.

He stood and Skye stood as well. The girls had given them a direction; and whether a respected professor might be involved or not, he could tell them more about the area.

And people in the area.

Maybe there was a student who was taking it all too seriously!

And then again, maybe the professor was involved himself.

Stranger things had happened. There were, she knew, two people involved. And the children were alive, as were Patricia and Jane Howell.

So, how could these people be holding the prisoners while going about their day-to-day work or existence? Unless, perhaps, they had a way of containing their prisoners.

Or even a third conspirator, whose job it was to hold the prisoners.

"We'll be in touch," Zach promised the girls. "And we will talk to the professor."

"He wouldn't just admit he was a kidnapper, right?" Holly asked.

"It's most unlikely that anyone would do so. We have our ways of talking," Zach said to her. "And again, of course, if he isn't guilty of anything other than being a dramatic professor obsessed by the history of the region, he may lead us onward. Anyway, we thank you all!"

"No, no," Holly said. "We thank you."

With smiles, Skye and Zach made their exit.

In the car, Skye turned to Zach. "Well?"

"Honestly? I have a bad time thinking that a professor who has kept his job can be in on this, but the whole thing is so absurd, who knows? We do need to talk to him. And hopefully, he'll be somewhere—"

"Wait! You have the brush."

"I'm driving!"

"I can drive."

"Of course, you can, I know. But I'd like a minute to sit with it. Concentrate. My talent doesn't always just jump forward the way yours does. And I know about the darkness through Jeremy's little toy, but I may get a view on things through Patricia's *older* mind."

"Okay. Then I'll call Lieutenant Bruns; he seems ready to

help at any turn. He can set up a meeting for us with the professor," Skye said, looking at her phone. "Ah! A message from Detective Cason. One of the rangers found a little green army man in the forest, too. Halfway between the shack and a rough road that's near the coast." She frowned and looked at him worriedly. "Do you think that they might have spirited away these women and children in a boat?"

He shook his head. "Absurd. That's the true situation. But because it's so absurd, I think it all has to do with this area. And that's just thinking. I could be entirely wrong."

She smiled and called Gavin Bruns. The detective immediately put a call through for them and was back on the line with Skye in just a few minutes. She put him on speaker so that Zach could hear what he was telling them.

"Well, I'm thinking that this will work out for you well. I hope so at any rate. Professor Isaac Stanley is heading out to dinner. He's happy to help you in any way, but hopes that you'll join him at the Village Tavern. It's a great restaurant, so you can have something good to eat while you're getting to know and question the man."

"Sounds great, thank you, Lieutenant Bruns," Zach told him. "Thank you so much."

"If anyone is going to solve this thing, it's you," Bruns told him.

"Hey, like Hillary Clinton's book said, 'It takes a village,'" Zach said.

"Keep me up on anything," Bruns told them. Skye could almost see the man hesitate, before he told them, "Cason and Berkley have been assigned the fieldwork; I'm actually the detective in charge of a few cases going on. But frankly, I'd rather be on the ground with this one and working with you two."

"Sir, you've been great. The connections you make for us are extremely helpful," Zach assured him.

"Well, thanks. The restaurant is right on Essex Street. And it's one of my favorites," Bruns told them.

Zach smiled, glancing at Skye as he drove. "I've been there, sir, and I've got to agree."

They ended the call with the two of them promising to let Bruns know whatever they discovered.

Skye was thoughtful as she hung up.

"You don't want to go to the restaurant?" he asked. "Well, I guess late lunch and early dinner beat the days when we don't eat at all."

"Hasn't really happened yet," she reminded him.

"Not in your career?" he asked, grinning as he looked ahead. "Ah, but then you don't seem to feel the need to fuel up all that often."

Skye shrugged. "Often enough. You're bright enough to stop when we can, but I've seen you involved in what we're doing—and not thinking about food at all."

"Well, I'm sorry I made you eat fast food. This place is good!"

"I know."

"Of course. You've been in Salem often enough before."

She nodded, looking downward and smiling. He was proving to be okay, after all. He had a great look for an agent; his height, shoulders, and even the character of his facial structure allowed for his appearance to instill confidence in those needing help—and wariness for those causing the need.

In truth, of course . . .

He just had a great masculine and arresting look. He was a striking man, but she was discovering much more: his sense of humor, and a great sense of justice. He was also capable of offering tremendous empathy. In fact, she might be discovering that she liked him a bit too much, which annoyed her to no end—they had just met!

"Okay, going to park about a block off Essex Street," he narrated, sliding into a spot. "Down-to-earth, reasonable—"

"And they have great appetizers and salads, among other things," Skye told him. "Yeah. We should eat now while we've got the chance."

"You know, there are people—even law enforcement—who call it quits after so many hours and go home, have dinner, and go to sleep."

"I have a feeling you've never been one of those people," Skye said, shrugging as they walked to the restaurant. "The nature of the beast. But it's been my experience that when we get a break—we get a break!"

"That's true. And there's the restaurant . . . and there. A table near the window, a man who appears to be in his late fifties, white hair, mustache, and goatee—he's at a table for four and it appears that he's looking for someone."

Skye laughed softly.

"What?"

"He looks exactly like the stereotypical professor!" Skye said.

Zach smiled. "I guess he does."

They headed into the restaurant. Apparently, they looked like Feds, too, because the professor rose as he saw them, ready to greet them.

"Lieutenant Bruns gave me a call. I didn't get a chance for lunch today, so I hope you don't mind joining me for dinner."

"Ah, professors don't always get to eat, either," Zach said, glancing at Skye before shaking the man's hand and introducing himself, showing his credentials and turning to her to do the same.

"Thanks, Professor, seriously, and oh! This dinner gets to be on law enforcement's dime!" she told him.

"We've both been here before and love the place, too," Zach told the man.

"Ah, great! Well, I can make a few suggestions," Professor Stanley told them.

"Thanks! I've had their salads and I'll be going in that direction," Skye answered him, smiling.

"I guess I will, too," Zach said, making a face. "Bad fast food for lunch—and a late lunch."

"Ah, there's our waiter! We'll order and you can start asking me anything, and I'll do my best to help in any way."

They didn't get to ask their questions right away after their waiter left their table; Professor Stanley broke into a bit of a tirade.

"Not that it's not incredibly important history," he told them, "but the only history anyone ever seems to get into here is that about the witchcraft trials! Not far from here, they've found proof that the first indigenous peoples, ancestors of our current Native Americans, were here as early as nine thousand to twelve thousand years ago. In 1614, John Smith first surveyed the coast; in 1626, Roger Conant arrived here to start up the colony. The first burial in the Old Burying Point, or Charter Street Cemetery, was in 1637. Those are just dates. Important things happened here. In 1636, just the year before, militia drilled on what is now the Salem Common, beginning what we now refer to as the National Guard. War of 1812, all kinds of seafarers—some privateers among them, of course. Yes, yes, 1692, the Salem Witch Trials began, but the first supposed witch hanged in the Colonies was Alse Young, in Connecticut. But I'm guessing you two know that. What you may not know is that in Salem in the 1840s, the area began desegregating schools. In 1854, they passed a law 'prohibiting all distinctions of color and religion in Massachusetts public school admissions.' Admirable things happened here, too, but . . . well, I guess tourism thrives on ghosts and what was once evil. Nowadays the only so-called witches we have around belong to our wiccan community, and those people—"

"Would do no evil, lest it come back at them three times," Skye said, interrupting politely.

"And there you have it!" Professor Stanley said. "Just like—"

"True voodoo, demonized by Papa Doc and Hollywood," Zach offered.

Professor Stanley nodded, and they all gave their attention to their waiter as he arrived with their drinks—a scotch for the professor and coffee for Skye and Zach.

"Ah, on duty still, eh?" the professor asked.

"Yeah, pretty much so on duty unless we're sleeping," Zach said. "But we get time in there in between assignments. Sir, what we've been told is that you are a beloved instructor—kids like it that you give emotion with your lectures."

The professor laughed. "Ah, yes! I tell them stories about the deep, dark woods; what it was like to fear and to not understand the indigenous people—a people who knew the woods and the darkness. Today college-aged students just think that everyone in the village at the time had to be stupid. Which is odd, seeing how kids—and some adults—automatically believe anything they read on the Internet, but . . . anyway, yes, I get a little dramatic. I describe the darkness, the wind rustling through brush and trees . . . I try to explain that Puritans were devout and, yes, unaccepting of others, and that in their religion, any possibility of magic, demons, or Satan himself was something terrifying, and that those who might have been influenced by him needed to be executed."

"But you don't believe the devil is running around in the woods yourself, do you?" Skye asked him, frowning.

He shook his head, letting out a soft laugh. "No, I do not. Of course, I go on to explain how those who weren't really malicious in any way might inadvertently be guided by other things—fear of a person, even resentment against them for anything they saw as a hurt, or who knows? Some say that they might have been influenced by greed as well—that it might have been a land grab. The average person might have just gotten swallowed up in it. Or perhaps the average person was afraid of protesting, since they might be accused as well."

"There's a strong possibility that many were afraid to protest," Zach agreed. "Sir, of course, you know about what's been going on."

"Yes, of course, and it's horrible. The news, naturally, blasted all the information. Nationwide. And there have been unverified reports that police suspect someone dressing up as a witch, but not the human-form witches of the past, rather a movie or Halloween version of a witch."

Zach nodded. "We think it's possible. But as for the very idea of a witch—"

"I am a professor. I teach facts. Not characters made up in a book, no matter how wonderful a book might be."

Their entrees arrived and they all thanked the waiter. When he was gone, Skye leaned forward slightly and said, "Professor, we were hoping that you might know about someone who has followed the history too closely, perhaps someone who understood too clearly the Puritan version of the devil. Someone who . . ."

"You mean, do I know about anyone who could be doing any of this?" Professor Stanley asked.

"Frankly, yes," Zach said.

The professor frowned thoughtfully. "Not offhand. I can go through my files—I've been teaching for years, you know. Many of my students are Salem residents, or they live nearby in Peabody, Lynn, Swampscott, Danvers . . . the area, you know. Of course, people come to the university here from all over, but . . . we do have a lot of locals or a lot of students from Massachusetts. I thought that the wicked-witch thing was just a rumor or supposition, but . . . I will do everything in my power to help, I promise."

Skye glanced at Zach. He gave her a barely perceptible nod.

The professor seemed to be the real deal. Of course, his students did love his theatrics.

Still . . .

He was a fine dinner companion. He talked about the seafaring history of the area; how Salem men had served in the wars; how the Massachusetts 54th Infantry Regiment had been the second formed by voluntary African Americans in 1863, after the Emancipation Proclamation, and how they had then been followed by a creation of about 150 such units across the country.

He was proud of Massachusetts, proud of Salem.

"There will always be a few bad eggs in society, in groups, in states . . . and during certain years. The witch hunts, we see today, were horrid. Across the globe, they were horrid and remain so in a few places. A few bad eggs—malcontents—can cause real harm, and that's why it's up to the rest of us to stand strong against them!"

By the time dinner was over, Skye realized she admired the man. A lot.

And she silently prayed that her faith in him would be proven to be the right thing.

Back in the car, she turned to Zach as they drove the short distance to their rental lodging.

"I am really starting to wish I were a mind reader!" she told him. "Thus far, Patricia's roommates seem to be truly crushed and worried about her. Professor Stanley came off as sincere to me, just a man who is passionate about history. Mr. Howell couldn't have been pretending his near hysteria—understandable—over his wife and child. But we're not finding anything!"

"Not true. We know something," Zach said. "There are at least two individuals involved, and they like to dress up while kidnapping people. We know they did whisk Patricia and Jeremy through the woods—but probably to a back road. We found a shack they weren't using as any kind of a 'stay there' hideout—but they did use it in passing through. Skye, we never thought this was going to be easy. And we know the kids are alive. Now I have something of Patricia's. We'll get back to our place alone, and I'll see what I can see through Patricia's brush."

"What did you think of Professor Stanley?"

"He appeared to be passionate about Salem, the State of Massachusetts, and history. I have a feeling his dramatics are to try to get his students to understand how some of the people may have been feeling back then—and how many wouldn't have dared disagreed with the arrests of their neighbors because of their fear of being arrested. And let's face it, people become part of their society."

"It just seems hypocritical to me," Skye said.

"What's that?"

"Well, the Puritans wanted something different from the Church of England because they thought the ceremonies and other bits of practice were too similar to Catholicism. They wanted a religion that, in their minds, came straight from the Bible. Then many fled England for New England to keep from being persecuted because they were under fire from the Church and the Crown. Then they turn around and accuse people of witchcraft in their new colony?"

He turned and shrugged before grinning. "A group moved to Holland first in 1608, and then to Plymouth in 1620. The Puritans didn't think of themselves as 'separatists.' But they were incredibly intolerant."

"And they met up with the Native Americans," Skye murmured.

"Well, the world is still wretchedly intolerant," he reminded her. "But that's why our Founding Fathers were so insistent on freedom of religion being in the Constitution. And to this day, many people are intolerant of others."

"But they aren't hanging them as witches," Skye argued.

"Ah, but that's because it's not accepted in society—or under the law. We like to think we've made some progress in human relations!"

"Okay, good point. We've got a way to go on that, though. And we're here."

"We are," Zach said.

Zach parked and grimaced at her as he stepped out of the car. They headed on in and he said, "I'm going to sit—"

"Wherever is best for you—I can close myself up in the bedroom if you need to be alone—"

"No, if you don't mind, stay with me in the parlor. Oh, I may brew a cup of coffee first."

"I'll get the coffee going," Skye volunteered.

He nodded to her, reaching in his jacket pocket to pull out Patricia's brush.

He sat with it while she started making the coffee.

But he was watching her while he held the brush. Skye wasn't sure how that helped him *feel* or *see* anything through the brush, but . . .

"You drink it—" she began.

"Black. Too many places we wind up have milk or cream that's soured."

"True. And sugar—"

"You know the saying. I'm too sweet already."

"I might argue with that saying!" Skye teased.

That time, he didn't answer her.

The second the coffee was brewed, she poured two cups and came out to join him, taking one of the armchairs that sat by the sofa, and setting the cups on the little table between them.

He didn't look at her. With his free hand, he reached for his coffee cup and took a long sip.

She didn't speak; he was staring at the brush, thoughtful.

"Patricia is alive. She isn't hurt, but she is scared. She's by Jeremy; she's terrified herself, but she's doing her best to reassure Jeremy and . . ."

"And?" Skye prompted softly.

"She's telling him just to do what the witches were telling them to do; to pretend to listen to everything that's being said."

"What's being said?"

"I don't know, because they aren't being spoken to now. They've been sent to bed."

"Where are they going to bed?"

"I can't tell; it's dark. It looks as if there are . . . mattresses on a floor."

"But there is a floor."

He nodded. "I think it's inside. But there's barely any light. There are others in the room."

"Jane Howell and Sophie?"

He nodded. Then he suddenly set the brush down and looked at her.

"Jane and Sophie—and at least two other people."

Almost as if on cue, their phones rang. It was Lieutenant Gavin Bruns.

"I'll get it and we'll go speaker," Zach said, answering the call and telling Bruns that they were together and both listening.

"We found something," Bruns told them.

"Something that could lead us—" Zach began.

"No, I'm afraid not. But we've been doing the search of local areas. Two young teens disappeared from a dance in Saugus. That's about eleven or twelve miles—"

"Yeah, we both know the area," Zach said. "Detective—"

"Gavin, guys, just call me Gavin, please. This may prove to be a long journey we're on."

"Okay, Gavin. Specifics, please!"

"Allie Mason, seventeen, and Beau Carter, just turned eighteen, disappeared from a school dance two weeks ago."

"And this is the first we're hearing about it?" Zach demanded incredulously.

"Red flags didn't go off anywhere. The two teens had talked about eloping; and while their parents were furious, they were angry with the kids, not with law enforcement. They think that once they've gotten to a place where they can hide out, they're waiting for the next three weeks for Allie to reach her eighteenth birthday so that they can be legally married without parental consent. They've had trouble with the pair, which is a pity. Nothing horrendous, no alcohol or drug dependency, but a lot of rebelliousness. It's an ugly situation, of course. Mr. and Mrs. Mason are blaming Beau, and Mr. and Mrs. Carter are blaming Allie. Now, of course, we can't assume that these disappearances have anything to do with what's going on here; the two missing teens are older than the children who have been taken. Now, yes, Patricia was older, and Jane Howell is older still, but they were taken with little children. But I figured—"

"You figured right," Zach told him. "We're going to want to see where the dance was and speak with the parents, of course."

"And we'd also like to speak with the Bolton couple. We haven't done that yet, and while I know your detectives spoke with them . . ." Skye said, pausing briefly to glance at Zach. "I think it's important we have communication with everyone involved."

"Yeah, I should have set that up with you before," Gavin said. "All right—you know what? Screw desk duty. I have a phone. I'd like to take this one with you, if that doesn't . . . um, mess up your chemistry. I'll swing by in the morning at about nine, take you to see Mr. and Mrs. Bolton, and then we can head down to Saugus. If that's all right."

The two Feds might be better off alone, but they needed Bruns in the long run. He was the one smoothing the way for them when they needed something.

Zach gave her a barely perceptible nod.

"Of course," Skye said.

"Oh!" Gavin stopped them before they could end the call. "What about Professor Stanley? Did he give you anything? Did you find him suspicious in any way?"

"Just to the contrary. He was credible in all that he said, just a man passionate about Salem and his state and teaching," Zach answered. "But he has promised to go through his records and notes and see if he can find anyone who might have gotten off the path of the law and started off on some ridiculous blend of history and fiction."

"Well, good, maybe he'll come up with someone or something. Okay, I'll see you in the morning. I'm punctual. I'll be there at nine."

The line went dead as Gavin Bruns ended the call.

"Strange. Did the couple run away?" Skye wondered aloud.

"It would be a changeup from what's going on. But . . ."

"You said there were more people in the dark room with Patricia and Jeremy."

Zach nodded. "Okay, well, I've been theorizing that it's a brainwashing thing. I mean, Salem, where the major witchcraft trials in the United States took place, and then making a witch combo by dressing up. Maybe someone out there is trying to make a point? Prove that you can get people to believe anything by working with children or those who are vulnerable? If so, I'm not sure two rebellious teenagers fit the bill. Then again . . ."

"It's going to be important to see where they were last. And," Skye said, "we need to get our hands on objects that each of them owned."

He nodded. "It may be easy to see if they are just off some-where—or if they are part of what's going on. But . . ." Zach hesitated and went still, Patricia's brush in both of his hands. Skye stayed silent, watching him, waiting.

Zach looked at her at last, then closed his eyes and shook his head before he looked at her again.

"Patricia is just staring up into the darkness," he said. "I can see what she's seeing, darkness. I'm going to need to do this in the daylight to see what she sees. She's lying down by Jeremy— her little pallet, cot, or whatever, is right next to his. She's afraid, and she's confused, and she's still telling herself to pre-tend to believe it all; it's the only way she can make sure she keeps Jeremy safe. And she's worried! There's someone there she's worried about, another young girl, someone who keeps protesting everything that's going on . . . It's as if she believes their only way to survive is to behave exactly as they're told, to listen to every word that's being said . . ."

He broke off for a minute and looked at her before he spoke again.

"Patricia is very afraid someone else is going to die."

Skye looked at him, feeling as if something strange swept through her. She moved over to where he sat, taking a position next to him and putting her hands over his as he held the brush.

He looked at her and smiled. "I'm okay. I'm frustrated and I want to find Patricia, Jane, the kids—and whoever else has been swept up into this."

"We will find them. But you and I both know, we must find the clues, the leads, and track them down," Skye said.

"Yeah, I know," Zach said. He twisted to look at her and smiled. His eyes were really something; he could appear tall and indomitable, and then give her that smile . . .

"Okay," she murmured. "Okay." She forced a huge smile

herself. She didn't want to leap away from him, despite the fact she was realizing that she was an idiot for having come so close both physically—and mentally. Or through empathy, or . . . whatever it was that she was coming to feel. Friendship. That was it. Friendship.

But she felt as if there was electricity leaping through her . . . from touching him.

"Good, right! Okay, we'll get on it. That's what we need to do, and it's what we will do," Skye said, speaking to fill the air between them.

"Well, tomorrow we will start early!" he observed succinctly.

Skye nodded and then left. She didn't want to feel that she *fled*—but maybe at that moment, she did do so. What she was feeling was crazy!

But as she showered and got ready for bed, ridiculous thoughts kept sweeping through her head.

High-stress jobs. Hey, they could use stress relievers, like . . . Sex?

Oh, that was pushing it! And she really needed to get a grip on herself. Of course, she'd considered him attractive and impressive when they'd met. Handsome, striking, maybe. But now . . .

She considered him to be too handsome, too attractive, too . . .

Seductive.

She groaned aloud and grabbed her towel, glancing toward the door to her room. She imagined him bursting in, taking her into his arms, letting her feel that poor fire again.

The door didn't burst open.

Of course not. They were professional law enforcement agents working on a case, even if they were slightly . . . different.

He would never do such a thing.

She finished drying off and donned her comfy flannel night-gown and crawled into bed. She lay awake.

She groaned.

Had she been waiting? Hoping?

With a groan, she smashed her head into her pillow. She needed to sleep.

CHAPTER 8

Twenty minutes later, Zach lay in bed.

In the darkness.

He stared up at the ceiling, just as Patricia had been doing. But he wasn't holding the brush.

Maybe he was a little bit different in his talents or ways than Skye.

To stay sane, to keep working, he had to take the time to shake off what others were seeing and feeling.

He'd rid himself of the night wherever Patricia lay trying to sleep, and he even told himself he couldn't feel desperate—desperate that they solve it all immediately. Things like this were seldom solved immediately. Whatever was going on was a plan—a well-developed plan. One that considered the terrain surrounding them, the location of streets, roads, even cities, in the area. Law enforcement, DNA, fingerprints . . .

Security cameras.

Yep. It was hard to identify someone in their regular appearance when they painted themselves green.

Were they using something to do with real and tragic history? Or was it nothing more than a disguise, and there was something entirely different at stake?

And why choose those who had been kidnapped?

If they had just been looking for children, they might have taken Patricia to help with Jeremy, and Jane because she was Sophie's mother.

He gave himself a mental shake. Sleep. Then he could look at everything with fresh eyes in the morning. Sleep, think of anything but . . .

Maybe that wasn't such a good idea, either.

He found himself thinking about Skye, wishing that he'd met her . . . well, doing anything other than what they were doing. At a party, a bar, a bowling alley . . . even online. There had been that initial standoffishness between them. Natural. They had just been called into this. No way out of the fact that in a way, they were on trial. They had been chosen for this, and he knew that Jackson Crow was hoping for more, but . . .

So there were defensive walls up at first, and then more defensive walls, but with admiration and wondering if he could be as useful.

Then there had been the first laughter between them, her understanding that he didn't doubt her in the least, that he believed in her, and her strange ability; and he truly hoped it wasn't as painful for her as it could be.

She'd been attractive from the get-go, of course. But he'd worked with dozens of women in the office and in the field who had been young and attractive. Maybe not quite *this* attractive.

And he hadn't felt anything more than simple desire, and relationships that were totally uncomplicated since . . .

He gave himself another mental shake. He'd been so young when Melanie had been killed. They had just entered their twenties, but they'd been old enough and wise enough to know that they wanted a life together after college.

Then there had been that awful night . . . tragic and terrible beyond belief.

He tossed over, no longer wanting to stare at the ceiling.

And he almost smiled at himself, and perhaps bizarrely whispered a little prayer that Melanie might forgive him. Because in life, there was sex. Simple biology.

And if he wasn't looking at the world through other eyes or reliving his past, he was thinking about Skye.

There were different ways of feeling in life; there was the desire that went along with biology; then there was the different thing—feeling, sense, whatever—that went along with regarding someone when they began to touch the soul with laughter, understanding, respect; and there was simply liking someone and everything about their personality, their integrity, work ethic, and so much more.

And . . .

Great. They were sleeping in the same house.

He groaned and tossed around again.

Exhaustion had to help. Their days were exhausting, not so much physically as mentally, but they were on it every hour when they were awake.

He twisted, turned, and tried every position known to man. And eventually, he did sleep.

And once he fell asleep, he slept soundly, not waking until his alarm went off at seven.

He hurriedly showered and dressed and headed out to the kitchen. Skye was already there, dressed and ready in business attire, a handsome pantsuit, her hair in a queue at her nape, almost rigidly pulled back.

The severe mode of style only enhanced the beauty of her face and hair.

She smiled at him.

"Omelets. Tomorrow I'm going to change it up. I make a mean French toast, the secret being that before you drench the bread in egg, you heat olive oil in your pan. Then, of course, when it's cooked, you add butter and syrup to taste," she told him.

"Hey, I'm on the receiving end here. Grateful for whatever you create!" he assured her.

She smiled. "Thanks. But tell me if you don't like something—I won't waste time on it, though it keeps me moving, which is good."

"So they paired me with a galloping gourmet."

"One armed with more than a spatula," she said, indicating the place beneath her jacket with her holster and her Glock. "Not exactly. I do a few things well," she added.

"When this is over, I'm going to grill for you!" he promised, nodding and indicating his own weapon beneath his jacket.

"Grill me or grill for me?" she teased. "I will be delighted if you're good with a grill!"

"I'll get coffee and juice and set the table."

"Oh, and will you push the button for the toast, too, please," Skye said.

He did so. In a matter of minutes, they were at the table. She grinned at him, watching him as they settled into seats across from one another at the table.

"What?" he asked.

"It just seems so odd. I feel that I've known you a long time, but it's been just a few days. Then again, sometimes when you know people, even for a long time, you only see them now and then, or for a few hours here and there, but we've had—Well, lots of hours of together time."

"That we have. And yeah, it's strange. I feel like I know you really well, too. And you're right—hours and hours. And this, too," he added quietly, "being able to see not just what an incredible talent you have, but how you've chosen to use it."

"You too," she said quietly.

"We should eat these!"

"Yes, indeed."

They ate quietly for a minute. "I do think, however, that when you have something like this . . . For me, it was a lot of the reason I wanted to go into law enforcement. We've been incredibly lucky to be noted—well, by Jackson Crow and not the people who would lock us up or dissect us. I couldn't imagine going through life not being able to speak with anyone, to share what I'm seeing." She laughed. "All through school, as you can imagine, I excelled in local history."

"I can well imagine!" He laughed. "People seldom let you hold historical treasures, so I might not have excelled so much."

"You didn't sneak a few touches in at museums when you were growing up?" Skye asked.

"Cameras. Cameras are everywhere. I tried not to get kicked out of museums on school trips and the like."

"Never cheated?"

He shrugged. "Define 'cheating'?"

"Wondered about something in the Smithsonian or—"

"I held the skirt of a dress once from the 1790s at the National Museum of American History at the Smithsonian," he admitted.

"And?"

"It belonged to a very sweet young woman who was at a dance, and she wore the dress when she became engaged. It was a nice vision."

"But you never shared your visions with friends. Or a girlfriend? I know you're not married, because I read your company bio, but I don't know what else is going on in your life. I mean, you could be engaged—"

"I'm not."

"But there could have been someone—"

He shook his head. "Once. Long over."

He wasn't sure if he snapped the words; she frowned and quickly apologized. "I'm sorry; I didn't mean to pry into your life."

He shook his head and let out a soft sigh. "No, no, I'm the one who should be sorry. I was almost engaged once, over a decade ago now."

"And what happened?" she asked, quickly adding, "I'm sorry; it's none of my business."

He gave her a weak smile. "It is your business. We're partners in an unusual way. We didn't break up; no one left anyone. She was caught up in a random shooting. Single bullet to the back of her head. We were on the street. I wasn't hit; she pitched forward in my arms, killed instantly by the force and trajectory of the shot."

"Oh, my God! Zach, I am so, so sorry!" she whispered. "So very, very sorry!"

"It was over a decade ago," he told her. "I'm sorry because a beautiful life was lost. Melanie was an amazing person filled with kindness for everyone. But please, that's why I don't like saying anything. I don't want people to be sorry for me. Time has gone by; I've had my share of flings. I'm fine; and yes, I went to therapy."

"I'm glad. I hope it helped you," she said gently. "Your share of flings—"

He winced. "Okay, a lot of one-night stands. But always with complete honesty with women who weren't looking for involvement. I like to believe that I've never been a jerk."

She grinned. "Hopefully not!"

"All right. Tit for tat. What about you? Is there Mr. Perfect out there somewhere?"

She laughed. "There might be a Mr. Perfect out there somewhere, but not in my life. I dated a guy named Elijah in high school. We had fun together. He went off to become an archaeologist, and I went off into criminology."

"And after high school?"

She shrugged and then winced. "Okay, well, there was Clive for a bit in college. I guess we were a thing for a while. A friend of my cousin, about three years ago, and not much of anything since."

"Bad breakups?"

She shook her head. "I, uh, had to get out. I was never really honest; I never believed that I could be really honest, and I would back away if things started getting too serious."

He nodded. "I get that. And that's why all this is so . . ."

"Amazing?"

"Yep. And oh, believe it or not, it's getting late. Gavin Bruns will be here soon. Let's—"

"I'll throw out our paper and fill the to-go coffee cups. You'll wash up the pan and whatever else," Skye suggested.

"Um, things fit in my pockets okay, but you always carry that shoulder bag—"

"I'm happy to carry the brush, zebra, and little green army man. It's better if I have them; you can take them at the right time and place, when needed," Skye said. "And now, we divide and conquer!"

Zach procured the objects and washed the pan. Skye thrust the objects into her bag and went about clearing up their trash and wiping down the counter.

They were done quickly, but just in time. There was a knock at the door; Gavin Bruns was precisely on time.

Zach opened the door. The detective had donned professional clothing as well. He was ready for the day.

"Hey, I'm just down the street if you're ready—" he began.

"Of course, we're ready," Zach told him, grinning. "You told us nine!"

Skye was right behind Zach.

"Nice!" Gavin said. "So lock up!"

Once Skye had stepped out, Zach locked the door, keying in the alarm. Then they were on the way, walking down the street to find Gavin's car around the corner.

"I'll slide in back," Zach said. Skye smiled at him and took the front; Gavin slid into the driver's seat.

"We're not going all that far. And I'm going to need to release the house to Mr. and Mrs. Bolton in the next few days; though, honestly, they haven't been rushing me," Gavin told them. "I don't blame them. Go home to where your five-year-old lives, but remains missing; and for Justin, where his grandfather was murdered. But our funds only stretch so far, and you've been in the house, my detectives have been in the house, and a forensic team has been in the house . . . It's time for us to let it go."

"Of course," Skye said.

"We will probably go back at the tail end of today," Zach said. "One last go-through. And I'd like to get back to the costume shop—it's still closed?"

"Mr. Howell has kept it closed; he's still spending his days running around different forests in the area by himself. He was going to burn every witch costume he had, but Detective Berkley pointed out they were sold all over the place. But, of course, we'll get you back in before he reopens, if you think that there's possibly anything at all that you can get back there. And we're here. Could have walked, just about," Gavin said. "But we'll need the car to head to Saugus."

They exited the car. Zach paused a minute, looking at the street. He'd had a friend who had lived nearby when he was a kid. Their parents had been friends, so they had spent a few days with Josh, now and then. And as teenagers, they'd once purchased a "fart machine" from a local gag shop and taken it on a ghost tour with them, convincing a couple of people that the ghosts were farting—until they'd been kicked off the tour by the knowing tour guide. Still, according to Josh, they'd had a "wicked" good time.

In this area, a girl could be *wicked* cute. A concert could be *wicked* amazing.

"Zach?"

Skye looked back at him.

"Sorry, sorry." Gavin was looking at him, too.

"Memories," he said. "I'd hang out here sometimes as a kid." He grimaced. "Not always a good kid!"

"Ah, the things we've done in our youths!" Gavin said. "But

please let me know anytime you need to stop, feel something, see something, okay?"

It seemed more and more possible to Zach that Lieutenant Gavin Bruns had to know about Jackson Crow and his Krewe of Hunters. He knew they offered an "unusual" way to investigate, and he was apparently willing to oblige their needs. But how much did Bruns actually understand?

"Of course," Zach said.

They headed to an apartment building.

Zach saw a car in front of the place and immediately determined that it was an unmarked police car.

Mr. and Mrs. Bolton were still being guarded. Because, of course, logically, they might be the ones who had really been under attack when Mike had been killed, and Jeremy and Patricia had been kidnapped.

That wasn't the case, Zach thought.

But watching over them was logical police work that fit in with procedure.

"Yeah, they are guarded," Gavin said.

Zach nodded. "Good. Of course."

Gavin indicated the walk and the little pathway that brought them through the section of ground-floor apartments.

He knocked at the first door.

Justin Bolton opened the door, looking at them anxiously. He was a man in his late thirties, with a receding hairline and anxious hazel eyes.

"Detective, thank you. I mean, we're feeling desperate. We can't believe you haven't found them yet; and every hour, we're more and more worried that—"

"They're alive, Mr. Bolton," Skye said. "Patricia and Jeremy are alive. We've found enough clues in movement to assure us that they're still alive."

"For how long?" the man wailed miserably. "We read the papers and watch every scrap of news on the TV, on the Internet! They are reporting that they were kidnapped by a green witch. Can that be true? What the hell! I mean, everyone saw *Hocus Pocus*. A cute movie, makes good use of the city's history in a fantasy vein, but . . . what if those kidnapped are wanted for a strange ritual—as sacrifices? Doesn't every single moment count? And . . ." Justin paused, looking from Gavin Bruns to Zach and Skye. "I'm sorry, I . . . I'm Justin Bolton and this is my wife behind me, Alicia."

"We do apologize," Alicia said. "But you must understand—"

"We do understand," Zach assured her. "I'm Special Agent Zachary Erickson, and this is my partner, Special Agent Skye McMahon. We have police and the federal government working on this, doing everything in our power. And, sir, ma'am, we're here today because we will leave no stone unturned. We're hoping you might have an idea about people in the area who may be up to something. We believe they're keeping the children in a forest or somewhere very dark. They are necessarily scared; but from everything that we've gleaned, Patricia will be guarding Jeremy with everything in her, making sure that he's alive and well until we're able to find them. But please think—think hard. Is there anyone you know who might—"

"No one has a grudge against either of us, I swear it!" Justin said, shaking his head, his face a mask of worry and pain.

"The question is really this," Skye said gently. "And think, please; do you know about anyone who might be taking stories about the devil being in the woods too seriously, or even someone who might gain from getting others to believe so?"

Alicia and Justin looked at one another for a long moment.

"Have you done a ghost tour lately?" Alicia asked.

"You know tour guides?"

"Well, there's a new tour group that started up recently. They pride themselves on being the spookiest tour out there, working off the distant past and the more recent past," Alicia told them.

"Yeah. They'll probably get our place on one of their tours

soon enough. We can't stop them from being on the road or on a sidewalk, but they'd best not step one foot on our property!" Justin announced.

"Well, your place is a little out of the center of town," Zach reminded them.

"But they're going to start up a trolley tour. I mean, there are already all kinds of tours, but . . . well, we know that Patricia and some of her friends took one of their tours recently. Patricia was all excited about it. She always said that history was sad and tragic, but that what people liked to twist it all into could be a lot of fun," Alicia shared.

"Fun, yeah. Make light of the awful things that happened in the past," Justin said. "Patricia is young, and sweet, and . . . today's teens should get to be young and sweet. I'm sorry. That's all we've got. But if you're looking for weirdos, those tour operators might be just where you want to start!"

"Thank you so much for your help," Skye said sincerely. "And we will investigate the tour company, we promise."

Justin and Alicia both nodded solemnly.

"All right, we're back to work," Gavin vowed. "And, of course—"

"You'll keep us up on whatever you learn!" Justin said.

"Of course," Gavin said.

They left the apartment building and walked the short distance to the car. Zach leaned forward and asked, "Gavin, what do you know about this tour company?"

"They're called Ghastly, Ghostly History," Gavin said, glancing back at him through the rearview mirror. "The company was opened by Ted and Laurie Sizemore about six months ago. The Sizemore family and Laurie's family are old-time residents—who knows, if you guys were hanging around here as kids, you might have come across them. The Sizemore family used to own a place on Congress Street that sold all kinds of potions. Ted's dad had owned the place and operated it as a shop that sold camping equipment. That was before Ted was born, sometime in the 1970s. Anyway, by the time Ted grew up, witchcraft shops were the rave, and so he turned it into a potion shop. He and his wife have done really well; they have a local wiccan, Linda Marino, who pretty much manages—and mans—the whole place herself, leaving them time to start up this new company. They've done all the right legal stuff to be legit."

"Anyone getting into business of any kind would want to do the right things to keep law enforcement of any kind out of their lives," Zach said.

"Zach, the problem here is that they may be entirely innocent of anything except for loving the lore and creating a business from it," Skye said.

"And then again . . . you two need to take a tour!" Gavin asserted. "I mean, they'd know me. I've been around too long. But they don't know you, and it's unlikely that any tourists who sign up for a tour will know you. You're a cute couple; you're in Salem! Naturally, you'll want to take a cool tour."

Skye groaned softly.

"And you . . . no shenanigans, Special Agent Erickson!" Gavin said lightly.

Zach frowned. *It's almost as if Gavin Bruns knew what I'd been thinking when we had parked before walking the last few steps to see Justin and Alicia Bolton.*

Interesting.

"All right, I'm looking up tour information now, except . . ."

"Except?" Zach asked.

She looked back at him apologetically. "Sorry, I went down the old rabbit hole." She glanced over at Gavin as he drove, explaining, "Since we've come here, I've tried learning everything possible—from different sources—about the trials. This is kind of sad. Tituba was arrested first. The girls probably blamed her because she'd told them stories to entertain them, and since she hadn't been raised a Puritan, her stories might have been a bit ghostly. They really aren't sure about Tituba's background. She might have been taken as a slave from Barbados . . . No one really knows. She was married to an indigenous man named John Indian. But, okay, think about it. Winters without our modern heating devices, dark as dark can be. The Puritan hardcore belief in evil, in the devil . . . So she confesses to witchcraft," Skye continued, paraphrasing from her phone. "Sarah Good and Sarah Osbourne are accused—by Tituba, according to many sources. Okay, now as far as the girls went . . . Betty Parris and Ann Putnam. They started having fits. The doctor couldn't figure out what was wrong. Really? Shocking that a doctor in the late 1600s didn't have every available diagnostic tool possible. Of course, if he couldn't cure them, it had to be something evil! And so, it all began.

"But I'm reading a great article that stresses how much these trials had to do with the way we learned that we had to create laws that stopped mass hysteria, possibly fueled by wrongs, imagined or real, that could bring about the executions of so many. Oh, yes, nineteen hanged, Giles Corey pressed to death—and at least five, possibly many more, who died in the disease-ridden and filthy jails! Here's what I don't get: Why wasn't anyone worried about the fact that, if they were indeed witches, they could have struck all their accusers down with a bolt of lightning?"

"They were afraid of their powers—thus the many people in jail who were chained—and charged for their chains," Gavin reminded them.

"No spectral evidence," Zach murmured, looking at Skye. She turned to look back at him and smiled. "Law enforcement. Even if their gifts allowed them to suspect someone or even see the truth, they needed proof."

And thus, they made their way through the academy; they worked cases with other agents before they might be approached by Jackson.

And it was right. No innocent man or woman should ever be condemned. Being in Salem brought that home more than ever.

"Okay, we're here," Gavin said, drawing into a parking lot.

There was a large convention center–looking building in front of them. It appeared to be relatively new, and, of course, nice—a great place for a senior dance.

"They didn't have the dance at the school?" Skye asked, exiting the car.

"The school is older, decent, but the rooms here are larger, better suited for having a DJ and the crowning of the king and queen for the year, all that," Gavin told them. "There's nothing going on this morning; but by tonight, employees of a giant tech firm will be taking over. So we need to see what we can see now."

"Great. Thanks for arranging this so quickly," Zach told him.

"Of course," Gavin said. "This way. I have the code to the side door. Come on in, follow me."

They didn't go through the large entry doors, handsomely flanked by columns and a sign that welcomed people to the new facility. Instead, they walked around to a side entry where Gavin used a code to open a door, keying in a second code once they were inside to prevent any alarms from sounding.

Every move they made seemed to cause an echo.

"Wow!" Zach commented. "I have never been in a place this size with no one else in it before."

"Hey, Gavin and I are in it!" Skye corrected.

"Eh, you know what I mean," he retorted.

"This is just a breakout room," Gavin told them. "Come on through here; I'll show you the main convention hall, the stage, and the side kitchens."

He took them through. The place was sparkling clean.

"They must have the best pickup detail known to man," Skye said.

"Yes, they do a good job," Gavin said. "All these are break-out rooms, then that archway just ahead leads into the main hall."

They stepped through the archway. The hall was huge, with a high stage that appeared to be well-equipped.

"I spoke to the local police chief," Gavin told them. "They have a giant party here Halloween night with costumes, prizes, music, food, cash bars . . . He said that it's insane, but it brings people here when they don't fit in Salem for the holiday."

"I guess a big Halloween party in the area is a money-maker," Skye remarked. "It really is a great place. That stage is huge. And I'm willing to bet that it's equipped with the best in lights, curtains, rigging, you name it. Do they have a theatrical company—"

"A local community theater is involved right now, and very happily involved. They're looking forward to becoming pro-fessional. And, of course, it can be rented out for concerts and all kinds of venues. Follow me. We'll take a look at the kitchen and prep rooms and then we can split up and wander at will, if you like."

He walked them through the kitchens first, then an enor-mous pantry, then a prep room that also contained numerous refrigerators and freezers—and even microwaves.

The main kitchen offered ovens, stovetops, and grills, and numerous counters that sat under lights for plates ready to be taken out to guests who were seated for an elaborate dinner, or for servers to carry out on appetizer trays they might offer around the room when the dance floor had been cleared and the setup was for a more casual evening.

"It's an amazing place," Skye commented.

Zach wondered how they were going to shake Gavin. There was little he could do here—the place had obviously been scoured since the teenage dance. But Skye . . .

"So you should wander at will," Zach murmured.

"Right," Skye replied. She wandered out of the kitchen and into the main hall.

She stood for several seconds, staring ahead. Then she turned toward the stage, but she didn't head toward the steps that led up to the raised floor.

She just looked ahead, keeping her back to both Gavin and Zach.

Then she turned around and said, "We're parked in front. But is there a back alley, loading docks, anything like that?"

"Yeah, sure, of course," Gavin told them. "We need to go back through the kitchens. Right behind the area with all the equipment, there's a sliding door that leads to a wide entry; when necessary, a truck can drive up a ramp and right in to make deliveries."

"Nicely done," Zach whispered.

They followed Gavin as he showed them where a ramp could be set up and a truck could drive right on up to the concrete.

"Interesting, considering the weight of a truck," Zach said.

"The ramp is concrete—it comes up from beneath the ground," Gavin explained.

"Okay, that makes more physical sense," Zach agreed.

"The door opens back there; and to the side, you can find some steps. I'll get the sliding door—wait!" Gavin warned as he saw Skye heading to a handle on the metal doors. "Let me put the code in!"

"Oh, thanks, I'm sorry!" Skye said quickly.

She looked back at Zach as Gavin went to open the delivery doors for her.

She had seen something; out here, she would see more.

"Okay, thanks!" she told Gavin, heading for the steps.

"Hey, Gavin, maybe you could show me—" Zach began.

But Gavin was already following Skye. Swearing softly beneath his breath, Zach swiftly followed Gavin as he followed Skye.

There was a wide alley in the back, framed by a scruffy field. There were scattered trees about, but not thick enough to allow for the ragged field beyond to be called a forest.

But Skye wasn't looking at the empty growth to her side.

She was starting down the length of the alley.

He'd need to be alone with her, somehow, and soon.

"Gavin, I think we should head back in and take a look around the main hall," Zach said. "Or the loading area, see if anything was left anywhere—"

"No, the action is here. They disappeared from this alley," Gavin said with a grin, turning to look at Zach. "Here, right here. Skye is seeing something—and we need to know what it is, when she's ready to tell us."

CHAPTER 9

"Pardon?" Zach asked, frowning, staring warily at Lieutenant Gavin Bruns.

The officer just smiled at him and shrugged. "Well," he said, "did you think that I called Jackson Crow just because I like federal involvement in cases? Skye is seeing something. You know it and I know it. And . . . well, do you know what it is that she's seeing?"

"No," Zach said flatly. "We're just going to have to ask her." Still frowning, he stared at Gavin Bruns. "And what do you mean, she's 'seeing something'?"

But Bruns smiled and shook his head.

"You had to figure I knew all about Adam Harrison and Jackson Crow, and, of course, about Jackson's special division of the Bureau," Gavin said.

"I figured you respected Jackson because he got a case closed," Zach said, shaking his head. "Does Jackson know that you know?"

"Honestly?" Gavin asked, shrugging. "Probably not. And I'm not even sure if what I believe is the truth. After he was here on a case, I went online and pulled up everything I could about the 'special' unit. Still, sometimes . . . but I've spent my life wondering about myself, always afraid to be honest, and—"

"You see and speak with the dead, souls who remain in their spirit form?" Zach asked.

"No."

"No. But you know about Jackson and the Krewe. And you know Skye is seeing something. Okay, I'm sorry, I'm completely confused."

Gavin took a deep breath. "Okay, at first, I thought Jackson Crow was certifiably crazy. I thought he was talking to a tree. I had been behind him, and he hadn't known I was there; but when he turned around, he had an answer to a mystery that only a member of the Duarte family might have known, and . . . the last of the family had left here thirty years ago. So I guessed that he had a power—"

"You just believed that, without thinking he was crazy?" Zach pressed.

"You don't understand."

"You said that you don't see the dead," Zach reminded him.

"I don't. Neither do you. I think I have Skye figured out, but you . . ."

"Touch," Zach said. "A personal object. Sometimes I can see what the last person who held it is doing or where they are."

"But you don't know where the victims are yet?" Gavin asked anxiously.

"In the darkness. But they're alive. And wait a second, I was asking—"

"Minds," Gavin told him.

"What?"

"That's why I make a good detective," Gavin told him dryly. "Not always, but often enough, I can read the mind of someone I'm talking to. The problem is, of course, when I'm with several people, it's sometimes like a lot of shouting in a concert hall. And it's not a guarantee. But then, often in an interrogation room, I'm alone with a suspect. And I can read guilt or innocence, regret and resentment."

Zach nodded slowly, looking at him. "It's good to know. Does anyone you work with have any idea about this talent of yours?"

"Hell no. I make a point of keeping my distance from detectives like Berkley and Cason, because . . . they're both hardcore. There's very little gray area in anything that has to do with the two of them. I was promoted before the two of them; and they already resent that, so, well, I keep clear. And I watch it with the patrol team—and frankly, everyone else."

Zach smiled suddenly. "I know how you feel. But if you don't mind, I want to tell the truth to Skye, Jackson, Angela, and anyone in our unit who becomes involved in this. It is so much easier to work when you can be honest, and we're just learning that ourselves. Jackson . . . watches agents. He and Angela study them and their methods, and Skye and I are different from the Krewe he's already put together, but . . . the thing is, he knows that some of us do have something that helps."

"Too bad I'm not an agent!" Gavin said.

"Well, you could be. I can't imagine a detective with your record wouldn't do well in the academy," Zach told him.

As he spoke, Skye turned around and looked at him. She frowned.

Because, of course, when she'd been seeing what had happened here in the past, she hadn't heard a word he and Gavin had exchanged.

But she knew something had gone on.

She looked from Zach to Gavin and back to Zach.

"What's going on?" she asked.

"He knows," Zach told her.

"Knows . . . what?"

"That you were looking into the past," Zach said flatly.

Of course, she stared at him then, as if he'd lost his mind.

"Skye, please, it's not Zach's fault. I was explaining to him that . . . I knew about Jackson. That he talked to the dead—"

"And you just accepted that?" Skye said.

"I had my reasons," Gavin said.

"He's a mind reader who, like the rest of us, spent most of his life thinking he was crazy, so when he sees others . . . he's not so quick to judge," Zach explained.

"But if you can just read someone's mind, can't—whoops, sorry. I guess you can't just walk around town and ask people to stand still so you can stare at them and find out what they're thinking," she said quickly. But she half-smiled, and half-frowned, as she asked, "Does it work all the time? Of course not. No one can ever guarantee that a departed soul will be around to help someone. I have no guarantee that I will see the past at the time I need to see it. We can only hope our talents work. How do you keep it from your co-workers?" she asked.

"I keep my distance," Gavin said.

"I guess that's what we always did," Skye said to Zach.

"Right. We've established we're all weird. Skye, what did you see?" Zach asked.

"They left from here," she said, pointing at the exit to the alley. "I saw them at the dance, and they were whispering to one another. I couldn't hear them because the music was loud and there were so many people. It was growing late and people were beginning to spill out the front—only a few of the kids were slipping through the kitchen areas to get out to the alley. When the kids came out here, they were alone. And they stood here for a minute, saw a dark sedan out on the road, and ran over to it."

"So they did elope?" Gavin asked.

"I don't know if they eloped or not; I do know they hurried to the car that was picking them up. I tried so hard to see something about the car, but . . . nothing. I don't even know if it was black, dark blue, or dark green. And it was definitely a sedan of some kind, but what make or model I don't know. Maybe they were lured by someone, or maybe they had made arrangements with someone to help them . . . I don't know. All I know for sure is they saw the car, and ran out to it, hopped into it—and were gone. I wish, I wish, that I had seen something that was really helpful!" Skye said.

"But that is incredibly helpful!" Gavin said. "We know that they went willingly—at least at first—with whoever came for them. And it will be important."

"Thanks!" Skye said. She smiled and shook her head. "Sorry. This is so weird!"

"I see it as amazing and good," Gavin told them.

Zach grinned. "Amazing and good. You're right. But we still have kids to find!"

"Right! Time to move on to the parents!" Gavin said.

He turned to lead the way back through the convention center, keying in the proper codes to ensure the place was duly relocked.

Skye looked at Zach as they moved along, as if questioning him regarding Lieutenant Gavin Bruns.

Could it all be real? she wondered.

Zach believed the man. And he wondered how difficult it might be for him, having risen so far so quickly because of his ability to solve cases.

And having to work with detectives like Cason and Berkley, who certainly resented his quick ascension in the department.

"Well," he whispered to Skye as they walked ahead to the car, while Gavin assured himself that he'd indeed secured the place, "that explains a lot. He's the man in charge; he was the one who could call on us."

"Do you think he really reads minds?" she asked worriedly. "We aren't being played, right?"

"I sincerely believe that everything about the man is real," Zach assured her.

"Okay, then. That makes us a bit of a trio."

"Not a bad thing."

"No, not at all. Especially since he is local law enforcement and on our side."

Gavin turned around, arching a brow. "Rather rude to discuss me when I'm right here," he told them.

They looked at one another and groaned and looked at Gavin.

"Let's talk about him right in front of him, only makes sense!" Zach said.

But Gavin chuckled. "I'm not even reading minds. I'm reading your faces. You guys are both pretty cool. We're going to get to the bottom of this. Okay, so, which set of nasty parents do you want to start with?"

"They're nasty?" Skye asked.

Gavin made a face. "I don't know. Maybe they're usually all right. It's just that they're both convinced their little darling was swayed by the other little darling to cause trouble. Apparently, they've both been convinced that they are one another's true love—and that nothing matters except for the two of them being together."

As they got into the car, Skye mused, "But it doesn't really make sense. They're going to graduate this year. Beau Carter is eighteen and Allie Mason is about to be eighteen. They could just wait, graduate from high school, and if they were so eager to be together, they could just screw the concept of college, get jobs, and get married. Once they're both eighteen, they can be together all the time, whether their parents like it or not."

"True. Which is why, I'm sure, the parents are so upset. I mean, what parent doesn't dream of their kid going to college, getting a great job, and living happily ever after?" Zach said.

"I spoke with the local police, and they informed them we'd be by to speak with them," Gavin said. "Apparently, the two have been in trouble a few times already. Beau crawled through a window in Allie's house. They have an old place, an old Victorian house, nice big oak tree right outside, and it's no trick for a kid that age to shinny up a tree, find the right branch, and slide through a window. Then Allie was on a school camping trip and snuck him into the girls' section and . . ." he broke off, shrugging. "Teenage love and mischief or something else? Hard to tell."

"Will you know if the parents are telling the truth when we speak with them?" Skye asked Gavin.

"I can't guarantee it. But if I know, I know."

From the rear seat, Zach could see that he lowered his head. He wished he were a mind reader himself.

Gavin was disturbed by something, perhaps something caused by his ability or maybe just something he knew about because of his ability.

"Well, I believe your talent will come in handy," Zach said. "The problem with this case so far isn't too many suspects— it's that everyone we talk to seems to be innocent, determined that the kids and women be found, passionate that they be found, and decent, maybe even kind. But someone must know something."

"Heading to the home of Allie's parents, Theodore and Emilia Mason," Gavin said. "It's the farthest, so we'll start there and be on our way back when we drop by to speak with Art and Sybil Carter."

"It's a plan," Skye said.

Everyone was quiet for a minute; then Gavin asked, "Skye, did you see a witch—I mean, in a vision of the recent past, did you see a green witch? There was no disappearing comment on social media, right?"

"There was no comment on social media," Skye admitted. "Yes. In both cases—or all three cases, really. Also, there are two criminals—at least two—involved in these kidnappings. And," she added quietly, "the murder of Mike Bolton."

"Two or more," Gavin said. "And Halloween will be up and running soon. We always have our witchcraft stores up and running, and many of the restaurants use decorations—like skeletons, ghosts, *witches*—all year round." He paused, shaking his head as he drove. "Most of the time, it's tremendous fun. After the movie *Hocus Pocus* came out, we've had dozens of trios on the streets dressed up as the Sanderson sisters. Of course, we've had our share of modern-day-movie witches forever, too. But this . . . We've never had characters kidnapping people before, not to my knowledge! Oh, and we're here! That's the house right there. Beautiful, isn't it?"

The home was gorgeous. Victorian and lovingly maintained, so it appeared. Unblemished blue paint covered the house, enhanced by white trim around the windows and on the porch railings, as well as the two balconies that were visible from the street.

"And there's the offending tree!" Zach said lightly. "I take it one of those is Allie's balcony?"

"Easy for a kid in good shape to get up the tree and over to the balcony," Gavin agreed.

They exited the car, and Gavin led the way to the front door. He raised his hand to knock, but the door opened before he could do so.

The woman standing there appeared to be in her fifties, with her short hair dyed silver and coiffed beautifully into gentle curls that handsomely framed her face. She was about five-five and medium in build, but tiny next to the large bald man who came to stand behind her. "Thank God, you're here! You are the Feds, right?" he bellowed before his wife could say a word.

"Sir," Gavin said, "I'm Lieutenant Bruns from Salem. These folks are the Feds, Special Agents Erickson and McMahon."

"Come in, come in! Now, mind you, I don't know what to

think! The first cop we spoke to was simply convinced that my daughter and that fellow waltzed off together because of a plan that they'd made! But she's not eighteen yet, and I want that young monster arrested. You need to find them and arrest him. Allie was a good kid until she met that wretch of a boy!"

"Theo, please, we need to invite them in!" Emilia Mason said.

"Yes, please, of course, of course, come in!" her husband said.

The door opened wide and the three of them entered.

The parlor was exquisite, with period furniture, shining hardwood floors, and elegant throw rugs that matched what were certainly custom-made draperies. The mantel was large, created from marble, and covered with family photos flanked by two vases filled with red roses.

A group of chairs surrounded a coffee table behind the couch, and an additional set of chairs offered a view of the mammoth-screen TV.

The family was more than well-off—they were downright rich.

Which made Zach wonder. Allie had to be accustomed to all the best that could be had in life. She'd surely never wanted anything that couldn't be provided for her. She certainly had to fear the concept of her parents disowning her.

And trying to make a decent living as a high school graduate.

Then again, young love could be fierce. Maybe she was so in love with young Beau that she would give up everything.

Until, of course, she would discover that even food had to be paid for.

They all sat, and Zach quickly spoke. "Please believe that we will do everything in our power to find your daughter. But we believe there was someone in their lives with whom they went willingly from the dance. Perhaps an older friend, who was a student before them, and then again perhaps just a classmate.

We have a witness who saw them leave the dance by the back alley—and hurry to hop into a dark sedan. Does that strike any chords with you? Is there someone in their lives who might have influenced them—or promised them a place to stay?"

Emilia and Theo looked at one another, frowning.

"Well, there's that fellow I saw watching Beau at the game," Emilia said.

"At the game," Skye said quietly. "What game, and watching how? Did the two speak at any time that you saw?"

"I'm afraid it's no secret that we don't like Beau," Emilia said. "But I will hand the young man this—he's an amazing football player. Put their school on the map with his prowess on the field. Anyway, this man was in the front row one night and he just kept watching Beau. And I think they did talk, at least a minute, when Beau was on the field, before all the players ran together to congratulate one another. I had the strange feeling they knew one another. But when I asked Allie about him—if Beau had family in from another state or something, she just shook her head and told me that everyone admired Beau."

"We tried to forbid her from seeing him," Theo added. "After we caught him in the house one night. But Allie threatened to run away then."

Huge tears struck Emilia's eyes. "I don't understand! Threatening was one thing. But even if she meant to spend her life with him once she turned eighteen, why would she disappear with him now? They were both about to graduate, they could have had . . ."

"Everything," Theo said. "If we couldn't shake him, I would have helped him."

"How?" Skye asked.

"His family hasn't got two red cents to put together. I'd have helped him through college, and, of course, the kid had a dozen scholarships offered, I believe, as *he* persuaded Allie to go to college. The kid and I had already talked about it! That's why . . .

On the one hand, and to law enforcement who first showed up here, it seemed obvious they had run away. And I had to think about it. But the more I think about it, the more I just don't believe they chose to disappear all on their own," Theo said.

"Please! Married, not married!" Emilia said. "We just want to know that our only child is alive!"

"We promise to do everything in our power," Zach said solemnly.

"And these two are Feds!" Theo said, looking at his wife.

"We'd like some little thing that belongs to Allie," Zach said.

"What? Why?" Emilia asked worriedly. "When people want DNA, it's because they're trying to identify a body!"

"No, no, that's not why we need something. Having an object can help us when we're on a trail—we can use it to tell if someone came a certain way or if they've been in a certain place," Skye said easily. "You never know," she added. "There might be something left behind, DNA, cigarette butts, trash with fingerprints. And sometimes, just what you see somewhere."

There was something about her gentle words and her demeanor that always seemed to be reassuring to others when they spoke.

Well, her words were partially true. It was always good to have DNA, though they hadn't gone the DNA route yet—so far. It wouldn't have been all that hopeful.

And Zach prayed silently, hopefully, they wouldn't need DNA to identify any burned or badly decomposed bodies.

They are all alive so far, he reminded himself.

Except, of course, Mike Bolton.

And as he stood silently, waiting for Emilia to retrieve something of her daughter's, he wondered why it had been so necessary for the kidnappers to kill the man.

What had he known about them? Would he have known them, dressed up as witches or not?

Hairbrushes seemed to be the item of choice. Emilia disappeared and returned with a brush and handed it to Skye.

That was for the best. If the brush was going to tell him anything, Zach figured it would be good if he was away from her parents when it did.

Just in case.

And he didn't want to think about the "just in case."

"We know, of course, about the kidnappings; and we're praying for everyone out there!" Emilia said. "But . . . they're older, you know. So, yes, we do believe that they went off together—"

"But how?" Theo demanded. "I control Allie's bank card and her credit card, and she hasn't used them! That boy, he doesn't have . . . well, a pot to piss in, as they say. Right now, we just want to know that our daughter is alive!"

"Sir, we will do everything in our power. And we have teams of people across the state and beyond now. We promise to let you know as soon as we discover anything, anything at all. But again, if you think of anything, anyone who might have been hanging around them, persuading them that they should disappear, please let us know!" Gavin told the pair.

"Of course!" Theo vowed.

Five minutes later, they were in the car again.

Skye turned and gave the brush to Zach.

Zach held it and closed his eyes.

It wasn't dark, but neither was it light, because Allie was surrounded by trees. He could see the world that Allie Mason was seeing.

Beau wasn't at her side and that made her nervous. In fact . . .

She was worried. Trepidatious. Something had gone wrong; something wasn't as she expected it to be.

Someone was crying near her. He heard the words of a child.

"I want my mommy!"

"Shush, darling, it's all right!"

Allie couldn't see the speakers; she could just hear them. And she couldn't move because her hands were behind her back. She was tied to the trunk of a large tree. The oak was so large that the branches were weighing down all around her, obscuring the world with the richness of their leaves.

The vision faded.

"What is it?" Skye asked him anxiously.

He shook his head. "Allie is tied to a tree somewhere. One of the kids is crying—Jeremy, I think. Patricia is trying to assure him, to keep him behaving so that he'll remain safe."

"So, what the hell is going on?" Gavin muttered angrily.

"What did you get from the parents?" Zach asked him.

"Honesty, I'm afraid. They were both telling the truth—as they know it," Gavin said. "Trees and woods. We could search the rest of our days."

"We believe, from what we and others searching in the field discovered, that the kidnappers took Jeremy and Patricia from the Bolton house through the woods to another road—but they're heading to another forest somewhere. That seems to be what Zach and I are both seeing. We must figure out where; something, somewhere, must give us a clue as to what forest and where!"

"All right, well, we're heading back toward Salem, with a stop by Beau's parents' house. Maybe they can give us something!" Gavin mused.

"Or someone. We need a someone," Zach said. "Any idea how we can find out who this person watching Beau while he was playing football might be?"

"Maybe Beau's parents can give us an idea," Gavin suggested.

Skye sighed softly. "And maybe it was a college scout or just a friend of the family. We need to find a way to really get a handle on this."

"Beau's parents, next stop," Gavin told them.

* * *

The house was far different from the elegant old Victorian they had just left.

It was a two-story home, but the paint was faded and peeling. Tile steps that led to a small porch appeared chipped in some areas and broken in others.

The car that sat in front of the house was a minivan that had to be at least fifteen years old.

"I can see where Allie's folks might believe that Beau isn't up to their standards," Gavin observed.

"As if money or someone's background would automatically make the boy a bad influence. I'm assuming he's keeping his grades up if he's on the football team, and it sounds as if he was an important player," Skye said. She sounded angry.

Zach smiled inwardly. Of course, Skye would hate that the amount of money someone possessed would create a judgment regarding a human soul.

"'Never judge a book by its cover,' and all that," Zach murmured. "They know we're coming—"

"Yep!" Gavin assured him. He exited the car, and they joined him walking to the front door and knocking upon it.

This time, no one showed up right away.

"Think they hightailed it out of town?" Gavin theorized.

Zach pounded on the door. "Federal agents!" he called out.

They heard footsteps; someone was coming at last.

The door was opened by a tall, broad-shouldered man, one who was probably in excellent shape at one time, but was just now developing a little bit of middle-age spread. He had a full head of graying-brown hair and a face that appeared haggard and worried.

"I'm sorry, I'm sorry, just out of the shower," he told them. "I'm Artie, Artie Carter. My wife is in the kitchen; we've got some coffee on. Would you like some?"

Skye glanced briefly at Zach before uttering a friendly "Sure!"

As they walked in, Skye was the one to do the introductions, repeated when they reached the kitchen and met Mrs. Sybil Carter. She poured cups of coffee, and Zach glanced at Gavin then—who gave him a nod as Skye had become prone to do when they were asking themselves if they were making a good read.

The Carters were nervous and miserable, truly anxious to be as helpful as they could be. Sybil Carter had been brewing the coffee—which she set out with a plate of homemade muffins—because she was worried, anxious, and needed something to do.

"I wish, I wish, I wish, that we could help you! Please," Artie said, "ask us anything; we are so worried about our boy!"

"I keep telling him it's that awful girl!" Sybil moaned. She was a tiny, slim woman, maybe five-four at a stretch. Like her husband, she appeared weary and haggard, but once, she had been an attractive woman.

"And they try to blame things on our boy!" Artie told them, shaking his head. "Beau is eighteen. He's a good kid, I swear. Excellent grades, works so hard. While that girl . . ."

He shook his head again, his voice trailing.

"Artie," Sybil said softly, "I don't think Allie is that terrible. It's just that she was raised to think everything in life would be handed to her. And her parents! They think money makes the world; and since we don't have any, they think Beau must be a horrible creature. He's anything but! I know we're his parents, and we're prejudiced, but you ask his friends, his teachers . . ."

"And those idiots are so full of it!" Artie told them. "Beau is the one who is going to suffer for this. He was in the offing for a full scholarship to college!"

"Several offers," Sybil corrected.

"He's had several scouts after him from several colleges!" Artie said.

"Scouts, of course. We've heard he's an amazing athlete,"

Skye said. "We understand that at the last game he played, someone was watching him. Was that a scout?"

"The last game . . ." Sybil mused.

"Yes, yes, of course!" Artie said, enthused. "I only met him briefly. He was going to speak with Beau after the game, and I guess that he did. Beau was getting a ride home with a friend, and Sybil and I took off after the game."

"I'm a housekeeper," Sybil explained. "And I start early."

"As do I. Construction," Artie said. "But that's just it. Our boy has been scouted by big places—Tennessee, Miami, Pennsylvania. He has everything in front of him!"

"If his infatuation for that girl doesn't ruin his life!" Sybil said passionately.

"Unless it wasn't the girl at all," Artie told them. "I mean, we heard about the kids who were taken by a witch in Salem! Go figure. Do you think . . . Oh, my God, is our boy even alive?"

His wife let out a sob.

"We have good reason to believe that those kidnapped are alive—" Skye began.

"But someone murdered that man! That man—" Sybil began.

"Mike Bolton. Old fellow, killed in his bed, from what we saw on the news," Artie said.

"But we have found clues in the woods that suggest the children are all still alive. Sir, with your permission, of course, we'll check with the schools. Witnesses saw Beau and Allie leave with someone in a dark sedan after the dance," Zach explained. "We think they were lured away with a promise of something. Did you try to forbid Beau from seeing Allie?"

Sybil and Artie looked at each other, both shaking their heads.

"We didn't; Allie's parents did," Artie told them. "Except they didn't try to forbid Allie from going to school events. So, yes, she saw Beau at games; and they both went to that dance. Do you think—"

"We seriously think they're fine, and we're going to find them," Skye said, her voice gentle and assuring. "But here's the thing—we believe someone did get to them. Maybe this person promised they would just spirit them away to be alone for a bit, or gave them some other reason to go and get into that car."

She stopped speaking, looking from Gavin to Zach.

"We'll think. I promise, we'll think and think!" Sybil told them. "Beau has spoken with scouts at school, but why would a scout try to spirit him and Allie away?"

A scout wouldn't, Zach knew.

But someone pretending to be a scout might.

"We'll check into it with the school," Zach promised. "And anything—"

"We'll call you. We'll talk. We'll think of anything and everything!" Sybil promised.

Her husband set an arm around her shoulders. "We need our boy back. Please, we're begging you."

"And we won't stop," Skye promised. "Question, though. Did Beau really climb through a window at the Mason house—"

"Yes, and he was duly reprimanded," Artie said. "The kid is a teen in love! And her parents were so horrible to him! It was a chance to see her—and, not to mention, she told him to come over and climb through the window."

Teens in love. None of that part of the story seemed faulty.

In fact . . .

Zach looked at Gavin.

The Carters were telling the truth. The truth, as they knew it.

"All right. We'll be in constant touch," Zach promised. "By the way, though, do you have something of Zach's that we can take?"

He knew the look. The look of horror. Everyone assumed that they were looking for DNA—to compare with that on a burned or decomposed corpse.

"Helps us when we find little clues—we can follow people that way!" Skye assured him quickly.

This time, when Sybil disappeared and reappeared, she was carrying a T-shirt.

"I haven't washed it yet; he was wearing it right before he disappeared," Sybil told him. "Bits of DNA possible, maybe?"

"It's perfect, thank you," Zach said.

"We'll get on everything that we can," Gavin said. "And thank you so much for the coffee and muffins. They were delicious."

Zach and Skye echoed his thanks, and they managed to get out the door and headed back to the car.

"I'll get on retrieving information from whatever cameras there might have been at that game," Gavin said. "See if that was a scout or not—or if one of the scouts he saw previously isn't on record with the school. There will be security footage from the school. But techs will get on that, once I make the call. So, where do we go now?"

Zach was holding the shirt.

He closed his eyes. And he saw what Beau Carter saw.

He opened his eyes and spoke to Skye and Gavin.

"Into the woods," he told them.

CHAPTER 10

Zach took a breath, shaking his head.

"Let's get in the car and talk," Gavin suggested.

They did so.

Zach took his seat in the back, and Gavin and Skye both twisted around from the front to listen to him.

"I don't know what the plan or agenda might be," Zach told the two of them. "But the two didn't think that they were disappearing from the party that night. There was someone who, I believe, convinced the two of them that expediency was urgent; they had a full scholarship for Beau—football—that also gave him living facilities. And if he was given private living facilities, Allie could live with him. All she would need to do was talk her parents into giving her a little help; and if she couldn't, she could apply for financial aid and get a part-time job. Then they could be together. But it seems the people offering them the help turned out to be strange; they had to live in the woods and learn the ways of the master first."

"'The master'?" Gavin repeated.

"Yes. And . . . I think I heard that term from Patricia or one of the kids," Zach said.

"'Master'?" Skye said, too, frowning. "Okay, so the two of them agreed to go with whoever was in the sedan, but they didn't agree to be swept off wherever they are now."

He shook his head. "If I'm feeling what Beau is feeling, it's a mixture of confusion and anger. He and Allie are not being kept together; women stay with the children. And he's with . . ." Zach paused, wincing, trying to see clearly what he had seen through another person's eyes. "I think he's with a homeless man who has been weaned off drugs, but a man so broken and miserable he thinks that he's been saved somehow, that this master person saved him."

"None of this makes sense," Gavin said.

"Wait, in a way, it makes perfect sense," Skye told him. "Kidnap children—and a mom and a young woman who is a perfect nanny and loves kids. Put them with children. Threaten the lives of children, and adults will agree to almost anything. They're being brainwashed. This master is trying to create a village, or a group—"

"A cult!" Gavin snapped. "Playing on the devil in the woods in Salem. It's—heinous! I mean, I love this community. The history is horrible, but those who choose to identify as wiccans here are good people, and the others . . . either just stay here because they're from here or they have family here, or because they can have fun and make a lot of money with creatures, even when it's not Halloween."

"I share your feelings," Zach told him.

"Are you certain—"

"I'm not certain of anything, except that whoever is doing this is keeping the people alive. He—or they—want something from them, but they need to be able to reprogram them. Deny people enough, scare them enough, you can do a lot with the human psyche," Zach said.

"In a strange way, it makes sense," Skye said. "You said there's someone with Beau in the men's quarters, or whatever. That means this started before anyone knew. The people selected were addicts or mentally ill, probably on the streets, having no family to miss them when they disappeared. And I believe they're using drugs themselves to control those that they are stealing from houses, shops—or even teenage dances."

"All right," Gavin said after a minute. "We believe we know what is going on, even if we don't know exactly why."

Zach shrugged. "Well . . . revenge for a slight, real or imagined. A simple psycho. There have been some wacky politicians out there, but I really don't think that this is a way to run for office."

"Who knows?" Skye said. "All you do is convince people who lean toward an idea that anything against it is a lie, and you can move mountains—or millions of people. But that would need to be something far in the future. How they possibly think they can get away with this forever—"

"They've done a good job so far," Zach said.

"The tour," Gavin said suddenly.

"What?" Zach questioned, sincerely confused for a minute.

"The tour! I never booked it." He had his phone out.

"You are the one who can read minds. I still think you're better suited to take it," Skye reminded him.

"No. Like I told you before, I'm known in Salem. Not by everyone, no; but if someone recognizes me along the way, on one of the stops . . . well, it needs to be you two. And if you suspect anyone, I'll make a point of meeting them when they can't keep their distance from me. But I do think it's important for you to find out what is going on with that, discover if someone on the tour said something to our missing teenagers," Gavin said.

"I guess we're going on a tour," Zach told Skye.

"Sure, sweetie, a ghost tour of Salem. I'm going to love it." Skye laughed softly, looking at Gavin. "You know, we were both here many, many times during our growing-up years. Not together! We just had families who loved Salem or lived here at one time or another."

"Then you'll know when the lies and exaggerations come in," Gavin told her.

"True. I'm not so sure tour guides like it when you correct them," Zach noted.

"Don't correct them; you'll just know," Gavin said.

He'd been busy pressing buttons as he spoke. He looked up, smiling at them. "You're all set, Mr. and Mrs. Elijah Smith."

"Smith? You could have just made us John and Jane Doe," Skye said, groaning softly.

"Sorry. Smith just occurred to me. I thought Elijah would mix it up a bit"

Mix it up a bit? A name from Skye's past?

"And, Skye, you're Sheila."

"Sheila Smith. Okay, then," Skye said. She frowned suddenly. They'd started at nine, but there had been the drive out, the time at the convention center, and then visiting both sets of parents. She looked at her phone at the same time Zach looked at his.

"Four o'clock already. And—" Zach began.

"He needs to be fed. Mr. Smith needs fuel," Skye told Gavin.

"Yeah, and I know you've already eaten in town, but there's a great place near here with New England scrod, which is delicious, with buttery breadcrumbs on top, and there are crab dishes, ribs, chicken, even Maine lobster," Gavin said. "And guest what, Mrs. Smith? I rather like having some fuel during the day at some point, too."

Skye chuckled softly.

"I think she's a camel," Zach told Gavin.

"A camel?" Skye protested.

"You know, a camel can go for miles and miles without water."

"We had omelets this morning and then home-baked muffins!" Skye protested.

"Hey, I only ate one," Zach said.

"And I didn't even have one muffin, I was busy . . . listening," Gavin said.

Skye laughed. "Guys! I have nothing against a meal. And I guess we couldn't get too deep into any woods with the time we have before the tour."

"It's a trolley tour," Gavin told them. "You won't need to do too much walking. From what I understand reading about the six o'clock tour, there's some walking on Essex Street and near the Witch Museum and walking at each of the stops. The tour doesn't include entry to the attractions, which are naturally closed at night, but it does give the attendees coupons for discounts on many attractions. But you'll go by a lot of major sites, and you'll hear whatever the tour guide has to say."

Skye looked at Zach and shrugged. "Well, we can get our bearings refreshed on what is where, while getting a nice ride on what will be a nicely temperate evening."

"Let's eat; then you two need to change! You look like Feds!" Gavin told them. He turned and started the car. "Look the menu up on your phones so we can go right in and order—no! We can call ahead."

Zach didn't care what they ate. He was still holding the shirt. He didn't close his eyes; he'd seen what he needed to see for the moment. The strange feelings were still with him.

While he drove, Gavin called the police department, saying he needed to keep people in all the surrounding forests. He believed there had to be something like a compound hidden somewhere deep within the woods. They needed to find it.

When he finished his call, Skye asked what they wanted.

"Make it easy. We'll all get the scrod," Zach suggested.

"Sure, fine!" Skye said. She made the call, saying it wasn't for pickup, and that they'd be there in a few minutes.

They were.

And the food was served as soon as they were seated.

"Good planning," Zach told Gavin.

"I try."

"All right, I have Beau's shirt. I told you what I got," Zach said, looking at Gavin. "Were they telling the truth—were they telling us everything they knew?"

Gavin nodded, pursing his lips grimly. "That's just it. Both sets of parents were telling us the truth, as they knew it, of course. And it's natural they'd want to blame one another's child."

"Such a . . . shame! They didn't have that far to go," Skye said.

"I was thinking at first that they were idiots," Zach told her. "But here's the thing. This person who talked to them seriously convinced them that he—or she—could make everything come up roses for them. Give them a place to live together, let them both get a good education, whether Allie's parents disowned her or not."

"I guess that does make sense. They knew they were both about to be of legal age to do what they wanted, but neither of them wanted to alienate their parents if they didn't have to, so . . . yeah, I get it." She was sitting next to Zach and looked across the table at Gavin. "That puts us back to this—someone local must be involved!"

"Please don't tell me that it's the area witches," Gavin moaned.

"Never. We've both known true wiccans by having been here a number of times ourselves, and that's not it. The costume might be that of a horrible witch, but that's not the game," Zach said.

"You sound certain," Gavin said.

"I am certain. This is Salem and someone thinks it's fun to twist history and legend; and as we all know, it really goes crazy at Halloween. I think that if anyone with this tour group is involved, it's to rub right in our noses the ease with which they're getting away with everything. But you still need to be licensed to be a guide, right?"

"You do," Gavin said. "And the company, naturally, employs several guides. So we can't be sure which guide you're going to get, but that doesn't matter, because we don't know which guide you'd want to get."

"Well, I can work on that a bit as we drive," Zach said. "And," he added, "I think this may be the best scrod I've ever had."

"Delicious," Skye agreed.

Back in the car, he held on to Beau Carter's T-shirt.

He closed his eyes and wished he could combine his strange sixth sense with what Skye possessed.

He needed to see the night that Beau and Allie had gone on the tour, but he knew he couldn't do that. But he could see Beau.

Beau was sitting on a log as dusk began to fall. There were others around him, but they seemed to be forms in a mist. Zach couldn't tell how many people there were, what their ages might be, nor could he begin to see their faces. There was something off about Beau, and Zach quickly realized what it was.

He had been drugged.

And he was staring at a man who was speaking to them, but the words he heard were jumbled.

The speaker was there, in front of Beau.

But his face was as much of a haze as everything else Beau saw.

Then . . .

The man was gone and someone else was moving in, ushering those who had been watching and listening along.

Then . . . nothing.

* * *

"Zach?" Skye asked softly.

"They are drugging the older kids and the adults they've taken. I don't know what they're giving them, but it makes them pliant. And I imagine, it sinks into their psyches so that they believe anything that they're told."

"Some personalities will resist that," Gavin noted.

"They will. I was in Patricia's head last night, and she was very afraid that someone was going to die."

"I so desperately hope you learn something on the tour," Gavin said. "I'll drop you at the Old Burying Point, or Charter Street Cemetery. They start there, then head down Essex Street, where they point out the Peabody Essex Museum and some of the other shops and attractions there. Next they move on over to the Salem Witch Museum and talk about Salem Common, and then point out the Hawthorne Hotel and a bit of history regarding Nathaniel Hawthorne, before heading into the trolley to drive out by the House of the Seven Gables. I think they drive out to the Rebecca Nurse Homestead and the Witch House—sorry—"

"Yeah, yeah, the Jonathan Corwin place, it's one of only a few structures still standing that had to do with the trials, since Corwin was one of the judges," Skye said. "We got it, Gavin, honest."

"Well, good, then. I'm going to drop you where Essex Street becomes strictly pedestrian. I don't want to chance being seen. I mean, I don't want to take a chance of being seen with you."

"You know, we've been around here, too, talking to Fin and just doing a few things on the street," Skye reminded him. "We've probably been seen—"

"But not with a police lieutenant," Gavin reminded her.

"True," Skye agreed.

"So we're going to hope you don't run into anyone who

might have seen you as anything other than tourists," Gavin said. He grinned. "Mr. and Mrs. Smith, dropping you off here. You can give me a ring when the tour is over, and I'll pick you up—"

"Gavin, if they drop us off where they pick us up, we can walk with no problem—"

"Except that I'll want to know what happened," Gavin told them.

"All right, all right. We'll call you!" Zach groaned.

Gavin had pulled over on Hawthorne, leaving them near the entrance to the pedestrian area of Essex Street.

Zach and Skye exited the car, with Zach handing Skye Beau's T-shirt. She gave him a nod and slid it into her shoulder bag.

And as Gavin drove away, Zach looked around them. He had always loved the city so much. From history to the present.

"What is it?" Skye asked.

"Salem. This is such an amazing place; what's happening is making it so that . . ." He shrugged, his words trailing.

"That you're infuriated by what's going on, anything that hurts the city like this?" Skye asked.

He laughed softly. "One of those old sayings I got from my mom. 'When life gives you lemons, make lemonade.' In my mind, Salem has rather managed to do that. 'Witch City.' But what always impressed me most was that the events had such a strong influence on the legal system created by our Founding Fathers. I mean, think about it! Anyone could get on a witness stand and say that they were tormented by the spirit of a person—when that person was right there in the courtroom. No spectral evidence! Innocent until *proven* guilty, instead of guilty just because you were accused. Freedom of religion. Laws came into being that kept mass hysteria from causing the deaths of innocents. Anyway . . ."

Skye set a hand on his shoulder. "We're going to stop this!

So let's walk through the pedestrian mall and cut back over to the graveyard. We have a few minutes. There are shops here that I love! Starting right there around the corner. Crow Haven Corner! I love that shop. Laurie Cabot used to own it, and she had another shop on Pickering Wharf—the Cat, the Crow & the Crown—but she closed it more than a decade ago. Laurie has done such amazing things that fall right in line with what you're saying. After the movie version of John Updike's *The Witches of Eastwick* came out, she established the Witches' League for Public Awareness. I mean, that's just it—we get things in our heads. Ideas that we don't know about or agree with and we turn them into something evil!"

"Such passion. Are you a wiccan?" Zach asked.

She laughed softly. "No, I just respect the beliefs of anyone who intends goodness and no harm to others!"

"And what's going on has no relation to any religion—unless someone's religion is to create grandeur for themselves!"

Skye nodded, taking his hand. "Come on, Mr. Smith. Now we are running out of time! We can run in and out of shops and get to the graveyard."

Zach smiled and opted to stay on the pedestrian way as he watched Skye do an amazing job of flying in and out of shops.

"Hey! Deciding what I might want to go back and see! There's a great place on movie monsters—"

"But nothing as elaborate or as complete as the Howells' shop, right?"

Skye shrugged. "Rents right here on the pedestrian area of Essex Street must be high; it's central, easy access . . . but Swampscott is a bit off the main, but it gives them tons of space and allows them to cater to the locals and those in the know when it comes to the best selections around Halloween. Somewhere along the line—though I'm not sure why—I'd like to get back to that shop and see if I can't get a better view of whoever it is dressing up as witches."

"More than one. And they're keeping protestors quiet and pliant with drugs," Zach said wearily. "Which I hope is working on whoever it is that Patricia is so worried about."

"You know, we could solve this easily," Skye said.

"How?"

"Have the entire population and all visitors speak one-on-one with Gavin—and he can tell us if they're telling the truth or not!"

Zach groaned. "Did you learn nothing in the academy?" he demanded.

She laughed as they came to the Old Burying Point, or Charter Street Cemetery. They had spent more time on the street than either one had realized.

By the time they reached their meeting point, the tour guide was there collecting names of those on the tour and checking them off on his tablet.

"Hey!"

It was a young man in his early twenties who was leading the tour. Unruly light-brown hair fell over his forehead. Medium in height and build, he appeared to be the least-threatening human being possible, especially when he smiled. His hazel eyes lit up; his face appeared to be a mask of friendship.

"We're the Smith couple on there," Zach told him. "I'm Elijah and—"

"Your lovely wife, Sheila! Welcome. First trip to Salem?"

"First trip when we've had a chance to enjoy it!" Skye told him, catching Zach's arm and holding close to him in an affectionate gesture. "And we're together, just in case it gets a little too spooky for me!"

"I'm Nick, Nick Sandoval," the guide told them. "And," he said, "this is mostly a history tour. But it is night, and things can get a little creepy! We'll be getting started in one more minute!"

He was true to his word. He pointed out the oldest gravestone remaining in the cemetery, the Cromwell Stone, placed there when Doraty Cromwell had passed away in 1673. The graveyard had been laid out in 1637, but Doraty's was the oldest remaining stone. No, those executed for witchcraft were not in the Old Burying Point; their bodies had been treated like rubbish. It was assumed, though, that in some cases, the families of the deceased had gone by cover of night to retrieve the bodies of their loved ones.

They spent time looking at the memorial at the graveyard, stone benches that commemorated each of the accused. Then it was time to move on. He took them along Essex Street, speaking about the growth of commercialism in the city.

He talked about the Hawthorne Hotel, opened in 1925 and named after Salem's son, the great Nathaniel Hawthorne. The site was near Hawthorne's birthplace on Union Street, and not far from the House of the Seven Gables.

They learned about events on Salem Common and were given a glowing review of the Salem Witch Museum. Then it was time to hop aboard the trolley and head out to see the Witch House, once the property of Judge Corwin, and then onward to the House of the Seven Gables, and, for the finale, a drive out to the Pioneer Village.

As they moved from site to site, Zach and Skye split up to stare with awe at different things, chatting with the guide when they could, studying the others on the tour. There was a trio of teenage girls on the tour, and it seemed the guide was spending most of his time with them whenever possible.

Natural? He was a young, good-looking guy. And the girls were young, too, cute and giggly, and ready to flirt.

But it seemed that at times Nick was leaning in a little bit too close to the girls to simply be answering a question one of them might have asked at a particular moment.

And at one point, he thought he saw the young man brush the hand of one of the girls.

"Giving her something?" Skye whispered to him.

"Drugs, maybe," Zach whispered back. "We need to keep watch. He seems to be getting especially close to that one girl. The thin girl, with the reddish-blond hair. I think one of her friends called her Cathy."

"Should we—"

"We can't just bust him on drugs," Zach said.

"We need to see where it goes from here, follow them when the tour is over," Skye said.

"Maybe it's natural. A boy flirting with a girl, supplying her with a bit of encouragement so that they get together after?"

"Hm. Natural," Skye murmured.

And then maybe not. Maybe a possibility, while others were culled as well.

Their guide was also spending time with a woman on the tour who was with a little boy of about seven or eight.

Zach's instincts, and all that they had learned, came to credence when they were on a remote road by the Pioneer Village.

The driver, a man of about sixty, suddenly seemed to have a heart attack, driving the trolley a bit off the road, sliding into the embankment.

"Oh, no! Hank, Hank!" Nick Sandoval cried.

There were screams and chatter coming from the rows of seats on the trolley.

Of course, Nick immediately began to apologize and worry, asking everyone to sit still or call for a pickup if they could; he'd be getting an ambulance out himself.

"I can solve this!" Zach told Skye, hurrying forward with her at his heels.

"What if it's real?" she murmured.

"It's not!" he assured her. "But we'll find out."

"Nick, Nick," he said, rushing forward. "I'm a doctor. I can—"

"What?" the guide demanded.

"Let me get to him," Zach said, reaching over to touch the driver's face.

The man's eyes immediately opened wide. As he stared at Zach, they could hear those on the trolley speaking with concerned anguish.

"My cell is saying there's no service," a woman cried.

"Mine too!" a man replied.

"You're a liar!" Zach told the driver.

"No, no!" the man protested.

"Zach!"

He turned and saw what Skye saw; she was already racing into the forest, running after the guide, who had called himself Nick Sandoval.

And one of the teenage girls, with whom he'd been flirting, It was hard to tell exactly what had happened. Had he grabbed her and dragged her into the darkness of the forest as well?

There was no telling what she might face. Nick Sandoval didn't seem like much of a danger himself.

But he was just a player in the game—whatever the game might be.

"Get help, keep an eye on him!" Zach shouted, his own phone out.

No service.

Their guide and the driver had known exactly where to stage their little emergency!

It was insane! There's a whole tour group, at least another fifteen people, available to tell the authorities exactly what had happened. And the driver—

As Zach started his own race into the forest, he saw the man throw off all pretense and fly into the forest himself.

Hell no!

Zach went after him.

And while the older man might have known where he was going . . . he was *older.* And he'd never gone through some of the rigors of the academy, and probably didn't maintain a gym membership.

They ran through the trees.

There was no damned way that Zach was going to lose him.

And he was going to get him down damned quickly. No one should be chasing someone like their guide, with a possible victim, into the stygian darkness of the forest at night.

CHAPTER 11

Skye was fast. There was no way that the rigorous training she'd gone through in life wouldn't have taught her how to run—and run fast.

There had been a standard joke at the academy when she had been there. One of their fitness instructors had once asked them, "Don't you all watch crime shows? They run! They always run! Well, when they're not having a car chase, they run!"

So, while she might not have become any kind of a gymnast, she could run!

But the darkness in the forest . . .

It had been night, of course. Night in the city, with city lights. Even night on the road, with lights from the trolley.

But here, where the branches obscured whatever light might have come from the sky, it was a darkness like nothing she had ever known before.

Thankfully, she could hear them running ahead of her. Naturally, she wondered where they thought they were going.

She paused for a second, just stopping herself from crashing into the trunk of a giant oak.

Rustling, ahead of her. Rustling, ahead and a little to the west . . .

She started to move again, quietly, but then she paused again, listening.

"Wait, wait, wait! I can't . . . I can't . . ."

It was a young female voice speaking. The girl sounded winded and confused.

Drugged.

"No, no, come on, just a little bit farther! And then I'll have you far and away; we can talk then, and you can rest, and you'll never need to deal with any problems again. Come on, now. Come on. Just a little bit farther. I was confused like you before, but now I know all about the world. I can bring you to the best people, and we can be together, and it will be wonderful!"

Nick Sandoval was the speaker.

Could he really believe what he's saying? And how would they go on after that?

The tours would need to be over! A crashed trolley and a disappearing girl and her guide? Who would ever sign on again?

But maybe it doesn't matter; maybe it just segues into something else. But what about the people who started the tour, who owned the company?

That was something they would have to follow up on later.

Right now . . .

They had paused, so Skye started to move in the direction of the voices, going as silently as she could, hoping that whatever small sounds her movements created might sound like the natural rustles of a forest.

She was close. There were a possibility: she could just follow them through the forest, as far as they went, and discover just where Nick was taking the girl, where he was going to wind up.

And she didn't think that she was heard—at least, not as a human being trying to sneak through the forest. Because Nick spoke again, his voice beginning to betray impatience and aggravation.

"Now, come on, now! Just ahead!" he said.

"I can't! I can't! I'm dizzy," the girl moaned.

The girl sounds weak, broken, as if . . . she's been given too much of something?

"I'll carry you!" Nick cried, no longer pretending he was anything other than purely angry.

He'd managed to be quite personable when they'd checked in for the tour; now it was evident that he was capable of being anything but.

The girl was moaning softly, as if she didn't even have the strength to cry loudly, to protest.

Skye winced inwardly. They might have come so close, but now . . .

And it was time to stop Nick's advance into the forest.

She drew her Glock and quickly covered the distance between herself and the two, despite the tangle of trees and brush in the way. As she reached the small clearing, where Nick had just tossed the girl over his shoulder, Skye came to a dead stop, aiming the weapon at him.

"Put her down. Now!" Skye snapped.

He stared back at her and smiled slowly, apparently not about to obey her command.

"Sheila Smith, eh?" he said. "A member of the corrupt few governing the rest of us, ignoring all the true tenets. You're another devil worshipper! And no, I will not put her down. You shoot me, you shoot her!" he said, laughing as he held the girl closer, making sure that she was covering his chest.

Nick Sandoval was suddenly so startled that the girl slid from his grasp.

Skye was equally surprised herself; Zach was there. He had come up behind Nick and held a gun directly to the boy's head. "Step back! Let her be!" he commanded.

"Cops!" Nick roared furiously, letting the girl slip the rest of the way to the ground. Crying, terrified, but under the influence of something, she clawed desperately at the earth and tree roots, trying to get away.

"Not cops . . . Feds," Zach corrected him.

Skye ran to the girl, hunkering down, lifting her to her knees and saying, "You're all right. We'll get you to a hospital and you'll be safe."

The girl didn't answer; she was just crying. But Skye was able to get her to her feet. Glancing at Zach, she saw he had Nick in zip cuffs, and the young man was staring ahead belligerently.

"Where were you taking her?" Zach demanded.

"Into the woods; that's all. You know, get a little alone time," Nick said.

"In the middle of a tour? Sure, right," Zach told him.

Nick just smiled. "Yeah, I needed to get lucky."

"What did you drug her with?" Skye demanded.

"Me? I didn't drug her with anything," he said. "I can't help what people bring on a tour!"

"You gave her pills. I saw you," Zach told him.

"Wow! What kind of a Fed are you?" Nick demanded, laughing, even though Zach was pushing him ahead, aiming him back toward the road and the trolley. "You think you saw me giving an awful drug to a girl, and you didn't stop me?"

"Where were you taking her?" Zach roared again.

"Zach," Skye said.

He turned back and looked at her. And the girl. *Cathy,* Skye thought.

She was worried; she did want to take the girl to a hospital.

He nodded, understanding, and pushed Nick forward. Without having to veer through the brush, trying to hear what lay ahead, they quickly made their way back.

Skye saw that Zach had caught the driver. He had left him sitting in the back of the trolley—also restrained with plastic cuffs—under the watchful eye of a man in his late thirties or early forties.

"We got a signal through—asked for police and an ambulance!" he said.

The two other girls who had made up the teen trio saw

Cathy coming from the woods, stumbling as she walked, even though Skye was all but carrying her. They ran over to her, anxious, too worried to be afraid. Skye had to put up a hand, warning, "Give her space, please. She needs to breathe! And what the hell drug were you all taking?"

"We weren't—" one of the girls began.

"Do you want her to live?" Skye demanded.

"It was just supposed to be a little low-dose bath salt," the girl admitted. "We didn't take them; Cathy took one. I have them—"

"I need them. Now. Please!"

They heard sirens; police cars rolled up, along with the ambulance. Skye looked at Zach and he nodded again.

He knew that she'd go to the hospital with the girl and that he'd be left with the driver, the tour guide, and an explanation.

But, of course, a young cop started to crawl up into the ambulance as well.

"FBI," Skye said quickly. "Meet me there!"

The officer nodded. "Meet you there."

"These are what she took!" Skye said quickly, handing the pills to the EMT. "The girls think that they were low-dose bath salts. What they really are, I don't know!"

"Gotcha," the EMT said, calling in the situation as the other EMT worked on the girl.

The night had seemed so still and dark.

Now it was alive with the sound of the ambulance's siren as they drove; the city lights came into view and then the lights of the hospital.

Of course, when Cathy was rushed into a room with the doctor on duty, Skye had to step back.

The young officer arrived as she nervously prowled the hospital waiting room.

He didn't arrive alone.

To Skye's surprise, he had somehow known to contact Gavin.

"What happened, exactly? Seems like heading out on the tour right away was a good decision," Gavin said. "Oh, by the way, this is Officer Ben Chambers. He happens to be one of my younger cousins."

"Ah!" Skye said. "Ben, Officer Chambers, nice to meet you." She looked at Gavin.

"He knows something is going on in Salem," Gavin explained. "And when his car got the call . . . he called me. So, what did you get?"

"Hopefully, the chance to keep this young lady alive. Her name is Cathy—"

"The officers on the scene got her name, and her parents have already been notified; they should be here soon. And her friends are being brought to the station. They're not guilty of anything because Cathy is the one who accepted the pills, sharing them, of course, and I was told—"

"Yes. I got the pills and gave them to the EMT," Skye assured him. "Zach stayed back with the driver and our guide—a fellow supposedly named Nick Sandoval—"

"That is his name. We've already been on that; he's been brought in on drug charges and attempted kidnapping. The driver is claiming that he was really having a heart attack, or thought that he was having a heart attack. Unless we can prove something, we can only hold him so long. I'm still trying to imagine this scene as it happened," Gavin said.

"Well, we went on the tour. Our guide was filled with great information. He was articulate and charming. We saw him spending time with the girls, might have even seen him hand the pills over, and then, as you know, the driver suddenly veered off the road and onto the embankment. And once he did that, Zach accosted him. Nick took off, grabbing Cathy, and started running into the woods. Zach caught up with the driver, while I went after Nick and the girl. Found him, and he tried to use her as a shield when I drew my service weapon, but Zach was behind him. Nick let her go, and here we are!"

Gavin started to speak, but Cathy's parents had arrived. Naturally, they were extremely upset, desperate to know if their daughter was going to be all right.

"I've got it," Gavin said softly, approaching the couple and leaving Skye with his cousin.

"I thought the right thing was to let my cousin know what was going on," Ben explained to her.

"Yes, definitely!" Skye said.

"Was Cathy going to wind up missing, too?" he asked. "I mean, it's getting so strange. Kidnappings and . . . and a guy running off with a girl from a tour? Not good. I know they're contacting the owners of the company, but I'm willing to bet, jail time or no, the two of them won't have jobs anymore. But where did he think that he was taking her?"

"Officer Chambers—"

"Ben, please. Obviously, my cousin thinks the world of you and your partner."

"Ben," she said, nodding. "That's the one thing I truly wish I knew. I even wonder if it was a mistake, stopping him when I did. He might have led us somewhere."

A doctor appeared; Skye watched with Ben as he spoke to Gavin and Cathy's parents.

Cathy's mother collapsed against her father.

For a minute, Skye feared the worst.

But as the husband assured his wife, Gavin excused himself and came over to her and Ben.

"She's stabilized. Thank God. He said that if she hadn't received Narcan when she did, she might not have made it. They're going to need to analyze just what's in those bath salts—more than the usual. But she has been stabilized; they're hydrating her . . . and she's going to make it; and if he had gotten her wherever he was going, well . . ."

Gavin's voice trailed.

Skye nodded, lowering her head.

They had saved the girl.

But what about the others being held?

She didn't get a chance to worry long; apparently, someone told Cathy's parents that she had been the one to make sure Cathy was helped immediately. She was drowned in a sea of tears and hugs and words of thanks. Skye accepted them as graciously as she could, assuring the couple that the EMTs, the police, and the doctors deserved the thanks.

Eventually, Gavin and Ben were able to get her away; Cathy's parents were going to stay with her then.

But before they could leave, Skye pulled back, staring at Gavin.

"We need more than her parents," she said.

"What?" Gavin asked her.

"Gavin, we caught a minion tonight, just someone following someone else's orders, bringing her to them to become part of whatever is going on. What if they believe she might know something? Sure, she was just on the tour, but whoever is behind this might believe Nick said something to her and . . . Gavin, she might not be safe."

He sighed deeply. "The department is being run ragged and thinned out!" he said.

"Call the state; or I'll call Jackson—"

"Right now, we need something fast. I'll—"

"Gavin, I can stay on. Get me spelled sometime by the morning by someone so I can get enough sleep to be cognizant before going back on duty, but I'm up for this. I was on the scene; I came straight here. The parents have seen me—and I've seen the staff and know how to check them out," Ben said.

Gavin smiled and nodded. "Good. Thank you. Skye?"

"Thank you, Ben," she said. "I could be wrong, but I come from the school of being safe rather than sorry."

"Of course, agreed," he said.

Skye looked at Gavin. "We can't talk to her yet, right?" she asked.

He shook his head. "She's completely out of it right now, and the doctors want her that way. Maybe her would-be kidnapper thought she'd take just one pill, but she took a few or something. But we can't talk to her for hours yet, so . . . come on. You and I are going to get over to the station and see what we can see, what we can discover."

"Right, time to get to the station and find out if we've learned anything from the driver or Nick Sandoval," Skye said.

When they were out of the hospital and on their way to the station, Skye looked over at Gavin and asked, "Does your cousin have something of your talent?"

"I don't really know yet. The kid went through the police academy like a true pro. Maybe, and maybe he's one of those people who just naturally has a sense about other people."

"He seems great."

"He is."

"Okay, so, on to the problem at hand. What about the owners of the tour company?"

"They've been summoned to the station," Gavin assured her. "And from what I understand, they're horrified. Oh, by the way, whoever the driver is—we're working on his identity—he wasn't supposed to be the driver tonight. Ned Bailey of Peabody was supposed to be working the night tour. We haven't been able to reach him. The man isn't married, but his live-in girlfriend thought he was at work. She didn't like his work arrangements, either, and said that he worked with a 'kook'; and from what's gone on, I'm going to assume that the 'kook' is Nick Sandoval, though that doesn't explain what happened to Ned."

"His girlfriend said he left for work as usual?" Skye asked.

"She did."

"I wonder if Zach has had any luck with anything that he's discovered," Skye said. She glanced over at Gavin.

"We'll know soon enough," Gavin said, nodding ahead.

They'd reached the station.

When they entered, the officer on desk duty nodded to them and indicated they go on through. Entering the hallway and passing by the offices, they were soon stopped by an officer who said the captain was in the observation room, and Special Agent Zachary Erikson was speaking with Nick Sandoval.

"What about the driver?" Gavin asked.

"Interrogation room 2, cooling his heels, I guess. He's being left to stew in his own juices for a while, so I've been told," the officer said.

"We'll see what's going on," Gavin said, looking at Skye for agreement.

"We'll join the captain in the observation room," she said.

He nodded and the two of them headed in to observe Zach's interrogation of Nick.

"Special Agent McMahon, pleasure to meet you and grateful for the help we can get!" the captain told her as she and Gavin entered the room. "Captain Claybourne," he added, offering his hand.

"Thank you, sir!" she said quietly, taking his hand for a solid shake. Claybourne was fifty-one, a serious man with clipped white hair, about six feet tall, with a sturdy frame. He had worked his way up through the ranks Skye knew, because it was her nature, when she could, to research everyone involved in a case or a place.

He gave her a mirthless smile and indicated the interrogation room, where Zach was questioning Nick, and they were all silent as they observed them.

"No!" Nick was saying passionately. "You don't understand. I was trying to save that girl!"

"She almost died. If we hadn't gotten her to the hospital when we did, she'd be dead now. No good to you for whatever you planned for her. What was in those pills?"

"Just a little happy juice. It's not my fault she took too many!"

"Where did you get the pills?" Zach asked.

Nick just sighed and looked at his hands. "Listen, I'm not going to answer anything. You're damned. You will reside in hell forever. That's what happens when you join with an evil conspiracy—when you dance with the devil in the woods!"

"I haven't done any dancing with the devil—in the woods or otherwise," Zach said without emotion. "I think you've been dancing in the woods with the devil. Only the devil would nearly kill a girl."

"We're trying to save her soul!" Nick announced indignantly.

"Well, let's see. You failed. So, who are you working for?"

Nick sat back, shaking his head. "The master will know all, see all. And if you hang me by the neck until dead right now, it will not matter because I will rise above all this. I will live in eternal bliss as one of the master's chosen few!"

Zach groaned. "No one is hanging you by the neck—or otherwise. Just locking you up for attempted kidnapping; and you'll get a trial date—and you can get an attorney. Those are the things that the people who formed this country knew to be important, not falling prey to the wacko preaching of any would-be messiah!"

Skye watched as Nick stared at Zach; for a moment, he had to wonder if Zach was telling him the truth.

But then Nick gave his head a serious shake.

"No! I will not fall to the lies of the devil!" he proclaimed.

"Others may die," Zach said quietly. "And if you're listening to a false messiah, their deaths will be on you. So, how about this—who killed Mike Bolton?"

"He was sent to his demise, lest he ruin the future grace of those who might see the true way," Nick told him. Then he suddenly said, "Oh, yeah, right! Lawyer!"

Zach stood immediately. "Your choice. You sure? I could maybe help you."

"No. You dance with the devil."

Zach nodded, clenching his jaw. The words seemed to be something of a motto for those in a mind warp around here.

He walked out into the hall, where Skye, Gavin, and Captain Claybourne met him.

"Brainwashed and beyond," Zach said. He looked at Gavin. "I didn't know you and Skye had gotten here. It might have been good if you'd gotten into him before he'd said the 'lawyer' word. What's scary, though, is that it seems he believes everything that he's saying; and that, at least, gives us a better idea of what's going on here."

"I admit, I'm still baffled!" Claybourne said. "'The master'? What the hell?"

"From what I've seen and heard, sir," Zach told him, "someone is planning something big in which they need a little army to help them. They're taking children, teens, and those they think they can force to be pliable."

"You think it's a cult—" Claybourne began.

"No, sir," Zach said. "I think they're planning on a heist or an attack, one in which they need obedient servants who believe that they're helping a great messiah. And everything about Salem that was suspected in the past was true—people were witches, they made pacts with the devil, and they must be the ones to fight against all the witches out here."

"That's so crazy," Claybourne moaned. "How do we know

what they plan to attack, or what they think they will rob? And how does a five-year-old or any child help in a heist?"

"Shields. No one is going to want to hurt a child. He—or they, from what we've come to believe—will use the children to keep others from reaching them," Zach said. He looked at Gavin. "You want to have a go at the driver?"

Skye knew Zach hoped Gavin would see into the man's mind—and through him, find out what the depth of the plan had been.

"Right. Going in," Gavin said, looking at his captain for acknowledgment.

Captain Claybourne nodded. But as Gavin stepped out of the observation room, they all saw a young policewoman who had been about to tap on the door. "They're here, sir. The tour company owners. They're waiting in reception."

For a moment, they were silent. Gavin, Zach, and Skye looked at one another.

Skye felt she was useless in what they were doing here. There was nothing that she could "see" at the station that would help.

But maybe . . .

"Where is the trolley now?" she asked.

"Out back, in our lot," Captain Claybourne said.

"I may see if there is anything we missed with the trolley," she murmured, heading out the back quickly. Gavin, Zach, and the captain might glean more from the couple who owned the company, or from the man who had driven the trolley.

The trolley was lined up right behind the station, along with several patrol cars. Skye did wonder what she thought she might get from it, but there was no way to find out until she tried. She climbed onto the driver's seat and closed her eyes and then opened them. Nothing. She set her hands on the wheel and tried again.

And then she saw an event unfold. A recent event.

A different man from the driver they had known, sitting at the wheel, checking his watch, just waiting.

Then . . .

There was the green witch again, the damned green witch, striking the man hard over the head.

He fell forward instantly, and the green witch dragged him out and away, and then the driver they had met appeared, sliding into the driver's seat.

Skye leapt out of the seat; they needed to find the man who was supposed to have been driving the trolley on the tour.

He'd been hit hard, but maybe . . .

She rushed back into the station; glad she was coming through the back. She hurried to the observation room, hoping that Zach would be there with Gavin.

They were both there, and they were alone.

She rushed in.

"He's out there, somewhere. Wherever the trolley parks before it's time to come in and sweep people up for the part of the tour that isn't on foot. I mean, I think he was just thrown aside after he was attacked, but he might be alive and . . ."

"Near dead," Zach said quickly. "Gavin—"

"You two go. I'll cover it with Captain Claybourne," Gavin promised. "We just talked to Claybourne—apparently, Laurie and Ted Sizemore are beside themselves, worried about their regular driver and grateful that nothing happened to that poor girl, who is in the hospital now. If you—"

"You believed them?" Skye asked Gavin.

He nodded solemnly. "I was watching from here, but . . . yes. Anyway, head out of town to the road that borders the heavily forested road out toward the Rebecca Nurse Homestead. Ted Sizemore said the trolley driver watches the time and waits off to the side of the road there until the guide calls to tell him to head into town. It's not that big a thing, but it has about four little cars, so it needs a bit of space without messing with Salem central traffic."

"We're done—we don't have a car!" Skye said.

"I've got Gavin's keys," Zach said. "We're borrowing his unmarked car. Let's move!"

They headed out, Skye worried they didn't have much to go on. "I know you can drive," Zach said, trying to put a tiny bit of levity on the situation. "But you know what we're looking for—I know where we might find it."

"Sure. Whatever," Skye murmured.

They were quiet as they headed out, but it wasn't long before Zach said, "Just ahead. You can see where the trolley has flattened all the grass there. I'll pull off; we'll start looking behind the closest trees!"

"Maybe they dumped him farther, maybe—"

"Let's be optimistic—I doubt if they bothered. I don't think this guy who took over knew he might be part of a murder plot. If what he is blubbering about is true, he thought he was hired as an actor. He thought the whole thing was kind of a show and that when the cops and ambulance came . . . he panicked? True or not, I have no idea, and I don't think Gavin was even sure. Thing is, I don't think there was time for anyone to do anything other than throw a body quickly in the woods."

"Then where did the green witch go?" Skye asked.

But Zach had parked the car and was already getting out. Skye followed, pulling out her phone flashlight to cast a glow over the trees. Zach did the same, looking at the scene for a minute, then frowning and stepping back behind a row of trees.

"Call Gavin; he has an ambulance waiting with coordinates!"

She called immediately, rushing back to find Zach.

He was on his knees in the brush, behind a large tree and a

tangle of bushes. He was there with a man who was flat on his back, almost hidden by the foliage.

But she could see the bloodstain on his forehead, and she wondered desperately if an ambulance was going to happen or not.

But while not a mind reader, Zach was coming to know her. And he looked up at her and said, "He has a pulse! Skye, you might have just saved a second life in just one night!"

CHAPTER 12

Zach watched Skye at the police station, concerned.

She was thoughtful when they had finally returned to the precinct, and when Gavin drove them back to their quarters.

They were all tired, of course. Exhausted.

But while they hadn't solved the mystery of what the hell the perpetrators were up to, they had stopped a girl from dying and had gotten a man to the hospital, when a few more hours of lying in the brush without help might have cost him his life.

And there were the very cryptic things they were learning from Nick Sandoval, the tour guide.

"Gavin, were you able to get in to speak with the tour guide yet?" Skye asked when they parked in front of the house.

He nodded. "I did. And here's what is truly horrible—and not in the least helpful. He believes everything he's saying to us. Evil is really alive and well in Salem; it was real back in 1692; and most of us—including the couple who owns the tour company—are in league with the devil. In his mind, it started with the witch trials—and it was the devil who tamped it all down. The devil was furious that his reign on earth was being stopped; and since then, he's been turning people in this area so that they do his bidding."

Skye shook her head. "How does someone ever become that gullible, that twisted?"

"Well, you can take a stab at him tomorrow," Gavin said. "We're holding him as long as we legally can before arraignment—he won't be getting back out there."

"Thanks, yeah, I would like to try talking to him tomorrow," Skye said.

Zach thanked Gavin and headed for the house, holding the door open when Skye exited the car and came up behind him.

"Okay," he said, once they were in and the alarm was keyed in on the door. "What? What is bothering you so much?"

"Nothing."

"You can't lie to me."

"No, no, it's just that . . . my mind is really being torn apart. I know that it's a good thing we kept Cathy alive. It was the right thing. It's just if she hadn't taken too many of those pills, and if we'd just been able to go wherever Nick was taking her, we might have had a chance to break the whole thing sky high!"

"But we did the right thing. And seriously, Skye! The real driver owes his life to you. So be glad, be happy, that we managed something good—especially because of you," Zach told her.

She smiled at him. "Thanks for that. Logically, I know everything you're saying is right. It's not the logic that's driving me so crazy."

Zach was not sure what he was thinking now; he had always behaved in a perfectly professional manner with all co-workers. He stepped forward, drawing her into his arms. He looked down into her eyes, speaking softly. "It's frustrating. Cases will be frustrating. It's amazing to work with the truth between both of us regarding the, um, special things we can see and do sometimes; but even with three people now, each having a bit of a different sixth sense, cases don't just solve immediately. Ask Jackson, ask Angela, or ask any of their other agents. Cases can take time. But we may just solve this one, when others couldn't, before a real catastrophe does take place."

She looked up into his eyes, listened, and smiled slowly, leaning her head against his chest for a moment.

"Thank you," she whispered.

"You'll be there for me, too," he told her.

She drew back at last, nodding. "You know," she said lightly, "I actually like you! Hadn't been sure that I was going to!"

"Well, I can beat that," he told her. "I like you and admire you a whole lot, and I wasn't sure at all that I was going to."

She laughed at that and said, "Okay, thanks. So . . . bed. No. After today, a shower and bed. And then sleep and breakfast! I do want to talk to Nick Sandoval tomorrow."

He nodded, heading into the kitchen for a bottle of water to take to bed.

"Water! A gallon of something stronger might be good right now," Skye called after him.

"I can go out and get you—"

She laughed. "No, no, not tonight. I'm joking. But you can grab me a bottle, too."

He did so, tossing it to her, grinning, and saying good night as she turned to walk into her own room.

She was right about one thing: He had a lot of forest to wash off!

Hot water was good. He stood under it a long time, feeling the heat steam away the tension that had built up in his muscles.

But the events of the night kept playing out before his eyes. It was good that they had been on the tour. If they hadn't been, Nick Sandoval would have taken the girl through the forest. No one would have known the driver's distress hadn't been bought and paid for—and no one would have realized that the guide and the girl were gone until it was too late.

And yet . . .

It was true. If only they'd been able to follow the pair, they might have truly gotten to the bottom of what was going on.

He exited the shower and dried off, then realized that he had finished his bottle of water already; perhaps because of the steam in the shower, he wanted another one.

He walked out into the hall between the rooms.

And there was Skye, coming from her room as he was coming from his. She, too, was wearing a towel.

"Um, sorry, I was just going for more water," he said.

"Oh, yeah, sorry. I was just going for more water, too!" she said.

They were barely a foot from one another. She smelled like the clean scent of her soap; something that wasn't too sweet, far more perfect, like the beauty of a summer day when the sun was casting down on grass and flowers. Her hair streamed somewhat wildly around her face, washed and dried, but still a halo of stunning color falling around her shoulders.

"Water," she murmured.

"Honestly, water," he said.

"Yeah, me too, but . . ."

She took the single step that separated them, placing a hand on his chest. She looked up into his eyes.

"Providence?" she asked softly.

"The most stunning coincidence known to man!" he agreed. And that was it; it was all that he needed. He'd learned to read her eyes in the pursuit of their case, and he knew that he was reading her right at that moment.

And from there . . . it was the most natural thing in the world.

His arms slipped around her. Their mouths met, a touch of exploration; then something deepened passionately and, in that passion, their towels fell to the floor; the lengths of their bodies touched and a fire, which was like eternal lightning, streamed into his body.

He broke away from the hunger of their kisses long enough to whisper, "My room or yours?"

And she laughed softly. "Who the hell cares?" she answered lightly. "Whichever is closer!"

And it was amazing, so natural, so sweet and easy; the hunger and the urgency mixed with laughter and ease and maybe more . . . maybe caring, respect . . .

"Okay, I'm bigger!" he said, sweeping her off her feet and into his arms. "My room is at least six inches closer!"

Her eyes. He could lose himself entirely in her eyes.

They fell to the bed together and there was an incredible moment when he lay over her, his weight hiked on his arms, when they just looked at each other and knew—knew that they had both felt it, something building, unexpected, but forming between them.

Then their lips met again, passionately, hungrily, and then they moved . . . Kisses, whispers, touches—the sweetest foreplay. Intimate, incredible. And at last, they were together; and as it seemed in all things, they could soar together until the best conclusion joined with all else. And then they lay, side by side, panting, smiling, with no regrets touching either soul.

Skye adjusted comfortably against him.

They lay together, her head rested upon his chest, an arm around him as he stared at the ceiling and threaded his fingers through her hair.

"I'm sorry. This is so crazy," she murmured. "You know, I didn't mean to take advantage of you. I swear, I was just going for water!"

He laughed softly. "I could repeat that, word for word. Or I could point out that what is happening between us is not crazy at all; it's rather perfectly normal," Zach said softly.

He felt her smile. "Weirdos attract?" she asked.

"Healthy young human beings attract," he told her. "And

the attraction is enhanced even beyond the natural physical desire, because honesty is a beautiful thing; and enjoying something that is beautiful and natural, without worrying about the
lies you may tell in the future, is exceptionally"—he eased himself down and around so that he could look at her for a moment—"sexy and sensual and," he added softly, meeting her
eyes, "wonderful."

She smiled.

"I guess now is when I say that this isn't something that I
usually do," he shared.

"Ditto. But . . ."

"Okay, honesty. I wasn't even sure I wanted to be a part of
this at the beginning. When I was informed that I was having
an interview with Jackson, Adam, and Angela, I thought I'd
figured out how to work in a way that I could use what I could
do without letting the truth out—"

"Ah! Manipulate evidence," she playfully interrupted.

"No, I don't believe in manipulating evidence. I really believe in the law. Speaking of which, in the late 1600s—John
Locke, English philosopher and physician—"

"'Wherever law ends, tyranny begins,'" Skye finished for him.

"Exactly."

"I was scared, too," she admitted.

"Well, I wasn't *scared*—"

"Ah, come on."

"Maybe a little. And when I heard that I was meeting with
you, despite everything, I guess I had . . ."

"I was suspicious of you, too," Skye told him. "Worried. I
meant to observe and keep a very careful distance."

"We're not very distant," he said jokingly.

"Not at all!" she agreed. "It's amazing how things change!
Now, all I want to do is crawl all over you!"

He grinned. "Please feel free."

Someday, maybe soon enough in the future, they would talk—really talk. He'd tell her how she was the first person he'd really cared about in forever, that she had made the past slip into the past for him—never forgotten, but set where it should be within his heart, his soul, his ability to function . . . his life.

And she'd talk to him, he knew. He felt he understood what he'd learned from her: In her life, she'd known a different fear—a fear that the mask she wore for the world would slip, especially if she dared become too involved with a lover.

But that night, talking was something that would come later. The time they shared was, Zach determined, the best therapy.

Because for just a little bit of time, his mind shut off to the maze and the puzzle that stretched before them.

Soon enough, his alarm rang.

Skye leapt out of bed like a gazelle. "Shower. And it's day. Don't you dare—oh, wait! I have my own shower. Let's move!"

"Aye, ma'am, aye!" Zach replied. He rose and walked into the shower, drying and dressing quickly.

They were out in the kitchen area almost simultaneously.

"I want to call the hospital, see if Cathy and the driver are doing well. And, of course, if we're able to speak with Cathy yet. And—"

"Start by calling Gavin. If my instincts about him are right, he'll already be back in the office. I'll cook today. I can scramble some eggs and throw some cheese in them, and I'm excellent at hitting a toaster button!" Zach said.

"Great. Thanks!" Skye said.

Zach headed to the refrigerator and then the stove, finding the frying pan and starting the eggs. He could hear her speaking and thought he should have just asked her to put the phone on the speaker, but it didn't matter. They'd need to sit down and eat, and she could tell him anything she'd learned then.

"Okay, well, you started off being right—Gavin was in the office." She joined him in the kitchen, going for plates and silverware and glasses for juice. He poured coffee cups between stirring up his egg mixture.

"Thankfully, both the real driver and Cathy are doing well; he was already able to see the driver—the man knew nothing at all. He was simply attacked by a witch; and after his head was hit and he finally came to in the hospital, he was sure he imagined he was hit by a witch. And Cathy . . . Gavin said that she's a weepy mess. She's swearing she'll never touch drugs again as long as she lives. The Sizemore couple has halted all tours for the week. They're horrified by what happened and are ready to take a loss on the whole thing—and they're stunned that Nick Sandoval turned out to be a mental case, under the spell of someone, and they haven't a clue who that could be. Sandoval had been with them for a month."

"Seemed fine when we met him for the tour, too," Zach reminded her.

She nodded.

"But I guess that's how you get away with what you're trying to get away with—you target victims, but you find the right lieutenants to be beneath you," Skye said. "The thing is, Nick believes all the rubbish he gave us."

"All right. There is someone out there with a major plan. Somehow the plan has to do with kidnapping people who are vulnerable, or can be made vulnerable. At first, they're drugged—and threatened. We find out about more people being dragged into this all the time; except, of course, it doesn't seem as if anyone with real power has been swept up into this. Whoever the leaders are, they aren't taking chances with someone they can't drug or brainwash into complete pliancy," Zach theorized.

"Here's what's so aggravating. At first, I thought we had it! We knew that Patricia and Jeremy were brought through the

188 / HEATHER GRAHAM

forest. But that area was searched top to bottom, another little green army toy was found, and the answer is that they came through to the road on the other side—and drove somewhere. Then, last night. Of course, Ned Sandoval knew exactly where the trolley waited during the few minutes between the driver being on call and the guide letting him know that they were ready," Skye agreed.

"They are using the forests," Zach said. "And we have every ranger and every patrolman in the area aware of what is going on, and how it's going on, and still . . ."

Skye reached across the table and set a hand on his.

"Hey, you stopped me from getting too down last night, and we looked at the good, instead. We did save lives. We do have Nick Sandoval. And we, at least, put a good kink in the operation. What gets me again is that they seem to know what they're doing. Wearing the witch costumes—in Witch City, no less—and leaving no prints, no DNA, and somehow managing to avoid traffic cams as well. So that either makes one look in the direction of someone very familiar with law enforcement, like a cop, an officer, an agent—"

"Or," Zach said, "someone who really knows how to collect the right programs off the zillion things streaming online these days, easily available by computer or TV or even podcast."

"What do you think?" Skye asked.

"Okay, if someone is culling all these people, to what end? I mean, this isn't something where we're going to discover a cult leader like a Jim Jones or a David Koresh. Our suspect knows what they're doing is illegal. I mean, when you're trying to sway people to a way of thought, you do it through growing a ministry. This person—no, you've seen two. These people are planning something. And the only thing that makes sense is doing something drastically illegal and using the victims as pawns, as shields; or in other words, their hostages are their means to get away with what they're planning. That doesn't suggest a kid who learned how to make a bomb by watching TV—or even excelling in class."

"Someone frustrated with where they are in life," Skye said. "Smart, savvy about the world—and Salem and even Halloween."

"And movie witches," Zach added. "All right, we'll get Gavin on it."

"All right, Gavin, yes. But get him on *it*. Get him on what—exactly?"

"Finding out what a massive heist might be. And how innocents might be used as shields or pawns for the thieves to get away with it."

She nodded. "Good plan. Okay, let's get to the station. I want to talk to Nick Sandoval myself. Then go to the hospital so we can see Cathy."

"Pick up, head out," and Zach did so.

When they were in the car on the way to the station, Skye turned to him and said, "I don't know why, but I want to get back to the monster store. I'd just like to have more time."

"It's still closed; I'm sure we can arrange it," Zach said.

"And I've been thinking . . ."

"Always good," he said.

She grinned at him. "Sometimes good! But okay, we've been fixated on the forests. That's because they use the forests to slip away with people, to hide them. But we've had so many people out, people who know the woods."

He laughed. "Lots of forests. Just because you live in the area doesn't mean that you know the woods. Hey, I have a cousin who grew up in Homestead, Florida. Talk about places to leave a body—the Everglades."

"Well, I don't think they're going from Salem, Massachusetts, to the Everglades!" Skye said. "My point is that there are huge warehouses and such all over the area, some of them abandoned. There are some businesses that never did recover from the pandemic."

"If they are using an abandoned building, it's an abandoned building with woods nearby. I saw Patricia and Jeremy—they were in the darkness. Someone was speaking to them in the woods."

"Good point. Maybe there is a big warehouse or even a big house somewhere that's on the verge of the woods or in the woods . . . They're somewhere out there, Zach!"

"That is true," Zach agreed.

"Another plan," Skye said. "I think I said it before—though sometimes the downside is I think that what's in my head has come out of my mouth. I want to go through the woods in the direction Nick was taking Cathy last night and get out to that road. And if we're lucky, I may see whoever it was who was coming to get them."

"Right. We may see—sorry, *you* may see a car there, parked off the side of the road, waiting."

"Wow, and if we could get Angela and the team back home comparing a car, if we can find it, to traffic cams, we get a good enough shot for facial recognition on the driver and have somewhere else to go!"

"Okay," Zach said. They had reached the station. "How's this? I'll talk to Gavin; we'll both watch you with Nick from the observation room."

He hesitated before getting out of the car and he turned to her. "This is . . . I mean, somehow in the middle of this strange situation, you made the night the most beautiful I might have known in my life—and yet here we are, amazingly, right back, thinking hard, in, yeah, what I think of as our twisted mess."

She smiled and said softly, "Yeah, I must admit, I'm glad I was so thirsty last night! Never knew what a bottle of water could do for me."

He laughed softly. "Back to twisted life."

Out of the car, they headed into the station, running into Detectives Berkley and Cason, who were on their way out.

"Hey, you two, quite the night!" Vince Cason said. "And all we did was walk around and around the Bolton house, around and around the forest, talking to rangers—"

"Well," Connie Berkley interrupted, "we did speak with a number of rangers. We know that the witch who took Jeremy and Patricia walked all the way through to the road. It was almost a perfectly straight path—"

"As straight as you can be, through a tangle of trees," Vince interrupted dryly.

Connie groaned. "A straight path—looping around a ton of trees—from the house. They're driving somewhere with the people they kidnapped. And I guess that the kid last night was planning the same thing."

"We tried to talk to him; Gavin has talked to him. He's gone crazy as a loon," Vince said. "And gone for good, I'm pretty sure. I don't know if any therapy could ever help him. He told me that he'd rather die than betray the master, who will save us all. He will have a place of beauty without horrendous people like us around him. You going to take a stab at it? This whole case got so nuts that the powers-that-be have ordered Gavin to take over in the field, but I guess you know that. We all went off on what he asked last night."

"Yeah! You guys got a great tour," Connie said, grimacing.

"Oh, it was great," Skye said, grinning back at her. "So—"

"We're out. Off to a meeting with a group of forest rangers. We'll give them what we know, and maybe they'll give us something. We're reaching at straws—so if they can hand us a few, who knows? Something has to break this. Anyway," Connie said.

"See you somewhere along the way. Gavin is keeping us all looped in, so you don't need to worry. You'll get anything we have!" Vince promised.

192 / HEATHER GRAHAM

As the two of them went out, Gavin arrived from the back.

"I know you want to have a stab at our guest," he said to Skye. "But I wanted to let you know about something else. My cousin made some discoveries—fellow is so good on a computer he could have made big money somewhere, but . . . anyway. He's found three rehab centers in the area that have no idea where several patients went. But, of course, when something is voluntary or when someone had completed a program as ordered, they are free to disappear if they wish. But Ben has a friend who has an aunt who just needed help with depression, and who was supposed to go live with her mom when she got out, and she just seemed to walk away."

"Are all three centers voluntary?" Zach asked.

"Two are. One is more or less what you'd call a lockup—state- or federal-ordered addiction and psychiatric help. I have the addresses—if you want to go to them today. I know that—"

"We'll need to move quickly," Skye said. "May I get started with Nick Sandoval?"

"Of course. Come on back."

Gavin led the way down the hall to the interrogation rooms and the observation room that sat between them.

Nick was in one of the interrogation rooms, head lying on his arms, which rested on the table.

"Did you two want to take him together, or—"

"Skye is going in. I'm going to ask you about something that's a theory now, but that we'd like to expound on," Zach told him. "We think the witches are hiding people in a building near or in a forest, maybe one with shacks around it. Something that appears old, locked up, and ready for demolition. Maybe. Or not. But we're almost positive they're being scared by the darkness and being taught that Puritan people were right to be afraid of the devil and evil."

"All right, if you have a plan—" Gavin began.

"Well, we do have a plan, and it is logical and requires procedure—real law enforcement work," Skye announced with determination. "We want to go to each of the locations where we're pretty sure the kidnappers did whisk away Jeremy and Patricia, and where Nick Sandoval was probably headed last night. If we can get to both locations, we might be able to see a car and people waiting, ready to drive away—"

"Driving away at the one, and having to give up on the other when Nick didn't make it out with his target," Zach elaborated, fleshing out Skye's plan.

"Hey, you drive; I'll hop in the back," Gavin said. He looked at Skye.

"I'm going into the interrogation room; we want to get to the hospital to speak with Cathy, too."

Gavin nodded. "I'll get my people looking for abandoned properties."

"Or just properties where you might hold people, when you're not drugging them and dragging them out into the darkness," Zach said.

Gavin nodded, and Skye slipped out.

And they watched as she took a seat opposite Nick Sandoval.

He didn't lift his head, but Skye waited. She appeared to have all the time in the world. When he kept his position, she yawned and leaned back in her own chair.

Curiosity apparently got the best of Nick.

He raised his head and stared at her. "So now—you!" he said wearily.

"Now me," Skye said lightly.

"You know, you look like you could be nice. You're really a beautiful woman, but don't you see? That just can't matter when you live beneath the devil!"

She shook her head. "Nick, I'm so sorry, and I don't know who told you that; but what's being done here, the people who are ordering you to commit crimes—"

"It is no crime to save a girl, to bring her to the way of the master!" Nick told her.

"I'm sorry, Nick, but it is a crime. And you're going to be arraigned for kidnapping, for drug possession, and possibly other charges," Skye said gently.

"And you may shackle me and put me behind bars. I will not betray all that I know to be good and just and right."

"The master is lying to you," Skye said just as gently.

"The master does not lie. He brings us to feel the night; to understand the darkness; to know that if we listen to you who play with the devil and all his demons, we will know nothing in the coming life except for darkness. He helps—"

"No, he doesn't help anyone. He takes little children from their parents. He threatens people that he will kill their children or those they care for if they don't listen to him. That's not listening to goodness, to seeking beauty and grace in an afterlife. That's just practicing cruelty here in this world."

"I know you will say these things. I know you will lie and lie. Because you don't know. As I said, it's a pity, because you could have been a wonderful asset to the tribe, to those of us who have been chosen to know the truth, to live the way, to bring others into the fold. You may beat me, you may hang me by the neck until I'm dead, but I will never betray the master."

She smiled sweetly at him. "But you already have, Nick. You failed him!"

"What?" Nick was stunned, taken aback by her words.

"Oh, Nick! You led us right to the road," Skye lied sweetly. "Of course, you didn't realize what was going on, but we judged exactly where you'd been and where you were going . . . It's only a matter of time now." She lowered her voice and whispered, "And I've heard that if someone fails him, or if he fears someone, they die! Maybe they go on to wherever it is that the master talks you into believing you're going, but in this life, they die. Poor Mr. Bolton. I believe he killed Mike because Mike might have guessed who he was. And, of course, there isn't one master; there are two—"

"No! No! Only one master. He has those of us who love and follow him—"

"And charm and kidnap young girls for him, dress up in costumes, and kill for him."

"He only kills evil!"

"But you failed him, so . . . well, he could see you as evil now. And if what you're saying is the truth, why doesn't he let the world see him? Why doesn't he spread his word on television or through the Internet?"

"Because people are stupid! They're sheep. Something has been believed, so they just keep on believing it. He very carefully chooses those to teach, to give the gift to, the gift of truly divine life, truly forsaking the devil!" Nick announced. "And just because you find the pickup spot, that doesn't mean you'll find him!"

Skye sat back, shaking her head. "Here's something you should think about. You believe there are witches—or whatever—who truly dance with the devil in the darkness of the woods. Well, here's the thing. Think about it. If the poor innocents tried for witchcraft in 1692 really were evil, all cozy with the devil, why didn't they just call on him to save them from the ropes? Maybe the devil and the master are the same! People believed those in cahoots with the devil deserved to die. Maybe this person convinces others that there are people being evil along with something like the devil and therefore, they deserve to die, too." Skye leaned close to him. "I have it on good authority that the master does kill if he senses someone might betray him in any way, shape, or form. You got any friends back there with the master? Even they could be in danger. Or you could see that they're safe now?"

She stood then, smiling at him.

"Think about it, Nick, please. Just think about it."

She turned and left the room. Nick Sandoval just stared after her.

And Zach knew. She had gotten to him. In a few hours, they just might get something from him that would lead them in the direction they needed to go.

CHAPTER 13

"Every once in a while, I wish that torture were legal," Gavin said stoically.

Skye smiled. As little time as they'd been working with Gavin, she knew that he would never go beneath the law. He wouldn't torture anyone. But she could understand he was frustrated.

They had someone who could probably give them what they needed in order to find the children and the missing people.

But they could get nothing from him.

The interesting thing was he hadn't asked for an attorney yet, though he had been read his rights more than once.

"For some reason, we've been big on quotes lately," Zach said. " 'Wherever law ends, tyranny begins.' "

"And someone out there is practicing tyranny," Gavin said. He chuckled softly. "We're into quotes? These people are practicing a different quote. 'When injustice becomes law, resistance becomes duty.' "

"Thomas Jefferson," Zach said. "Except that the Thomas Jefferson Foundation says the quote was never from him. But true or false, no real difference in a world where the Internet has given everyone the right to belief without facts. And then again, we, as human beings, have always believed what we want to believe."

"True," Gavin said with a sigh. "So, now—"

"We're off to the hospital to talk to Cathy," Skye reminded him.

"Okay, I'm with you," Gavin said.

"We'll take both cars," Zach told him. "That way, we can divide and conquer, if need be."

Minutes later, they were on the way to the hospital.

The officer on duty, watching over Cathy's door, assured them that no one had been in her room except for her parents and the two friends who had been with her on the tour, Sheryl Dunn and Melinda Seymour. Gavin told his officer he'd hang by the door; the officer should go grab a cup of coffee while he could.

The officer was happy to do so.

"I've already spoken with Cathy and her folks; I'll wait here, not cloud the talk, mess up any mojo, and give that guy a break in the meantime!" Gavin said quietly as his officer walked away.

"Sounds good," Zach said, and he and Skye walked into the room.

Mr. and Mrs. O'Hara, Cathy's concerned parents, Joe and Marlene, were in the room with her, anxiously looking over their daughter. Skye wondered if she was putting pressure on law enforcement resources by asking that Cathy be guarded— the teen's parents might have been the best possible watchdogs themselves.

They were determined that they would be with her until they were able to take her home.

Cathy was awake, pale, and worried as she saw Skye and Zach chat with her parents, explaining that first, they wanted to make sure Cathy was doing well, and then, naturally, to find out if there was anything she could tell them about Nick Sandoval—and what he had told her.

"People—cops—have already been in here to speak with

our daughter," Mr. O'Hara told them. "But you are the two who saved her life! Cathy—"

"I'd be happy to tell you anything!" Cathy told them, sitting up on her bed, but leaning back against a pile of pillows. "As I told my parents, I swear—this might have even been good in an odd way—I will never, ever take drugs again!"

"Nick Sandoval supplied the pills, right?" Skye asked.

Cathy nodded solemnly. "Yeah, he told me that he could take us to a really cool party after the tour and that we just needed to be a little bit happy for it! But everybody thinks that I took too many. I didn't. Just a couple. And I guess . . . when the trolley kind of careened into the embankment, I felt sick! But Nick took my arm, looked back at Sheryl and Melinda, and then just shook his head and told me it would be just the two of us, that we needed to get away before someone came for the trolley and got us all involved in something that would last all night. But I . . . I could barely walk. And it was so dark, and I was so confused . . . and finally . . . you helped me." She glanced over at her parents. "And I know how close I came to dying, and I'm really grateful to be alive. I do want to live! So, thank you, thank you!"

"Cathy, we're just grateful to see you doing well," Zach assured her.

"Before you caught up with us," Cathy continued, "he kept telling me that we just had to go a little farther, and that I was going to wind up so happy. We weren't just going to have a good time; we would learn 'the way' for the rest of our lives." She shook her head, glancing at her parents again. "This has all been my fault! I'm a lucky kid. My parents are super people. They taught me all about stranger danger, and the real downside of drugs, but . . . Nick didn't seem like a stranger, and it just sounded as if this party he was talking about was going to be amazing!"

"But your friends didn't want to come?" Skye asked.

Cathy sighed. "Sheryl has an older sister, who has had some trouble with drugs, and I know she just held on to the pill that Nick gave her, and I think Melinda was trying to make sure that she watched over her." She hesitated, frowning. "And while he offered the pills, I don't think that Nick ever wanted them to come, and maybe they thought that he wanted me especially, or . . . honestly, I think he intended that they not go all along."

Skye glanced at Zach. "Sheryl's sister has had trouble with drug addiction? I'm sure it's in the records from the events last night, but has her sister been in any rehabs? Has Sheryl seen her sister lately?" she asked.

"Um, I don't think so. Her sister is twenty-three years old and has been coming and going for years, but . . . Sheryl's parents are good people and love her to pieces; they're always trying to help her, so I'm assuming they're expecting her home soon. I'm sorry, but does that have any, um, relationship to this, to what happened to me?" Cathy asked.

"We don't know, but thank you," Zach said honestly. He handed her a card and added a second one for her parents. "If you guys think of anything—"

"Wait!" Marlene O'Hara said. She looked confused and concerned. "I'm not really sure that I know the relevance, either, but I can call Loretta Dunn and find out if she's seen Bella—that's Sheryl's sister—lately."

"Sure, that would be great," Skye said. "And if you don't mind, can you find out where she was going to rehab?"

"Of course," Marlene O'Hara assured them.

She put through her call. Everyone else in the room watched her. They could hear a nervous voice on the other end talking before Mrs. O'Hara could talk.

Marlene O'Hara sweetly tried to calm down the woman on the other end of the line, assuring her Cathy was doing well and then asking about Sheryl and then Sheryl's older sister, Bella.

Marlene O'Hara listened, and then tried to assure the woman on the other end of the line that everything would be all right.

She didn't look so confident herself when she ended the call, then looked at Skye and Zach.

Marlene shook her head. "Bella was supposed to have come home last night. They spoke to the rehab, but found out that Bella had lied to them. She'd checked herself out more than a week ago."

"Oh, no!" Cathy moaned.

"Apparently, Bella is an adult, and she has the right to check herself out. She was in there for help, not because she had been court ordered," Joe O'Hara said. "She could be fine; she could be trying to make it on her own, or . . . Well, addicts— she could be off doing drugs again."

"No, I really don't think so," Cathy said. "Dad, we're all friends with that family. You know Bella, and she's not a bad person."

"Honey, sadly, lots of good people fall prey to addiction," Mr. O'Hara said gently.

"Not Bella!" Cathy insisted. "If she said that she was coming home, she meant to do so! Maybe she meant to surprise her parents, coming early, and got swept up, instead, by the monster doing all this!"

Maybe indeed! Skye thought.

"Please don't fret. We'll put Bella Dunn on our list of missing people," Zach promised, "and we'll do everything we possibly can to find her."

"Thank you!" Cathy whispered.

"And thank you, Mrs. O'Hara, you've given us information that may help save Bella, and give us other answers as well," Skye said.

"Right. Again. Thank you! We'll do everything that we can to find Bella," Zach said. "And get to the bottom of it all."

Cathy spoke from the bed. "Please, please, do! She's had trouble, but she's not bad, I swear it! She just gets depressed, and so she tries to take stuff to cheer herself up. She's so talented, a super singer with a beautiful voice. She gets jobs easily enough, but she never feels that she's good enough. She did need help, and . . . oh! Now I'm worried about Sheryl!"

"Cathy, don't worry, thanks to you and your family, we're on it," Zach said solemnly. "And thank you. Thank you so much for your help and feel better."

"I'm better already," Cathy told them. "I'm alive!"

They smiled at her, nodded another silent thanks to Joe and Marlene O'Hara, and headed out of the room.

The officer on guard duty had returned. He and Gavin were speaking softly, casually, Skye thought, and they broke off as Skye and Zach emerged, ready to move back into business.

But apparently, while Gavin had seemed to be friendly with the young officer on duty, he didn't want to talk in front of others.

"All right then," Gavin said. "Time for us to head out. Thanks, Trevor."

"Thank you, Lieutenant! My giant coffee is great!"

The man nodded at Skye and Zach, and then they and Gavin managed to head for the elevator and exit the hospital.

"You don't trust that man on duty—but we're leaving him to watch over a young girl?" Zach asked.

Gavin shook his head. "I trust Trevor completely. Good cop. I just don't know who he might talk to and . . ."

"And," Skye finished, "you don't want to admit it, but you're worried that someone in your department might be involved."

Gavin looked completely uncomfortable. And miserable.

"Hey," Zach said softly. "More quotes. Not sure where it came from but 'a few bad eggs' doesn't mean your force—"

"If I'm right, it is corrupted," Gavin told them. "And it means you might be right on several points, too. As in whoever this master is, he and his co-conspirators are planning something big. We need to figure out what it is. Okay, did Cathy give you something that we didn't have before?" he asked.

"Cathy O'Hara went on that tour with two other girls, Sheryl Dunn and Melinda Seymour. We just discovered that Sheryl has a sister who was at a rehab, probably among those your cousin discovered that had missing people, or people who disappeared after they checked out," Skye said.

"Makes sense," Zach added. "If you're creating an army of shields using pills and darkness to control them, where better to start than with a few addicts?"

"So, did you want to head out to any of the rehabs? Which one was Bella Dunn at?" Gavin asked.

"We didn't push our luck with the O'Hara family. They were helpful enough; and when Mrs. O'Hara was on the phone with Loretta Dunn, Sheryl and Bella's mother, the other was so distraught that . . . Well, she ended the call when she ended it. But—"

"I can find out," Gavin said. "So, should we head there—"

"Here's where we divide and conquer," Skye said. "You get the information on the rehab and go talk to whoever is in charge, find out anything you can about Bella Dunn—and make sure they're telling the truth. Zach and I will head out to the areas where we believe the witch brought Jeremy and Patricia to be picked up, and then to the place in the road where we believe Nick Sandoval was headed with Cathy and see . . ." Skye trailed off, wincing.

"See if she can see the past and get a make on a car so that we can trace a person or maybe at least make a discovery on the vehicle through a traffic cam," Zach said flatly.

Gavin smiled. "Great, all right, attacking it all from different positions. We have Vince and Connie still working with rangers; you're on the possible escape routes; and I'll find out if there was anyone who came to see Bella, or if she said or did anything that would point to someplace she might have gone, or someone she might have wanted to see. Among all of us, we may get something, somewhere, that gives us a clue."

"Keep in touch," Skye said, turning to head for the car.

"Will do!" Gavin called, heading for his own vehicle.

Then they were off again.

"You've said a couple of times you wanted to get back to the costume shop," Zach said as he revved the car into gear. "First, we'll head to the road where Jeremy and Patricia were probably picked up. Going the other way, we'll be closer to the costume shop, and we can get more done in the least amount of time."

"Sounds good," Skye said. She grimaced. "And then again, maybe I'll see a face nice and clearly, and we won't need to go anywhere else!"

"That's a great 'maybe,'" Zach told her.

She shrugged and said, "It's beginning to make sense in an odd way. Steal people and make them believe that even if they die, it's going to be for a wonderful reason. The only problem being that reason is not the great wonder and reward they've been led to believe exists when you battle a world that's been tainted and controlled by the devil in the woods, but rather making a few people incredibly rich or powerful or both."

"And," Zach told her, "they've gotten too full of themselves, pushed it too far. In all of this, there's a mistake. And we're going to find it."

"Oh, speaking of which, I'm going to call Angela. Somewhere there will be a better notion if there's going to be a huge event or a massive money exchange, or anything like that, in the Salem area," Skye said.

"Good plan," Zach said. "And . . . we're on the road, and I believe that orange tie on the tree ahead marks the spot the rangers and detectives determined to be the exit through the trees from the Bolton house."

"Right. Okay, and . . ."

"And?"

"I was just wondering. Why kill Mike Bolton? He wasn't even in the main house. He was too old to put up much of a fight—"

"Don't kid yourself. I know a few people about that age who could still flatten many a younger person," Zach said. "But you're right. He was in the back apartment, the in-law quarters, or whatever you call it. The witch could have gone in the main house and gotten away with Patricia and Jeremy without Mike ever having known about it. So—"

"Maybe—despite the green makeup and costume, hat, et cetera—Mike might have recognized the person if he would have looked out a window, opened a door . . . done something. He was killed with drugs forced into his system, not a gun, not with a knife, not even with strangulation or suffocation," Skye said. "I think he might have known what was going on—and that he did what he was told to protect his grandchildren."

"So now to add to the mix, we need to find out who was in town that Mike Bolton knew," Zach said flatly, pulling the car over onto the embankment.

"Half of Salem, probably. He was eighty!" Skye said.

Zach nodded. "Yeah," he said quietly. "Well, we're here. Time for you to pop out and rise and shine."

She groaned. "Quotes and expressions! 'Rise and shine' is a good expression when you're waking someone up."

"But you must *rise* out of the car and let your strange talent *shine*."

Still groaning, she exited the car. He did so, too, letting her sit on the hood of the car; then he stepped back and stood at a supportive distance.

The day was beautiful, and the sun shone down on the trees and the road . . .

She closed her eyes. She willed it to be night.

At first . . . she just saw cars.

She opened her eyes, closed them again, and concentrated on what she knew about little Jeremy and Patricia.

She saw the green witch in her mind's eye . . .

The witch was emerging from the woods. Pushing Jeremy and Patricia ahead, toward . . .

A dark SUV. The automobile was coming toward her.

It was being driven by . . .

A witch. Someone also facially painted green, a prosthetic nose added on and wearing a pointed black hat.

The vehicle . . .

She needed to see the plate and the make and model of the vehicle!

She turned, trying to see as the SUV took off with its burden of people and raced past her heading toward town.

The license plate! It had been covered by mud; it was impossible to read.

Not a natural spray of mud from going through mushy ground . . .

No. Whoever owned the SUV had very purposely seen to it that the license plate couldn't be read.

Her eyes flew open and she turned to Zach.

He waited for her to speak. "This was the place, all right. And I'm beginning to believe more and more that someone in law enforcement—maybe a cop, an attorney, or even a judge—

might be involved. They knew to completely cover the license plate in mud."

Zach nodded. "Of course. What kind of a vehicle?"

"Black SUV."

"That will help on the traffic cams. Anything else. What about the driver?"

"You're going to love it. Another wicked witch."

"Of course. Once you turn green and have prosthetics on your face . . ."

"Still, if we could get a picture, a close-up of a face, maybe the facial structure could give us a person, a name—a suspect at the least."

"Possibly. Let's get to our next destination and see if *you* see the same thing, the same vehicle waiting on the road. If it's there waiting for any length of time, the person might have stepped out of the car—and that will give us a better idea. In the meantime, we'll get Angela on a search for black SUVs," Zach said.

"Maybe we'll add 'dark' to the description," Skye said thoughtfully. "A dark car in the dark . . . I thought black, but maybe something in a deep, dark blue or green."

"All right. You drive this time. I'll call."

She slid into the driver's seat; the keys were in Zach's pocket, but the car's sensor knew they were near, and their vehicle started right up when she hit the ignition button.

She listened as he made the call, explaining to Angela what they were doing and sharing the bits of information they had gleaned.

"Can you do some deep dives on people up here, too? As in, people that Gavin works with," Zach added on the call.

When Angela had all the information that she needed and Zach had ended the call, Skye mused, "'A few bad eggs.' But here is what I don't understand—if Gavin can read minds, why hasn't he—"

"Okay, think about it. Just because I'm holding an object, I don't get an automatic read. Every once in a while, something just pops in, yes. But that's rare. Usually, I need to concentrate; and from what I've seen, it's the same with you."

Skye nodded. "But, still—"

"He can't go around to everyone in the department—and every prosecutor and defense attorney and judge—in the area and stare at them and do what he can to get a real read on them."

"But he's watched people from the observation room and—"

"Skye, it's not Gavin."

"Because you don't want it to be Gavin?" she asked.

"Do you really think that it could be Gavin?"

She sighed, staring at the GPS in the car's dash, following the directions Zach had fed into it.

"Skye?"

"No. No, I don't. Because he's been with us when a few things were happening—or, I should say, we have verified information on where he's been at certain times. And I like him; he seems to be decent, and he's done amazingly well without getting himself into an uncomfortable position or . . ."

"Being committed?"

Skye laughed softly. "Exactly. Anyway . . ."

"Right now, let's keep going on what we can do that others can't," Zach said.

"Right. Okay . . . this area is bigger than one might think. When you want to be somewhere in a hurry, anyway."

"Okay, trivia as we drive. What now-deceased but incredibly popular animator and creator was related to someone hanged as a witch?"

"What?"

"Sorry, hanged during the Salem Witch Trials."

"Uh, which witch?" she asked.

He laughed softly. "The one who said the Lord's Prayer before he was hanged—something a witch wasn't supposed to be able to do."

"George Burroughs?" she asked.

"Yep."

"Okay, I haven't a clue."

He smiled. "According to genetic research, Walt Disney was Burroughs's sixth-great-grandson."

"Oh, hm. Well, I'm glad George Burroughs had kids before he was executed, since I was a kid in love with just about all things Disney!"

"Got any for me?" he asked.

"Why did Nathaniel Hawthorne change his surname from Hawthorne?"

"Easy! Because his great-great-grandfather was John Hawthorne, one of the judges responsible for the twenty people being executed for witchcraft!" Zach said. "Hey, I was one of those kids who read everything."

She laughed softly. "Me too. But it sounds like you know more trivia than I do!"

"All right. A fellow named William Towne arrived in Salem with his wife, Joanna, in the 1630s. They had eight children altogether. I imagine it was lucky for the couple that they died before the trials—three of their daughters were accused of witchcraft; Mary Towne Eastey and Rebecca Towne Nurse were among those condemned and hanged. Only one survived in jail until after the insanity had ended. That was Sarah Towne Cloyce—and one of my favorite actors, and one of the most eloquent of all time, was one of her great-great-greats. He was her and Mary Eastey's seventh-great-grandnephew. And, therefore, the seventh-great-grandson of their sister, Rebecca Nurse."

"No clue."

"Vincent Price! Yes, he's been gone awhile; but thanks to

the wonders of streaming, young people across the world can see *House of Wax, The Pit and the Pendulum, The Raven*—not to mention hearing his voice in *The Great Mouse Detective*—a Disney classic."

Skye laughed and groaned. "Man, have you been studying up on this!"

"Couldn't help myself," he told her. "Art imitates life. Actress Sarah Jessica Parker played one of the three Sanderson witches in *Hocus Pocus*. And she's the tenth-great–granddaughter of a woman, Esther Dutch Elwell, who was accused of witchcraft, but who also survived the insanity."

"Life imitates art, art imitates life!" Skye agreed. "Wow. Hm." She laughed. "Thankfully, my parents were both first-generation kids, so—"

"People move around, you know. And think of what went on in other countries."

"I don't really want to. But feel free to keep going with silly trivia."

He kept it up and kept her guessing and laughing.

And being amazed by the number of known descendants who had ties back to a time of such tragedy.

And then she realized that they were arriving where they needed to be.

She pulled the car off on the embankment.

They both exited the vehicle. Once again, Skye sat on the hood. And she realized she was grateful that he was there behind her. She was almost always able to snap back quickly from a vision, but it was still so wonderful to have someone there— someone who understood; someone who could catch her, if her mental images caused her to fall too deep.

Once more, she saw nothing at first, just a slow drift of traffic. Blinking, she tried again.

Night fell. The darkness, the sound of crickets, very little traffic on the road. And then . . .

Then a dark SUV pulled over on the side of the road. It sat . . .

And it sat.

And then the driver emerged.

The person appeared to be tall. Even as he leaned against the car, she thought that he was tall. But . . .

The sweeping black cape, the black pointed hat, the green face, and the prosthetic nose kept her from even beginning to wonder what he might have looked like without the makeup.

He waited, and waited . . .

Swore.

Still swearing beneath his breath, he pulled a phone from a pocket in the encompassing black cape he wore and stared down at it.

He was looking at the time. He'd been there way too long, and he realized that something was wrong.

He got back in the car.

And the SUV pulled back on the road, heading in the direction of the center of town.

"Skye."

Zach's voice lifted the darkness from her vision.

It was daytime again. And he was helping her back to her feet; she'd slumped down from the hood of the car to the ground and was leaning against the grille.

"Thanks!" she murmured, coming to her feet with his help. She smiled, feeling his arms.

He had really nice arms. And, of course, she knew that well now.

"Are you—"

She smiled at him. "I'm fine. And thank you. Thank you for being with me. It gives me a better feeling about . . . well, being me!"

"So—"

"If anything, I'm frustrated, Zach! He waited. Got bored. Got out of the car. He was angry! He was there, waiting—and waiting—and he was angry. And once again in costume. I mean, don't they worry about people thinking that they're deranged when they run around the city in those costumes?"

"He, he, he?" Zach queried, a brow hiked.

"Tall, the description. Possibly a woman, but more likely a man!" Skye said, groaning softly.

"Well, they get them off before they get to the city, or they go to wherever it is that they take people before they do anything else. That must be where they dress up as well."

Skye nodded. Of course, it was Salem. But still, if they were seen by many people in such a getup, wouldn't it surely be noted by someone, somewhere?

"Zach!" she said. "They can't let Nick Sandoval go; and they need to make sure that someone is guarding him. He failed—and I'm afraid that the price of failure in this thing *really is* death."

"I'll give Gavin a call when we're at the costume store. While you're doing your thing," Zach said.

"Maybe you should do some things. Try picking some things up?" she suggested.

"The problem with the store is that items have been touched by so many people!" he said. "But I can walk around and do a bit, too."

"Is Mr. Howell going to be there?" Skye asked, wondering why she hadn't checked on that important bit of information.

Apparently, though, Zach had.

"No. Gavin texted me the code; we use it to get in."

They arrived at the store.

Zach used the code, and they entered; inside, he coded in

the numbers to see that the store remained locked while they were in it.

Skye wasn't sure where she wanted to go or what was it she was expecting to find. She walked to the little room where Sophie Howell did homework and played on school days, while her parents finished their workdays. Skye closed her eyes.

Sophie was seated on her little bed, playing with a doll she'd created from a build-a-doll kit. Her mother entered the room, looking terrified at first, then trying so hard to smile, to convince Sophie that she was fine, while telling the little girl they had to go.

Skye blinked. She knew what Sophie looked like, and she knew what Mrs. Howell looked like, but what was it here . . .

Skye walked back out to the main body of the store.

Zach was standing by the register.

He was holding something in his hand. He was intense, staring at it . . .

Seeing something.

She didn't know whether she should let him continue, or . . .

As quietly as she could, she walked in his direction. He didn't move; he just kept staring.

And he appeared to be intensely disturbed by what he was seeing.

She moved closer.

He shook his head and set the object down. It was an apple. A golden apple, with a little sticker on it, describing it.

It was a poisoned apple from a little display on Snow White's evil stepmother.

"Zach, are you—"

He smiled. "Fine. My turn. I'm fine. I just . . ."

"What? What did you see? You didn't take a chunk out of a poison apple, did you?"

He smiled.

"No. In fact, I idly picked it up. But then, I saw someone who was standing right here, holding this, holding this for a long, long time."

"Who was it?" Skye demanded.

He hesitated. "A bad apple, I guess. Skye, it was Detective Constance Berkley."

CHAPTER 14

It didn't mean anything, Zach determined. Of course, Connie Berkley had been in the store, probably standing restlessly at the counter forever, while . . .

While what?

Forensics had been there, yes. But it was a store, a place where people came and shopped, all kinds of people, some just looking, some buying things.

Skye was staring at him.

He winced, shaking his head, thinking he should not have spoken those thoughts out loud already.

And Skye was staring at him skeptically.

"So," she said dryly, "you're thinking Connie Berkley is 'a bad apple,' and she might be one of 'a few bad eggs'?"

Zach shook his head. "Ouch. No, I mean, there was every reason in the world for her being here. The apple was here *before* and *after* Mrs. Howell and Sophie disappeared."

"When the green witch spirited them away," Skye murmured. She hesitated. "Well, we could see if Gavin could speak with her, one on one. Since we've been here, I haven't seen Gavin with either of them. Gavin is the one in charge of managing the case, but he seems to send out orders and spend much more time with us than he does with Berkley and Cason."

"I think he has more faith in us finding an answer," Zach told her. "But before we go to Gavin . . . I know she was holding this apple. And for a while. Maybe you could see what she was doing, what was happening, while she held the apple?"

Skye nodded. "Of course, I can try."

"I'm going to be right here," he told her.

She smiled. "I know," she said softly. "I'm going to stand in front so that I have a pretty good view of the store itself, the register area, and a few of the aisles. You know she was standing there for a long time; we don't know what else was happening in the store."

"Right. She could have been just standing, while a forensic team was seeing if there was anything at all that they could do. I mean, Connie . . . Okay, so apparently, she and Vince Cason can be rude and hardline as detectives, but that doesn't make either one of them a criminal, a witch, or . . . a murderer," Zach said.

"Okay, here we go."

Skye took a position just inside the shop with her back almost against the door. She closed her eyes and opened them.

Nothing, just the store.

She closed her eyes again, concentrating, thinking about the store, her visions of Mrs. Howell with Sophie, the register . . .

Then time seemed to sweep by.

There was Detective Berkley, just standing at the register, holding the apple, moving it impatiently in her hands, waiting, just waiting.

No one else seemed to be in the store.

There was a silence so complete that . . . as the saying went, it was almost deafening.

Then the detective set the apple down and the silence was broken.

Her phone was ringing.

She looked at it anxiously, then looked toward the back, toward the little room, where Sophie played and studied.

A look of confusion and fear crossed the detective's face.

She reached to the holster at the belt of her pantsuit, drawing her service weapon. But then she turned and fled, the image of her race to the door and out of it was so strong, Skye felt as if she'd been slammed back . . .

She had been, or she'd leapt back as the woman had raced for the door.

Skye's vision of the past disappeared as the sound of the glass rattling behind her brought her instantly back to the present.

"Okay, what the heck happened?" Zach asked, standing before her, taking her by the arms and drawing her gently to him. "Seriously, this time, are you okay? I've never seen you react so physically!"

She smiled at him, glad of his warmth at that moment, and of the sense of security his presence gave her.

Of the caring—the deep caring.

"I'm fine. No, I will be fine. Need to shake that one off a little," she told him.

"Breathe," he said gently.

She smiled. "If all else fails, you could make a great Pilates instructor!" she told him.

He arched a brow. "Ah, but here's the thing. We will *not* fail."

"I hope not!"

"So, was Connie here to destroy evidence? Were there others around? Is she guilty of something? Is she innocent?" Zach asked.

"Well, here's the problem with what we've seen. Connie was here, just as you said. She was standing impatiently in front of the register, playing with the apple. I couldn't see anyone else

218 / HEATHER GRAHAM

in the store at all. Her phone rang; she drew her weapon. But then she bolted toward this door and out so quickly that it was as if I felt her hurtle herself against me!" Skye explained. "Zach, I just don't know! What could scare an armed detective so completely?"

"I think we need to ask her. With Gavin," Zach said.

"I'm going to get ahold of him and have him make sure she gets to the station, somewhere we can put her down in a chair and question her," Skye said. "I don't want to believe . . . All right, I can understand that a woman detective doesn't want to let anyone know she was frightened—"

"Anyone can be frightened," Zach said.

"Yes, but trust me, it's not something she would want advertised," Skye told him. "But we need to find her. We need to speak with her ourselves—and Gavin needs to speak with her."

Zach nodded and put a call through to Gavin, frowning as he did so. Things just kept twisting and twisting.

"What?" Skye asked.

"We need to get back to the station."

"What's happened?"

"Vince had the same feeling you did—that there might be something here about the kidnapping we had missed. Connie wanted to go home, but she told Vince she might get her car and meet him here last night. When he got here, she wasn't here," Zach told her. "He walked around, thought about ways they might have missed a witness, thought about where someone might have gone, but he didn't worry last night. He figured she just didn't agree with him and decided not to come. But when he couldn't reach her this morning, he got concerned. He went to her place and got no answer. He's been trying to call her, reach her online . . . and he finally called the department to report to Gavin that he couldn't find her."

"Did you tell Gavin what we saw—" Skye began.

"Yes," Zach assured her quickly. "And I told him we'd like

to speak with Detective Cason, and he needed to speak with the man. But apparently, Cason is a pile of nerves at the moment, and he took off to look for her and isn't replying to anything now himself."

"But if he was given a direct order—" Skye protested.

"No one got a chance to give him a direct order—he reported he'd be busy looking for her—and noted that we had been brought in specifically for the case."

"All right, then. Did Gavin say anything about his interviews with the rehab centers? Did he find out anything about Sheryl's sister, Bella?"

"He asked that we get into the station and take it from there," Zach said.

"Okay, okay, but wait! Just one more minute, let me see . . ."

"Right," Zach said. He knew what she wanted to do.

Find out if she could "see" what Connie had done when she burst out of the costume shop.

"Where do you want to be?" he asked her.

"Back on the road so that I can see the door, the parking, and the surrounding area," Skye told him.

He nodded. "I'm right beside you."

She smiled and nodded and headed out to her desired position. He followed her; and when she found her position, he stayed a small distance behind her, and a little to her right.

He watched as she stood still, looked at the entrance to the shop, closed her eyes, and opened them again.

She repeated the process.

She didn't fall or falter. She closed her eyes, and he set his hands on her shoulders and turned her to face him.

"What did you see?" he asked her.

"She ran out of the shop and raced for her car. She hopped into her car and got the ignition going, just as someone else burst out of the store!"

"*Who?*" Zach demanded, wincing at the sound of his voice.

But she didn't seem to hear the tone of his question. She was still caught up in whatever the surprise had been in her vision.

She stared at him directly. "A witch," she said wearily. "A person we've seen a dozen times, someone dressed up in green makeup and a black cape and pointed black hat."

"Why would an armed detective run from a perp dressed up as a witch?" Zach demanded.

"Probably because he was carrying an assault rifle," Skye said.

Zach nodded. "We've got to get to the station. We'll invent a witness who saw the witch go after Connie. Officers need to be warned; the public needs to be warned now. Someone is going to need to do a press conference, because everyone in Salem and the areas surrounding the city is in danger."

She nodded, then headed for the car, walking around to the passenger seat. She was shaken enough by what she had seen to determine that he was better suited to be driving at that time.

"She was running from a witch with an assault rifle," Zach said reflectively, setting the car into gear. "What did the witch do?"

"Stare after her."

"Run for a car?" he asked.

"No. The witch headed back into the shop."

"How the hell is this person getting into the shop?" Zach mused, shaking his head as he drove.

"Well, it's a code. And we believe someone in law enforcement is involved. Oh, my God! What if it's Gavin?" Skye suggested, looking at him with horror.

Zach shook his head. "Jackson Crow set us up with Gavin. Or, I should say, Gavin called Jackson for our help. But if Jackson didn't trust him completely, he wouldn't have sent us out here."

"But what if . . ."

"What if Jackson didn't know?" Zach asked. "He's Jackson

Crow. And he works with Angela. I can't believe for a minute that after all the years he's been dealing with the unusual, he wouldn't know."

Skye nodded after a minute. "I guess . . . Well, we're back to a witch. Because anyone in the station might have seen a scratched-out note, or someone's phone—somewhere that the code to enter the place was written."

"I would think only someone close to the department," Zach said.

"What about Gavin's cousin Ben?" Skye asked.

He didn't really have an answer for that, except . . .

"Gavin would know," he said quietly.

Skye sat back in the car, closing her eyes. "Traffic cams."

"Yes." He glanced at her and quoted stolidly, " 'ET phone home.' "

Skye nodded and pulled out her phone. She set it on speaker. Both Jackson and Angela were out of the office, but they were quickly connected with a woman named Michelle Bainbridge, one of the main techs at the office.

"We've been studying the footage, and we wound up with the good and the bad. Using our best manipulation abilities, we found a black SUV being driven by, yes, a wicked witch. The plates were, of course, obscured. Still, state and federal troops were put on it and they found the SUV."

"They found it!" Skye exclaimed.

"Abandoned right across the state line in New Hampshire," Michelle told them. "We still have forensic teams on it, but . . ."

"The witch or witches wore gloves and didn't leave a thing behind," Zach said wearily.

"Not that we've found so far," Michelle told them. "But our teams are still working, we promise you."

"Of course, thank you. And you know—" Zach began.

"Angela and Jackson are in the field, as I believe you know. But I have your numbers, and I was about to call you when you

222 / HEATHER GRAHAM

called in," Michelle told them. "Please trust me. I will give you information as soon as I have any."

They both thanked her, and they ended the call.

"Gavin must have a press conference," Skye said. "People need to know, especially now that we know a witch is running around with an assault weapon."

"I hope that's not it," Zach murmured.

"What do you mean by 'it'?" she asked.

"I hope they're not planning on using this community . . . shooting wildly to get away somehow, knowing that responders are going to need to worry about the fallen and the wounded. I'm worried the people coerced into this little tribe, having been drugged and brainwashed, are intended as disposable targets when the plan comes to fruition."

"We need to know the plan!" Skye said. She phoned the main office once more, asking for Michelle.

"Michelle, sorry, it's Skye and Zach again. Have you found anything in Salem, coming to Salem, or going through Salem, that could be the object of a heist? Not just gold, money, or diamonds, but anything?"

"I've been working with the major tech companies in the country, trying to find out if they're transporting any new technology, anything earth-shattering," Michelle said. "So far, there's nothing unusual. Banks are working as always, but nothing we know about would be seen as a major haul. I've spoken with a few heads of companies who have informed me their transportation of materials is classified—and I've got the director working on that, acquiring the federal warrants we need."

"Thank you again! We strongly feel that many lives are in danger," Skye told her.

"Of course. I promise you that we're working as hard and fast as we can here."

Once again, they thanked her. They were almost at the station.

Zach glanced at Skye. "Green witches with assault rifles. Oh, my God, Zach! What if they also have . . ."

"Bombs," he said.

"There must be a way . . ."

"We're here. At the station," he said. He turned to her before they could exit the car. "There's always a way. And we will find it. Let's get in and then determine our next moves."

They headed in, just in time to hear Gavin speaking to everyone in the office at that time. "One of our own is missing. We're good here. We've learned to deal with Halloween, with tourists, with expeditions, you name it. One of our own, people. And we're going to get out there and find Detective Constance Berkley!" Gavin saw that they had arrived. "I'm going to let Special Agents McMahon and Erickson tell you more about what they know; and from there on, it's all hands on deck until we stop whatever the hell is going on here!"

Zach glanced at Skye; she knew he wanted her to speak.

She was the one who had seen the witch.

And the assault rifle.

She headed to the front of the group to stand with Gavin. "We were able to find a witness who saw a car tearing down the street—and someone dressed up as a wicked witch in front of the shop. We believe Detective Berkley knew she was up against a person wielding an assault weapon, a person eager to use it on her. The witness, of course, turned and ran, terrified, and said we'd need to arrest them to ask them to come in and make a statement. They are, naturally, terrified of reprisals. What's most important is that we all realize what appeared to be a murder and a kidnapping has escalated into many kidnappings. Our fear is that people are being taken and drugged and brainwashed. We have one man in captivity who is so convinced of what he's been told that he'd rather die than give us information. He has, in fact, suggested that we hang him. He seems to be like any suicide bomber who is convinced of great rewards in another life for his loyalty in the here and now. But we are aware that these witches are heavily armed, and we believe they're planning something major. What that is, we're still trying to determine. If you encounter anyone suspicious, please remember how heavily armed they may be. Call for backup and take extreme care. And, of course, we believe Detective Berkley is alive—but probably in deep hiding."

She stopped speaking and looked at Gavin. He gave her a nod.

"All right, people, get out there. Lives are at stake, including our own, but we are the bastion between the criminals and the killers and the innocents, who put their trust in us. State troopers are on this; the federal government is on this. But Salem is our city, and we are the ones who know and love our city. Get out there!" he urged.

The meeting broke.

Zach joined Gavin and Skye, telling Gavin, "You must hold a press conference and warn the people that witches are out there carrying heavy armament."

Gavin nodded. "I've called it for thirty minutes from now."

"What about Detective Cason?" Zach asked.

"He's still not responding. The captain has left him messages. I'm getting worried both might have been taken and held, or might be"—Gavin paused, then shook his head—"or dumped in a ditch or a forest somewhere."

Zach indicated they should head into Gavin's office.

Gavin nodded and the three of them walked in; Gavin then closed the door.

"What's your feeling?" Zach asked him. "You know both detectives better than we do. And we know that Connie was at the costume shop waiting for Vince, and she didn't go home. We need to talk to him, to find out if he arrived after she was gone, or if he decided not to go, after all, thinking that she wasn't coming and that he really wasn't going to get anything else. And you need to talk to him, look him in the eye and talk to him, and find out if the man is telling the truth or not."

Gavin let out a sign, sliding into the seat behind his desk.

"I don't really know them. They've been partnered together for a few years. The partner I was working with before my promotion transferred down to Orlando—he was tired of the New England winters. I'd see them now and then in here, and they both have impeccable records. The captain was the one who decided they should be lead on what we thought at first was a one-shot kidnapping at the Bolton house, which has turned into a murder and kidnapping, and then . . . You know the rest. The point is, we weren't even on the same shifts. So I don't know either of them well."

"Is Captain Claybourne in?" Skye asked.

Gavin nodded. "He's preparing for the news conference." He stood. "I'll take you to his office."

He tapped on the door to Claybourne's office. The captain bid them to enter.

The man was tense, staring at his keyboard, but he looked up at Zach and Skye as they entered.

"You have something new?" he asked anxiously. "You've found something or someone?"

"Sir, I'm afraid not. We do know, though, that Detective Berkley was at the costume shop and—" Zach began.

"And that a witch came after her!" Claybourne finished, aggravated and rising. "With an assault rifle. This is a total disaster, you realize. Despite history, Salem isn't that big a place! We're usually a law-abiding town, absurdly tolerant these days, when you think of the past. Guns must be licensed and registered in Massachusetts, but assault rifles are against the law. God knows, someone could have driven in from somewhere else with such a weapon, but—"

"Captain," Skye interrupted softly, "this is truly painful to say—"

"I know!" he snapped back at her. "Bruns has told me you believe that someone within this department may be guilty!"

"Sir, it doesn't make the department bad—" Zach tried.

"No, just me and my judgment!" Claybourne told them.

He was in no mood, Zach realized, to speak calmly about his officers. But they needed to try to understand the dynamics within the department.

"Sir, Detective Berkley disappeared in terror. Detective Cason is now refusing to respond to you and to Lieutenant Bruns. Tell us about the two of them, please. We understand they have impeccable records. But is either having money trouble? Have they been through a divorce or a domestic dispute? Anything that might not be in official records?" Zach pressed.

Claybourne walked over to him. "I know you're a Fed. And you were asked in to help by Lieutenant Bruns because he was given so much help once by your Special Agent in Charge Jackson Crow. But you're not Crow, and you weren't given the lead in this case. You want to help? Get out there and find the real culprit and get off my detectives!"

"We're hoping to save their lives, sir," Zach said.

Claybourne looked down and mumbled, "I'm sorry. This has . . . this has gone beyond anything anyone might expect. But Cason and Berkley? No. They're stable. Neither is married—or divorced. Neither is a gambler. There would be no reason for either to be involved. I'm afraid that—"

"We don't believe that they're dead, Captain. But we're afraid they might be in deep hiding, and they've ditched their phones, lest someone manage to trace their movements," Zach said.

That seemed to calm the man down a bit. "Please. Find them. Safely," he said.

"Yes, Captain," Skye said. "And thank you. We feel it's incredibly important that the people of Salem be warned, and they not try to be heroes and accost any witches they might see on the street, but rather they should report any sightings when it is safe to do so."

THE WITCHING HOURS / 227

"We'll get out of your way," Zach said, nodding at Gavin.

Out of the captain's office, Skye told Gavin, "We still need to talk to you."

"Talk, please."

"Your office?" Zach suggested.

Gavin nodded and they followed him. Once they were in his office and the door was closed, Zach asked, "What did you find out at the rehab—or the rehabs? Did you get out to them?"

Gavin nodded. "I found out that a young man named Charles Durbin managed to leave the place where he had been ordered by the courts to finish a program. They believe he hid himself in dirty sheets and escaped via a laundry vehicle. They did, of course, report it; and if Charles is found, he will go to jail. Possibly had nothing to do with the occult. The other two places—including the one where Sheryl's sister, Bella Dunn, was working on getting and staying clean—are based on voluntary admissions. Apparently, Bella just disappeared from the lawn one day, but they weren't overly concerned because she'd been telling her counselor she was feeling great, and she just wanted to get out and start living her own life. Bella did some paperwork, and probably thought that she was done, and so she walked out on the grounds and was gone. "

"But no one has seen or heard about her since she left the rehab? What about visitors?" Skye asked.

"Yes, they were allowed visitors. But no, no one was visited by a witch with green flesh."

"You got a list of visitors?" Zach asked.

"I did. But I'm sorry to say—it doesn't mean much. They don't exactly do background checks at these places. If someone had an ID, they got in with that ID," Gavin said. "The people in charge reminded me that she was an adult with rights—and when she chose to leave, they had no right to stop her."

"They lose someone, and it doesn't bother them at all?" Skye asked.

"She had told her counselor she wanted to live her own

life—and as much as she loved her family, there were things that she needed to do on her own. They shared her words with Bella's parents, but . . . well, of course, her sister was extremely upset."

"Do you know if Connie or Vince meant to go by any of the rehabs?" Zach asked.

Gavin shook his head. "They've been on the forest connection. You're the ones who first led into the forests. Of course, we know the forests are being used as disappearing byways, but still . . ."

"The darkness. Yeah. Someone is dancing with the devil in the darkness," Skye murmured. "All right, then, do you know where they were last meeting with a ranger?"

"Yeah. There's a coffee shop, truck stop in a way, but nice, clean, even charming, really, across from an area where the state forest runs into unincorporated land. They were meeting a fellow there . . . Let me get my notes and I'll give you his name."

Gavin delved through scratch papers on his desk. "Don't worry, you two. I know how to use a computer. I just jot things down when I'm not at mine. There. They were meeting with Ranger Reggie Woodson. Good name for a ranger, I guess. I wonder if that came into his decision to go into the *woods*. Anyway, I'll text you the name and address of the place."

Zach and Skye smiled grimly. "Okay, we're going to head out there. But we will be on cell phones."

"I'll be attending the press conference with Captain Claybourne. Don't worry about him. He's a good man. This has just been . . . Well, he's dealt with robberies, even a murder or two over the years, but he hasn't dealt with anything like this. None of us have."

"Not sure we've ever dealt with anything like this, either," Zach told him.

"Nope," Skye agreed.

"Anyway, I promise you, Claybourne will get the right things into the press conference," Gavin said.

"Thanks," Zach said lightly. "All right, you know how to reach us."

"And vice versa," Gavin said, nodding grimly.

Zach and Skye headed out.

He looked at his phone after they'd gotten into the car and found the texted address and name of the coffee shop—one that made a play on words as well: **Out of the Woods Café.**

"Twenty minutes in light traffic," he told Skye.

She nodded, looking thoughtfully out the window.

"What?"

She shrugged. "I'm just curious. Connie was waiting for someone. She saw something, or heard something, from the back of the shop that I didn't. The witch, I guess. And maybe she was expecting Vince, or maybe even someone else. But maybe *not someone* who had dressed up in a witch costume. Could she have been involved—and then her partner or partners started to worry we'd be onto her, and she had to be taken out?"

"Either that or she saw the assault rifle and knew she had little chance of beating it if the witch came close enough for her to try to get off a shot."

"Too aggravating," Skye murmured. She was looking out the window.

"How about another quote—'a penny for your thoughts'?"

She grinned and answered without turning to him. "Trees. Trees, trees, and more trees. And bushes. I must admit that while we live in an age that came after the Enlightenment, and we supposedly know so much more, I can see how darkness and the endless woods might influence people."

"But now that we know that germs and bacteria and viruses

230 / HEATHER GRAHAM

cause a lot of sicknesses, we know that TB victims aren't vampires—"

"But we still know instinctive fear," Skye said softly.

"There's the café—ahead on the left," Zach pointed out, seeing its sign.

"Let's hope it's a café that serves good coffee," she said lightly. Then she frowned suddenly, closed her eyes, and blinked. "Zach!"

"What?"

"Pull over!"

"Why? What? Did you—"

"I just saw her! I just saw Berkley run into the woods!"

"In a vision—"

"No, no, in the flesh! Zach, pull over. We must catch her!"

CHAPTER 15

Once out of the car, Skye started to tear toward the woods in pursuit, but then again . . . "Zach!" she cried out.

If Connie was running into the woods to hide, it must mean someone was in pursuit of her. Someone who was farther back; she had to have had a lead to clear the road in such panic and so quickly.

"Looking for the source!" Zach yelled back to her, heading for the café.

She almost smiled as she cleared the road and ran over the embankment to the trees. They thought alike so very often, having nothing to do with their strange abilities. He'd barely come into her life, and yet she wondered what it would be now without him.

The situation at the moment didn't leave much time for such worry; the witch who had been after Connie at the costume shop had been carrying an assault rifle. And now, Zach might well be going after that same culprit.

Carrying the same assault weapon.

And she was just chasing a terrified detective into the trees.

Zach knows the situation. Zach knows how to be careful, how to watch for such a weapon. He knows how to move, how to calculate distance, variables . . .

"Connie!" she called, hoping that maybe the detective would answer her, let her know where she was.

Trees, shrubs, brush, and the earth itself, of course, had little respect for the boundaries created by man. The trees didn't care if they were on state land, federal land, or unincorporated land. They all just . . . existed and grew.

Beautiful, tall oaks stood so near one another that their low-dipping branches seemed to interlock, creating natural sections that seemed to embrace certain areas, making them places of quiet privacy—wonderful, perhaps, for private picnics, and yet so encapsulated and lonely that someone could hide there for-ever, ever shadowed by the extremely heavy canopy of the leaves overhead.

The detective could be anywhere.

She stood very still. Her so-called gift wouldn't help her right now. Even if she saw Connie running in terror, dodging trees, trying not to trip over the roots, Skye wouldn't know which way she had gone.

Skye just had to listen. To study the ground.

Branches! Like Zach had shown me. Look where the branches are broken . . .

But for a minute, she was determined to listen. She heard the rustling sound she was coming to know; trees and foliage moved along with the breeze.

Chirping . . . insects, of course.

A cry in the air, now and then.

As she stood there, she thought at first she was beginning to have a vision—then she realized that no, the day had begun early, but it had been long, and the darkness was descending around her because the day was dying. Dusk was coming on, and soon enough it would be total darkness in the woods.

There were things she believed completely. While she didn't agree with all aspects of any denomination, she knew there was a power much higher than man, and she knew the human heart and soul outlived the frailty of human flesh. She had known she wanted to be in law enforcement since she'd been a child. The law was a perfect place to make the strangeness that haunted her pay. She didn't scare easily.

And she doubted Detective Berkley scared easily, either.

But . . .

As Zach had said, an assault rifle could scare anyone.

But as she stood there, it was as if she could feel the woods around her. Feel the very growing darkness of the night.

And here she could imagine that in long-ago times, people living where the woods all but surrounded them might have had strange thoughts and had let their imaginations run wild, especially when they had been taught to live by the harshest of codes.

People didn't change.

They knew more these days. News—both true and fake—crowded the airwaves, and everyone got a bit of something the second they turned on their smartphones or computers.

Yet, standing here in the woods, Skye could imagine being under the influence of a heavy drug, perhaps treated to a strange light show, and told that the world had gone to the devil, and they must be the ones to fight what was happening around them.

Suddenly, there was something, a louder sound of rustling, ahead of her and slightly to the right.

She started to move again, carefully, keeping her eyes open, drawing out her penlight, because even dusk became so shadowed it was difficult to see more than a few steps ahead of her.

Then she heard the scream of surprise and terror.

Ahead, just ahead, but I have to be careful, careful!

Branches and leaves tore at her clothing and hair as she moved along, but she could hear clearly then.

Someone had taken hold of Connie. Someone laughing as she cried in terror.

234 / HEATHER GRAHAM

"You never can account for witches, eh?" a male voice demanded, his words filled with laughter. "Which witch is which, eh? Don't you know yet, you foolish woman? And you call yourself a detective!" He broke off, laughing again. "Run, run, run from a witch aiming an AK-47 at you, and run right into the arms of a witch with a lethal blade!"

Skye quickly theorized and calculated.

Did only one of the witches carry an assault rifle? The leader, or perhaps the leaders, and this witch was possibly just a . . . brainwashed devotee?

She drew her weapon and carefully moved forward. The witch had the detective caught in a hard hold against one of the trees; he had his arm across her throat—a powerful arm, most probably. Connie was just staring; the force of his hold prevented her from reaching for her weapon.

If she still carried one.

Skye saw the man had a knife in his free hand. Despite the shadows, the weapon glinted in the frail remnants of the dying sunrays that made their way through branches and leaves.

It was time to step forward. Glock out, she aimed at the man.

He didn't ease his hold on the detective or loosen his grip on the knife as he turned to see who stepped out from the trees. He might be drugged, but he wasn't stupid. He held still, staring at her.

"I don't really care which witch you are," Skye said casually. "Let her go, or I'll put a bullet through your head. I don't know what all you've been told; but witch, human, whatever— a bullet through the brain will end it all for you."

"You shoot me; I slice her throat," the witch told her. "That's a promise."

Skye shrugged. "You'll be dead."

"A martyr to the cause!" the witch said.

Skye smiled, hiding the fact she was desperately thinking, trying to remember everything she had ever learned in her training about defusing a situation and negotiating.

"That's really not true. There is no great cause. And you've been running around the woods a lot, I'm guessing. Have you had any encounters with the devil?"

"You don't know the devil!"

Skye smiled and laughed softly. "I don't? But isn't that the point? That the rest of the world—other than your *master* and your group, or tribe, however you identify—dance with the devil in the woods all the time? I mean, seriously, think about it. If I was in league with the devil, couldn't I just call on him to knock you on the head and take you out?"

The green-skinned witch shook his head slightly.

But he never loosened his hold. If his arm slammed against Connie's neck with any greater force, he might well suffocate her or break her hyoid bone.

"Ease up on her! Let's talk," Skye said.

He shook his head. "I ease up on her, you shoot me."

"I don't shoot you. I'm a law enforcement agent. If you just let her go, I am not legally allowed to hurt you. You see, there are laws. Laws that protect the innocent. You've been drugged. You've been given so much stuff that you do see things in the darkness, maybe your great master makes you think the devil is there, and only *he* is able to keep the devil away with his great strength. I won't shoot you. Let her go."

He shook his head slowly, confused, but still determined that what he believed had to be the truth.

Tears were streaming down Connie's cheeks.

She was a detective. But that didn't mean she was ready to die.

"Listen to me! Pay attention!" Skye begged again. "If I knew the devil, wouldn't he come and help me right now? But as you can see, I don't have a devil with me. The devil could come up right behind you—"

"No!"

But along with his protest, Skye heard a dynamic thudding sound.

And despite his protest, the man staggered back, let out a strangled yelp of pain, and dropped his knife.

As he staggered back, his foot caught on a tree root and he crashed down to the forest floor.

And to Skye's relieved surprise and amazement, Zach stepped out from around the tree.

"Not the devil. Just me!" he said, shaking his head as he looked down at the witch.

"Thank God!" Skye murmured.

The man on the ground moaned and mumbled a broken word: "Maybe!"

Connie was collapsing. Zach quickly caught her and eased her down to the ground before turning back to their witch.

But by then, Skye had already rushed forward, straddling over the man in the green makeup and the black getup, pulling his hands behind his back and cuffing him.

Zach was on the phone, swearing beneath his breath.

"What?" she asked, trying to get the heavy man back up to his feet.

"Nothing is getting through. We need to get closer to the road. Connie is going to need help, and I may have broken this . . . witch's jaw."

"Up!" Skye commanded, ready to assist the man she'd handcuffed.

"Why?" he cried. "Just kill me here!"

"We're not going to kill you!" Skye said. "Up!"

"I'm trying! Please, I need help!"

"Fine, I'm happy to help you," Skye told him. "You're under arrest for assault and attempted murder."

She proceeded to read him his rights.

But he did need help, and she gave it to him. His bulk seemed to be more from bloating than muscle—as if what he ate was very bad for him. Clutching his arm, she helped him shift his weight up. He stood, staggered again, but he found his footing.

"Lead the way," Zach told Skye. "Remember—"

"Follow the broken branches!"

It was impossible at that time to ask him what had happened when he'd gone into the restaurant, and how in the world he'd managed to get behind that tree, and to be right where she'd need him, right when she'd needed him.

It was logical, of course, that she move ahead. Connie was almost completely out of it; Zach had lifted her and was carrying her rather than trying to drag her.

But if she led, that left him able to react if their captive made any wild attempt to escape or attack them.

Skye realized Connie hadn't said a word since Zach had arrived. She had surely realized that she was going to live.

That she was back with the people with whom she worked.

But she was now just semiconscious. And once they got help to bring the man in for interrogation, after getting both him and Connie medical care, they could ask all the questions they wanted.

As they came closer to the road and the café, Skye heard Zach on the phone as he called in their position and situation.

They had barely cleared the last of the trees before she heard sirens. By the time they were back on the road, an ambulance and two police cars had arrived.

Gavin jumped out of one car himself, looking anxiously at them—and at Detective Berkley in Zach's arms.

EMTs were coming forward, looking for explanations.

"I don't know . . . I don't know," the detective said, shaking her head. "I don't know how, but . . . I can't . . . The witch, the other witch . . . they're so green. They blend in with the forest. But the one, I think, can breathe fire . . . that one. He was coming. I should have never thought that I had gotten far enough. I should have just stayed hungry and thirsty . . . I thought I could figure something. I don't know . . . I don't know . . ."

"She's been given something," a young EMT said. "And you don't know what?"

"No, but she was able to scream and talk about twenty minutes ago," Skye told him. "She took off from the café—"

"It was in the coffee! And then . . . then I saw him, and I knew that I shouldn't have been in there, that I should have stayed in the trees!" Connie said.

"I'll go with her to the hospital; Ben is driving the first patrol car. He'll get our witch into the station—"

"He might need medical assistance, too," Zach said. "I gave him a pretty good right on the jaw, had to get him to fall back, get his arm off Connie's throat, and force him to drop the knife."

"You didn't break my jaw," the witch said. "Take me, prosecute me, hang me!"

"Get him in the car!" Gavin said impatiently.

As he spoke, they noticed that people were coming out of the café. "Ben is in the car—have him take this guy!" Skye said, releasing her hold on the witch and looking at Zach.

"Send the officers in the second car to help!" Zach said.

Skye and Zach took off to head across the street.

"What happened when you came in here?" she asked.

"There was no one—just a waitress and the few customers who we're seeing coming out now," Zach said. "I asked the waitress what had happened, why a woman had gone running out. The waitress told me she had no idea—and the customers were all just as confused by what had happened."

They reached the area around the front door of the Out of the Woods Café.

"What's going on?" Zach asked quickly.

A middle-aged woman, with two very young children, answered, "I don't know! Nothing. We couldn't find the waitress, and that man over there looked in the kitchen and there was no one there. And that crazy lady had looked at the TV

and then went running out, as if monsters were after her . . .
Then we heard sirens, and I felt I needed to get my grandkids
home. It was getting weird. And we all saw that press conference with the captain of the police . . . I think we're all scared,
and we want to get out of here! We were just customers in that
restaurant. Please . . ."

"Yes, yes, but we'll need your name and address, just in case
we need to talk to you again," Zach said. Skye noted that a
young policewoman, along with her partner, an older police-
man, had come out of their car and had followed her and Zach
across the street—as Zach had asked.

"Of course, you can get the kids home," Skye said to the
woman, "just please give your information to the police officer." She raised her voice and spoke to the others who were
trying to move toward their cars. "Please! Help us! Just tell
these officers what you saw, or give them your contact information, and you're free to go. No one is under fire here; we'll just
take all the help we can get!"

"We've got this!" the older officer assured them.

"Something has gone on in there!" Skye whispered to Zach.
But what?

"Okay, no one saw a witch. But Connie thought that she saw
a witch," Skye said. "And now the waitress has disappeared,
but she couldn't have been working alone."

They paused in the café dining area, looking around at the
charming wooden tables and the artistic paintings on the wall—
most of them depicting cherubs and other mystical forest creatures, fairies in many, a few bumbling but charming ogres in
others.

"Do you think that a painting scared her?" Skye asked.

He shook his head. "No, the paintings are all too . . . fun.
Cute? It's a truck stop, but an area hangout as well."

A few of the tables remained clean and ready for guests.
Others had the remnants of meals on them—food just left

there, as the customers apparently decided it wasn't worth staying to try to eat.

"Kitchen?" Zach suggested.

"Yeah."

They headed back into the service area. Steam flowed above the kitchen's long grill.

Water still boiled, spilling over on a stovetop.

There was no one there.

"What the heck happened?" Skye remarked.

"There was a waitress here, a woman of about fifty, pleasant, and capable of moving fast, greeting people, never seeming to lose her cool—though she was confused as hell about the way Connie tore out of here. I came back here; the cook was reading an order the waitress had just brought in. He didn't even know a woman had jumped up in alarm and gone running out to the street. He was also ready to talk, to give me anything that I needed; but with no one and nothing here, I figured it was more important that I come out and see if I could find you or the detective."

"She's alive because you found us," Skye reminded him.

He nodded. "But . . . what the hell happened here? Where is the waitress I met? Where is the cook?"

"Not out front—we would have seen them. Out back?"

"There's got to be a delivery entrance," Zach said, heading toward a large freezer at the back of the kitchen. "Here!" he called.

She followed him. He opened double doors to a delivery area, where trucks could easily come in and out. Trash cans and recycle bins were lined up against the wall of the place, and Zach walked to them, frowning.

"Here!" he shouted. "Skye, keep the officers and get more ambulances!"

"Right—"

"I found the cook and the waitress."

He slammed a couple of the cans out of the way, hunkering down. "At least, the waitress has a pulse! We need help. Fast!"

Skye didn't go back in through the kitchen; she tore around the building to reach the front, where the police officers were still speaking with a number of the patrons who had fled from the café.

"Ambulance! Help, now, please!"

The young policewoman was on her phone immediately. The older officer nodded at Skye, asking, "Where? What?"

"Around here!" she said, showing the way, heading back to where Zach was working with the victims.

He was by the cook then, desperately performing CPR.

"Let me! I was a paramedic before I joined the force," the officer told him.

Zach nodded and moved.

Skye saw he had lifted the unconscious waitress and had moved her onto a little stretch of grass at the side of the bins.

There was a dumpster, too, at the end of the row of plastic recycling and garbage bins; she didn't want to look.

But she did.

To her relief, there were no bodies in it.

It seemed like the EMTs and an ambulance arrived in just seconds. Zach was explaining that the waitress had received a stab wound. He'd been able to staunch the flow of her blood; and she had a pulse, a weak one. The officer had gotten the cook's heart pumping again; but this victim, too, had suffered a stab wound in the thigh.

The officer glanced at Zach. "Luckily for this gentleman, our special agent friend knows how to tie a tourniquet."

The injured cook and waitress were quickly and carefully transferred to stretchers and the EMTs took off.

Zach looked at Skye.

"Hospital, I guess."

"Divide and conquer?" she asked. "Someone needs to get in there and talk to our witch from the woods," she reminded him.

"All right, wait—these two aren't going to talk for a while. And Connie may take some time getting her head clear. You're right. Let's go to the station. Let's go talk to our witch."

Zach turned to the police officer. "You guys finished up here? Forensic detail to check out the kitchen area?"

The older officer smiled and came over and shook Zach's hand.

"You know your stuff. That guy may well live."

"Ah," Zach said, "but I'm sure you far surpass my expertise with CPR."

"We both did good!" the officer said. "And get out of here, do what you need to do. I'm not sure what the heck we can get; but yeah, we'll have forensics come out."

"Thanks," Zach said.

Skye gave him a smile and a nod, and the two of them headed for their car. The young policewoman finished up with the last of the customers and walked toward them as they came around the building.

"Got them all," she told them. "Names and addresses, just in case we need them."

"Thank you," Skye told the female officer, handing the young woman her business card. "If you can—"

"I will get them emailed to you right away," she said.

They both thanked her and walked across the road to the car.

It was dark, Skye realized.

They'd run all morning, starting with the roads, heading to the costume shop. By the time they'd gotten to the station and talked to Gavin and his captain, the afternoon had come on.

The much-needed press conference had been given.

They'd come out to the café and found Connie and the witch.

They'd discovered the half-dead waitress and cook.

And, of course, it was now night.

She glanced at Zach and realized he had bloodstains on his clothing.

"We're so lucky!" she whispered.

He looked at her, arching a brow as if she were crazier than a loon.

"Lucky?"

"They're alive! Two people are alive because you know how to move quickly!" she told him.

He smiled, but his smile faded. "I'm grateful, yes. But there are more than just two people involved in this. The main person—or persons—target people in trouble with addiction or mental problems, or people who are desperate to keep kids alive. Whatever is on their agenda, it's coming soon. Skye, I think this was happening a while before the witch came to take Jeremy Bolton—and to kill Mike. Again, I'm not sure why Mike was killed, and I sure don't understand how no one saw anything but Connie—and someone decided they still needed to kill the waitress and the cook."

"All right," Skye said, theorizing with him, "so they were bringing people in before, maybe weeks before the Bolton murder and kidnapping. And they could have stuck with addicts and the homeless, or people they could easily control with drugs and brainwashing. But then they went to the Bolton house and the Howell costume shop. They did things that were guaranteed to bring attention to them. Of course, the witch costume might be part of the brainwashing, or it's just a way to do things without giving away their faces. Prosthetics do a major number on recognition, even in the best facial-recognition program."

"So, when they got to those measures, they weren't worried about the fact the police would get in on it?" Zach theorized.

"Because whatever they're planning is imminent," Skye murmured, "as you said and believe."

"Exactly."

"But what?"

"We'll try calling back to headquarters again," Zach said. "See if they've found any possibilities."

Skye nodded. Frowning, she looked down at her phone as it buzzed.

"What?" Zach asked.

"That was from the female cop we just met. Her name's Officer Lucy Carmichael. She forgot to mention one thing. There was an advertisement on the television above the counter in the restaurant. One of the local networks is going to be showing *The Wizard of Oz* several times next week."

"So, somehow, they drugged Connie; then she saw the TV . . ."

"And freaked out," Skye said. "Freaked out at the sight of Margaret Hamilton acting in the movie in green makeup and . . ."

"Ran across the road and right into one of Salem's contemporary wicked witches!" Zach said. But he glanced at Skye briefly before asking, "How in the hell did she go on the run? Just walk into that café—and wind up drugged enough to run from the sight of an actress on the screen and right into a real would-be killer?"

CHAPTER 16

When they arrived at the station, they were greeted by Captain Claybourne.

Zach saw that the man was grave and serious.

Claybourne was also glad to see them. Any hesitance he might have about his lieutenant inviting them in was gone.

Well, he was missing three of the people he counted on: Bruns, Cason, and Berkley.

"I've had the fellow in the interrogation room since he was brought in. First of all, we want to thank you both for finding Detective Berkley—and for saving her life."

"It's what we all do," Zach said. "All of us, right? But thanks. We're hoping they'll manage to bring her down into a sense of reality soon enough. When we saw her last—when we first got out of the woods—she was having flashes."

"Yes, Gavin phoned me; told me she was going in and out, most of the time just moaning that she doesn't know, she doesn't know," the captain stated.

"It will take time to clean out her system," Zach said. "Now, of course, we're hoping the restaurant staff survives."

"We heard about the situation in the back and it's horrible. More and more innocents just going about their lives. Of course, we're all hoping they'll pull through. Please, though, the witch in the interrogation room is all yours. He's been fingerprinted. But it doesn't show in the system. And he refuses to give us a name. To be honest, he's been cooling his heels for only a few minutes—he's been given one of our local jumpsuits after being sent into one of the station showers. At least, we can now see what the fellow looks like. We had the doc check out his face; but while he's swollen up, you didn't break his jaw. Which means he can talk just fine. Doc says he's about forty; he diagnosed he's been homeless, or living on the street, for a long time, since his skin and other factors point to a lack of nutrition."

"Sounds just like the target victim for our main witches," Skye answered.

"You can take a look at him from the observation room before you go in," Claybourne said. "He also doesn't want an attorney; he doesn't want to talk. Maybe one of you can do something with him."

"Cleaned up and ready," Zach said.

"Hey, we did put him in there and did just leave him. That often starts to make people nervous, good and bad. Oh, he was very offended; we tried to make sure that every bit of work with him was proper procedure, so we made a point about offering him an attorney again. He told the officer who was speaking with him that the attorneys were the worst devils of them all. And, of course, cops like us, we come right after attorneys," Claybourne said. "You know, of course, that Bruns went to the hospital with Berkley."

"Yes, sir, we know," Zach assured him.

"Bruns is a good cop, but more. He's a good man. He feels a great responsibility for those under his command. Anyway, it's late and you must be worn as ragged as the rest of us. See what you can do with this witch, and then get out of here—go home and get some sleep. No one in the hospital will be able to speak until then, not with anything that resembles truth or sense."

"Yes, Captain, thank you. I just feel that—"

"Something horrible is going on; people are in danger. Yes, Special Agent Erickson, I am well aware. And we do have people working around the clock."

"Of course," Skye said pleasantly. "You know how it is—"

"Yes, to be in the field, and feel that sense that you must keep going because you're so afraid you're failing people. We all work as teams, you know. All of us, here, members of this department—and with others when we work together."

"Let's see if we can get somewhere," Skye said.

"Together?" Zach asked her.

"That might be the right play—the two of us were the ones who stopped him in the forest," Skye said.

"I want to get a good look at this guy first," Zach told her.

"Come on, then. We'll head to the observation room. I'll want to watch when you go in, of course," Claybourne told them.

"Absolutely," Zach said. He wished Gavin were there, but he understood why the man was at the hospital.

But they could use Gavin's mind "expertise" with the man they were about to question.

Through the one-way glass in the observation room, Zach looked closely at the man. He knew he'd never seen him before; and what the doctor had told Claybourne appeared to be right—the man was fortyish in appearance; hair clean, but a wreck, with some graying and unevenly cut around his face; his actual complexion was pale and slightly splotchy, as if he'd spent a long time receiving little nutrition.

They'd uncuffed him. His hands were on the table. He just stared ahead, bleakly; his face was long and his expression rather like a depressed bloodhound's.

"Ready?" Skye asked him.

"Sure. Take the lead," Zach told her. "After all, you met him first. Seriously, I think he might respond better to you."

"All right."

But before they could go in, an officer opened the door, looking at the captain. "Sir, there's someone to see you—a couple and a teenage girl. They're agitated, but want to speak with you or Lieutenant Bruns. I thought . . ."

"You thought right," the captain said. "You two go ahead. Get started. It may prove to be a long session."

Captain Claybourne headed out to meet the waiting people.

Zach looked at Skye again.

"Let's do this," she said. "All we do is get nothing," she added dryly.

They entered the room and took the seats across from the man. His expression didn't change; he didn't look at either of them.

They sat in silence for a few minutes.

"We don't want to hurt you; you do know, though, you're going to be arraigned on serious charges. If you talk to us, we may be able to help you," Skye said quietly.

Nothing.

They sat in silence again until Skye said softly, "Believe it or not, we do want to help you. It would be nice if we could start out with your name, Mister . . ." Skye's tone was low and even, almost pleasant.

"Beelzebub," he said flatly.

"What? No, no, no—you think we're the ones in league with the devil. You're the one who claims to be fighting for good things, fighting against the devil," she said.

He shook his head dismally. "I failed the master. Now . . ."

"Your so-called master is an evil man! You were threatening to kill a woman," Skye reminded him.

"No! She was a witch!" the man said in distress, dismayed they didn't seem to understand the situation at all.

"No, I remember the situation exactly," Skye told him. "When I came into the woods, you were green and wearing a witch's hat and cape—holding a knife up to a very terrified woman."

The man groaned.

"You don't understand anything at all, do you?" he asked.

"No, we don't, so anything you can explain to us will be very helpful," Skye said encouragingly.

"All right, the world as we live in it is a mess. Surely, you see that. The rich can buy almost anything, including people. And then men and women get into power; and when they have power, they become drunk with it. They abuse it and they hurt everything and everyone around them. The problem is, years and years and years ago, someone stopped the people from ridding the world of those who did dance with the devil. That's why the world is still so corrupt. If you don't see that's what's happening . . ."

Skye leaned in close. "The world can be very hard. But how does hurting children and innocent people help that?" she asked.

"The master teaches; he never hurts anyone. And he is constantly thinking and looking for ways to stop all the devil dancers—ways that won't just stop evil here, but around the world!"

"Money—" Skye began.

"The master cares nothing for money!" the man said.

There was a tap at the door. Zach glanced at Skye, letting her know he'd slip out.

When he did, he discovered Gavin had returned to the station; he and the captain were in the hallway waiting to speak to him.

Gavin looked at Zach first, giving him a slight nod. Zach knew that Gavin had been watching for perhaps just a minute or two, and he was going to tell him what he had observed.

In front of Claybourne, Gavin would have a good physical or logical reason why he had his opinion.

"He's telling the truth about what he believes," Gavin said. "The man is completely brainwashed."

"Yes, it seems so," Captain Claybourne said. "The people

who arrived are the Dunn family. They'd heard about the commotion at the café, and they wanted to know if we had any news on Bella. Gavin got the idea to let them come into the observation room and look at this man, and Gavin's instinct was right on. They recognized him as someone who had been at Bella's rehab. Sheryl had met him when she visited her sister one day and knew his name was David."

"A quick call and we found out he was David Harrison, spent his growing-up years going from group home to group home, child of two drug addicts killed in a car crash. Aged out at eighteen, held a few menial jobs over the years, fell into drugs himself, and has lived on the streets for the last ten years or so. I figured that might help you—"

"It will, thanks!" Zach told the captain. He looked at Gavin and nodded. In their careers, most law enforcement officials came across excellent liars, criminals so good at spinning tales they should have gone into acting careers.

He headed back into the room and took his seat.

David Harrison was still sitting with his head just hanging down.

"David—Mr. Harrison—" he said, letting Skye know they had gotten the man's name and background. "I believe—"

"Beelzebub. Just call me Beelzebub," he protested, looking at Zach and frowning. "You're not getting it at all. We need to behave as the witches, the devil, and the evil, so that those around us can see that it is out there! We work against type, don't you understand? People are sheep; they believe what they see; and what they see can be so, so wrong."

"But your name is David," Skye said softly. She shook her head. "You're not any kind of a devil, David. We can see that you've spent a miserable, miserable life! And your supposed master knew that and offered you something better—food, a home, caring. And you were eager to listen to someone who wanted to help you."

"Because he knows!" David exclaimed.

"So, who is he? If he's so wonderful, you can tell us who he is," Zach said quietly.

David Harrison sat back, smiling. "He's the wicked witch!" he said.

"You don't know who he is, do you?" Zach asked.

Something flashed across the man's face.

He didn't know! But how is that possible?

"He's the wicked witch, teaching those who are truly evil the truth. He will win; he will take the power because he must," David said.

"Where does he live?" Skye asked.

"In the darkness of the woods, where he can fight the devil and keep him at bay," David told them earnestly.

"When you need to see him, you see him in the woods?" Skye asked.

David waved a hand in the air.

"When were you supposed to meet him next?" Zach asked.

David hung his head again. "I failed him! I was to have met him in the forest with . . . with the devil's woman."

"The woman you were threatening to kill?" Skye asked softly.

"Yes, she needed reconditioning. Badly," David said. "She needed to be brought into the light; she needed to be saved."

"Where in the forest?" Zach persisted.

David laughed. "Head in from the road, find the center, the large space in the midst of the star copse of trees. Except most people don't know the forest, and even if they know the forest, they'd never know the star!"

"Maybe we'll have you bring us there," Zach suggested.

The man sighed deeply. "I'd be . . . I'd be as lost as you. I just knew that I had to get the woman and start looking until I found it. Or until he found me."

"Where else do you meet him? What else do you do for him?" Skye queried.

"I'm earning my wings," the man said. "I . . . I bring people to designated places."

"People," Zach repeated. "Like Bella Dunn?"

David smiled then. "Bella is my friend. She deserves everything the master can give her, do for her! Yes, I brought Bella to him."

"Where's your gun? Did you force her?" Skye asked.

"No! I invited her. And only a few carry weapons such as guns!" David said, as if horrified by the idea that all of the master's followers might do so. "And only the master himself carries Eve."

" 'Eve'? An assault weapon, you mean," Zach said.

David shrugged. "She is Eve; only someone who truly gains their wings may carry a weapon such as Eve."

"How many have earned their wings?" Skye asked him softly.

He shrugged. "Perhaps a few. But there is tending to the flock; there is food; there is guarding those who, we fear, have not understood; who might try to take the innocents, who are learning, away from the righteous path."

He sat back, closing his eyes. "There is nothing more I can tell you. The master cared for me a long time. He made me well; he made me whole. But he is smart. He knows that the devil dancers can sweep us up, and he's careful that none of us can give him away. I can't tell you anything else. It's not that I *won't* tell you anything else. I simply can't, because he keeps places, people, and plans to himself. He knows that devils can be tricksters!"

Zach glanced at Skye; they both believed the man was telling the truth.

And yet . . .

They knew Bella had been introduced to the master, and she was among the "flock" that he was gathering.

They stood together. "Thank you, David," Skye said. "They

will take care of you tonight. They will see you have food and a bed. We aren't devils, nor do we dance with any. Hopefully, you'll begin to see the truth."

She wasn't waiting for an answer. She stood and walked out.

Zach stood and looked at the man. "Yes, thank you, David, for your honesty. And because I do believe you're a good man at heart, I hope for your sake the innocent people your master has taken don't wind up being brutally killed in defense of his lies."

The man looked at him. Zach thought something almost like fear touched his eyes. He didn't know, and there was nowhere left to go in the little room.

Zach headed out to join Skye in the hallway, just as Gavin and Captain Claybourne came out of the observation room.

"Connie? The cook and the waitress?" Zach asked Gavin immediately.

"Connie is coming around. She was still groggy and not very coherent, but the doctors say that may change. In addition to being stabbed, the waitress had a blow to her head; she's been put into a medically induced coma and may need further surgery to reduce swelling in the brain. The cook is out of surgery, stable, but still sedated. Tomorrow is the earliest we have a chance of talking to those two," Gavin told them.

"But Connie could . . ." Skye began.

"Bit by bit. She was hit with some heavy scopolamine, which was what the doctors believe was somehow put in her coffee!" Gavin told them. "Ironically, I'm told that scopolamine is also known as 'Devil's Breath.'"

"Ironic, all right," Skye murmured. "So, I imagine, when she was in there, the cook had probably already been struck. The witch slipped the drug into the coffee being served to Connie and waited for the waitress to head back into the kitchen. Maybe the witch was on the way out after Connie—with his

minion in the woods, ready to sweep her up—when the waitress interrupted him."

"Possibly," Gavin agreed. "And this guy, this minion . . ."

"We've been listening, but it's almost as if he's been speaking a foreign language. Do you think we have anything?" Claybourne asked anxiously.

"We know Bella is with whoever this master is, but that's obvious to all of us. At least, you can tell her parents that she's
alive," Skye said.

"At some point, we'll get back into the forest—" Zach
began.

"Well, the master won't be there now! He'll have known
that David failed, and he isn't getting Connie," Claybourne
said.

*Of course, Claybourne didn't know just what Skye might see
if they were able to find the star copse in the woods,* Zach considered.

"We know these people are being taken as pawns, as
shields," Zach said flatly. "This guy has doped and brainwashed the addicts, kids, and anyone he saw at the bottom of
the ladder as being vulnerable. Frankly, I think he killed Mike
Bolton because he might have had an idea of who he was and
what he might be up to. He took the Bolton kid—and Mrs.
Howell and little Sophie—to have small children in his number.
He also went for the obvious, instead of doing his usual—stealing a kid out of a group home or something like that—because
he wanted us spinning our wheels searching for them. I believe
it's because whatever the great plan is—it's happening soon.
We need to see Detective Berkley, which we'll do now and get
whatever she can give us. And maybe there's hope we can
speak with the cook or the waitress from the café, but I don't
think they'll be much help. When they're able to talk, they'll
say they were stabbed by a witch. If I'm right, the witch came
into that place through the back, trying to verify that Detective

Berkley was there. Maybe the TV freaked her out—or maybe she saw he had followed her into the café. The waitress and cook had to go because they were going to call the police. Captain, I think Gavin, Skye, and I will go to the hospital and try to speak with Berkley. Then we'll get some sleep after seeing to it that our best people, and your best people, continue seeking something that would make this man a king in truth—a gold shipment, a massive money exchange, something, perhaps the movement of tech or a serious military weapon—"

"A bomb, a bioweapon!" Captain Claybourne said with dismay.

"Possibly. And when he goes after it, the kids—the innocents—will be his shields. We must know what—and stop it!" Zach said. "So, Skye and Gavin, ready?"

"Incidentally, we've got another problem," Gavin said.

"What's that?"

"I'm afraid we're going to find Detective Vince Cason . . . dead," he said flatly. "He still hasn't responded. Either someone slipped him something, and he's in deep, deep hiding, or . . . or he's dead. He'd have responded by now if he could have."

Claybourne shook his head. "No. You found Berkley. Get out there and find Vince Cason, too!" He headed off to his office.

"I can drive," Gavin said.

"We'll take our car, too," Skye said quickly, glancing at Zach. She smiled. "We haven't eaten since breakfast, and now it's very late. So after we've spoken to Connie, we'll need to grab something—"

"And probably fall asleep in our soup," Zach joked. "But we'll meet you there, all right?"

Gavin nodded grimly. They all left the station and headed for their cars.

* * *

Skye walked to the passenger seat and Zach took the wheel. "This is getting scarier and scarier. I mean, the master apparently wants to be king of the world. Now, I love Salem, Massachusetts, but it's not the Hague, Paris, London, DC, New York, or Tokyo—though I hardly think the master is a linguist. And if he's trying to instill fear into the heart of every country, then it might be a horrific weapon he's after," Skye said, leaning back and closing her eyes. But she spoke softly again, saying, "This is . . . I mean, I thought we were looking for a simple murderer. There's really no such thing as a 'simple' murderer, but I still . . . a person or persons, maybe horrific cult killings, but to think that someone might start out in such a way, converting some, killing some, and seeking something that's much bigger, even more horrific . . ."

"Michelle has had the director speaking with the top brass in the military," he reminded her.

She nodded. "It's just that . . . there's something. Something big."

"We'll see what Connie knows," he said.

"And then eat!" She cast a glance his way. "I can't believe that you—and your determination we all need fuel—have been so patient!"

"Oh, I'm hungry. Today has been one thing after another, with no time to give in; and therefore, I've been ordering my growling stomach to be silent," he told her.

"And that works?"

He laughed. "No. One more stop, then food," he promised.

And then? he wondered. *We'd both be ready to crash, of course. That is . . . if something else didn't happen!*

"Let's get in there. Connie telling us what's happened to her might be the best break we get yet," he said.

They parked at the hospital. Of course, the visiting hours were over and they had to produce their credentials. They had arrived right behind Gavin and entered together. They were led to the room where Connie was alone—guarded by an officer in a chair just outside her door.

"You're back!" he said to Gavin. "Sir!"

Gavin smiled. "We'll just be a few minutes. Has she been in any distress?"

"I heard her mumbling a bit, but not in the last twenty minutes or so," the officer said.

Gavin thanked him and they went into the room.

She appeared to be sleeping peacefully.

Gavin perched at her side on the bed. He touched her arm gently, nudging her and saying, "Connie?"

She seemed to whimper; he shook her gently and her eyes opened. She stared from him to Zach and Skye. She let out a sigh of relief.

"I'm still so . . ." Connie began, her voice trailing.

"I know. Confused," Gavin said.

"*Scared!* Oh, my God, it was so awful. I mean, someone knew something! I thought I was going to meet Vince, but I was kind of irritable, so I went home. I had started to settle in for the night, and then decided I'd head back to the shop and meet him and try to make more discoveries, as he had suggested. I got there, figured maybe he hadn't come yet, and I'd give it a few minutes. Then I was at the register playing with some stupid thing there, and I looked up and . . . I saw . . . it! Big and green and whipping an AK-47 around, and I realized I'd stupidly put my gun in the safe at home. I ran and I heard this cackling, and I knew it was behind me. I couldn't go to my car, because it was cackling and swearing that I shouldn't worry, I'd just explode, so . . . I ran into the forest. I threw my phone away because Vince and I had both thought of the possibility a cop was involved, and another cop could have traced me . . . and . . . I got lost in the forest. I wandered and wandered; and by the time a whole day had gone by, and I saw the café, I figured I'd get coffee and ask the waitress if I could borrow her phone. I could call in and run back and hide in the forest again until someone could come out for me . . . It really wants to kill me! That awful creature wants me dead!"

"And there's no chance the awful creature can get you now," Gavin promised her. "We have a man at your door, and we have backup outside and in the waiting room. You're all right."

Tears streamed down her cheek. "Gavin, I don't deserve to be a detective!"

"Yeah, you do. You're still alive," Gavin said gently, reaching down to squeeze her hand.

"Why didn't I immediately ask to borrow the woman's phone? Why did I feel I'd be better and sound sane if I could just have coffee? I don't know where I walked from. I'm lucky I didn't startle any creatures . . . but I was terrified of being on the road where I couldn't hide! And then at the café . . . I sipped the coffee, and it was strong and good, and I thought I'd be all right until . . ."

"Connie," Skye said gently, "are you able to tell now if you were frightened of something on the TV—or something real? We know your coffee was drugged. Did you see a movie, or—"

She smiled. "I was aware of the television! I was thinking of the irony. But no, the coffee hadn't really gotten to me; yet . . . he was there in the back."

"The same witch?"

She shook her head. "I don't know. I just really don't know!" she said with dismay.

"And that's all right, it's all right," Gavin assured her. "That's the point—dress everyone up in the same costume, and no one knows which witch is which."

"The important thing is you're all right," Zach said.

"Vince hasn't been in to see me yet!" she said, and she frowned, studying Gavin's face. "Oh, no! Has something happened to Vince, too? Oh, my God, did the witch get him at the costume shop before I got there?" she demanded, growing more and more distressed.

"Hey, we think he's in hiding, too," Gavin told her. "He's smart; he's careful. He's going to be all right."

His words didn't convince her. She lay back again and closed her eyes, her face a mask of misery.

Zach squeezed her hand. "No, no, Connie. We heard from him after that—he was on a search for you. And now? We're going to find him. I promise you."

Was that something he was supposed to say? No. Something he needed to say at that moment? Yes.

"Connie, have faith in the man you work with!" Skye told her quietly. "He knew you would survive; you just needed the right people to find you, and we did. We'll find Vince, too, I promise."

They needed to leave; to let the patient go back to sleep.

"Rest," Gavin told her. "You've worked this; you've worked it hard. Now rest and let us do some of the heavy lifting."

She gave him a weak smile.

As they started to file from the room, Connie caught Zach's hand.

"Someone . . . Be careful!" she whispered.

He realized she didn't want Gavin to hear her words.

"Someone in the department is involved!" she said.

He gave her a smile, eased his hand from her grip, and assured her, "We know!"

He quickly rejoined Skye and Gavin.

Connie hadn't wanted anyone else to hear her—and that anyone else had included Gavin. Did she suspect him?

They were informed that the cook, Sam Astrella, and the waitress, Ona Patterson, were still sedated.

Cathy O'Hara had been released; her parents had determined that they should take her on a long trip out of state.

They said their good nights to Gavin, knowing they'd all meet again in the morning; hopefully, they would know more at that time, with tech crews and others working through the night.

In the car, Skye asked Zach, "What was she warning you about? That she wouldn't say in front of Gavin. Does she suspect him of being involved?"

"Probably," he told her.

"It's just not possible."

"We don't want it to be possible."

"I don't even want to think about it right now!" she told him, groaning softly. "Wouldn't it be cool if our brains came with on and off buttons, and we could rest our minds when we needed to?"

"That's what sleep is for," he assured her.

"But we're both starving."

"Get out your phone—find us something open all night in the area," he told her.

She did so, then smiled. "I didn't find an all-night restaurant that's close to us—there is one in Peabody. But there is a sandwich shop, with tables and chairs, right on our way, that's opened until two in the morning, so—"

"Put the coordinates into the car," he told her. "Please."

"Uh, not necessary. Just ahead, at the end of the block!"

There were a few diners in the sandwich shop, but not many. They were able to order quickly, and their food came fast. Besides sandwiches, it offered several platters as well; they both opted for seafood, with salads, rice, and corn on the cob.

Zach was hungry, but it was fun to see that Skye might have been even hungrier. Of course, she might tend to be more of a "grazer," and they hadn't had much of a chance to graze that day.

They didn't talk much; they were too busy eating.

Then they finished up, leaving the restaurant with two large cups of iced tea. And in another few minutes, they were at their quarters.

Skye looked at him as she tossed her bag on the sofa.

"Maybe we also need to feed our sanity!" she said softly.

She had a hell of an effect on him. He smiled.

"Who would I be to refuse to fuel our sanity?" he asked. "But . . ."

Long day. Playing in forests again, being at the hospital . . .

"My shower or yours?" she asked.

And it was good, because she made him laugh while sending little lightning bolts to sweep through him.

Later, holding her, he smiled to himself.

The days were brutal and long.

But the nights were amazing—a time when they could find a sweet sanity; and in the ugly world they were struggling against, moments of sheer beauty.

CHAPTER 17

Skye was half awake when the alarm rang.

She didn't want to rise. Of course, that was the problem with such an involvement. She liked being just where she was, feeling the warmth of his flesh beneath her cheek and knowing the beat of his heart and the soft movement of his breath.

She leapt out of bed.

They'd chosen his shower the night before, and so she hurried into her own room and showered and dressed quickly—that was one thing about her chosen line of work. She could truly shower and dress for the day within a matter of minutes. But a morning shower was always a necessity to her.

And then breakfast, because it seemed to be the only meal of the day they could count on to have anything that resembled a normal time.

She was surprised to discover Zach had moved faster than she had. He grinned at her from where he was standing by the stove.

"My turn," he told her. "Veggie omelets, maybe not as good, but . . ."

"I'm sure they're lovely."

"And there was raisin bread in the bread box, so it's in the toaster ready to be popped. I hope you like raisin bread?" he asked.

"Raisin bread is just great, and thank you. I'm sure you're an excellent cook—"

"Not excellent, but passable," he assured her.

"But it's morning, and . . . oh!" She felt her phone buzz. It wasn't even six-thirty yet, but she saw she was receiving a message from Angela: **So far, looking and looking, no bioweapons are being moved through the area. Nothing. Call me with any ideas.**

"They have something?" Zach asked her.

She shook her head, frowning. "I wonder . . ."

"What?"

"Well, we're moving in a brave new age of technology," she said. "I'm calling her; I'll put the speaker on."

Angela answered immediately. "I know you're busy," Skye said quickly, "but I did have an idea. And I'm sorry. Just how early do you start working?"

Angela laughed softly. "We have kids. Up with the sun or before it, depending on the season. I need to head out, but I kept thinking we weren't looking at everything someone could look at, but . . ."

"Things that connect to things!" Skye said.

"Like?"

"Maybe . . . tech of some kind? I don't know. Are there AI enhancements of a control somewhere that has to do with weapons, power, controlling the government, hacking into specialized systems?" Skye suggested.

"I'll do some digging myself," Angela promised. "And you—"

"Ah, we're going to start by doing some looking around in the forest," Skye said simply.

"Keep in touch."

"You know it."

She ended the call and looked at Zach. "So I want to head—"

"To the forest across the street from the café," he finished for her. "We can eat and head right out. We talked to Connie last night; and if the cook and the waitress are able to talk, we're just going to learn they were attacked by a witch. Eggs are ready—hey, you were supposed to push the button on the toast!"

She laughed. "Whoops, sorry. Doing it now."

She pushed the button and poured coffee as she waited. In minutes, they were set up to eat and were seated in front of one another.

"Two meals in ten hours, and we had sleep in there, and energetic physical activity, too," Zach said, grinning at her. Only his smile faded quickly. "This whole thing is so crazy that it should never have gone forward a single step. But now . . . there is something coming, and we both know it. And we know that if we don't find those people—"

"The star in the woods, the place where a copse of trees forms a star around a central clearing. We can find it, Zach. I know we can. And if the master witch was waiting there—"

"He was probably dressed as a witch."

"But he might have gotten frustrated waiting. This guy really wanted to get his hands on Connie. You don't fake that kind of terror. He wants her dead," Skye said.

"And Vince Cason remains missing."

Skye's phone buzzed and she looked at it.

"Angela!" she said, answering the call right away. "We're both here; you're on speaker!"

"Great," Angela said over the airwaves. "We found out about a small company there, Ballantine and Almeria. It was founded by two friends who graduated from the Massachusetts Institute of Technology a decade ago. Smart as whips—and they're working on special key cards that someone must possess, along with eye readings, facial recognition, a fingerprint . . . I'm not sure what else. But they're due a visit from the CEO and another think tank genius at the end of the week—from the bit I've managed to get off protected sites, Ballantine and Almeria will be giving a display of the tech, among other things. So your suggestion got me to thinking that it may be nothing, but what they're planning is something to present to the military. It could be something that could be used for great damage in the hands of the wrong people—for instance, it might be the way to open up and engage a weapon. I'm trying to figure out how someone could breach a meeting like that; but seriously, other than that, I haven't been able to find a big shipment of cash!"

"Thanks! But this will happen at the end of the week? That gives us a few days," Skye said. "It gives us something. And"—she paused, glancing at Zach—"we have a few ideas of where we're going and what we're looking for today."

"Thank you," Angela said. "We'll get back up with you as soon as possible."

"That's great," Zach said.

"Agreed," Skye added.

Angela laughed softly. "Sounds like you two have moved well without us. If we get anything else, we'll be back in touch with you immediately. I'm out in the field today, but Michelle knows everything to follow up. Naturally, keep the reports coming."

"Will do," Skye said, ending the call. She looked at Zach.

"Could this person be after tech? Am I crazy?" she asked.

"No. Drones and other weapons, even nuclear weapons, are controlled by tech. If these guys have some brilliant kind of key . . ."

"Then that may just be what we are looking for. After we find out what we can in the forest—"

"What you can find in the forest," he reminded her with a touch of amusement. "This one is you."

"Okay, well, when we find out what we can, let's head to the building where the company is, get a good look at it, and try and see if we can figure out how you would use a drugged-out group of kids and kidnappees to get what you wanted—and get away," Skye said. She hesitated. "I don't think we need to head into the station. Okay, let's face it, even Detective Berkley thinks Gavin might be involved. And Detective Cason may be dead!"

"I can't explain it, but . . ."

"I know. I don't want to believe it, either," Skye assured him. "But we must be open to anything."

He nodded. "Ready?"

"I'll wash; you toss?" she suggested.

He smiled and nodded. They quickly cleaned up and headed out.

"Hey, we moved this morning. It's only about seven-thirty. We managed to get right in all the morning traffic. Thankfully, nothing is all that far."

He was right. There was traffic, but they weren't in the center of town, and it didn't take him that long to reach the embankment across from the café.

"Did you want to pick up a couple of cups of coffee?" he asked her.

"From the café? No, I do not think so!" Skye countered. "Let's head to the area where I found David Harrison as a witch trying to drag Connie to his master."

"I know the way," he told her.

"Follow the broken branches," she said.

But she let Zach lead. They made their way through the thick growth of trees and brush, and Zach easily proved that he did know the way.

In a matter of minutes, they reached the same place they had been, the little clearing where Skye had finally come upon the pair.

"From here, he intended to take her to the star shape of trees around a clearing," she murmured.

"This way," Zach replied. "No, wait. There's almost a trail

there; it moves a little closer to the road and runs almost parallel with it, maybe . . ."

He started walking. She followed.

They were closer to the road. She could hear the running sound of a car distant and faint going by every few minutes, but close enough that she knew the road wasn't all that far.

She almost jumped when Zach's phone rang, loud and clear.

"There has to be a tower somewhere near us," Zach said, veering as the narrow trail made a turn into the deeper woods.

"Yes, thanks, we're near—we'll be right there!" Zach said.

But as he spoke, Skye saw it ahead—the clearing. And the position of the trees did make it appear as if they were in a star shape beautifully created by nature.

"Zack, what? This is it!"

"That was Ben, Officer Benjamin Chambers. He's at a small house about a mile from here. The owner called the cops because a kid wandered in, scared and terrified and wanting his mother; and he's saying the man they called the master hit his mommy. The kid doesn't know where his mommy is, but if I can get to him—"

"Go, but, Zach, let me stay here, right here. This is it! Go and talk to the kid, sit him on your lap or touch his shirt, and . . . maybe that will give us something."

"No, do your thing—"

"I can't under pressure! God. Our phones work here. Zach, we know our time is limited!"

He looked downward for just a second. "All right, all right, I'm going. But you are armed—"

"And I know how to use my Glock."

"And you've got me on speed dial—"

"I do. Go!"

He nodded and started back along the trail, moving quickly.

When he was gone, Skye stood still, feeling the sunrays that filtered through. She was listening for the sounds of nature:

chirping insects and birds, flying from branches to branches, letting out their calls. The breeze touched her face as it touched the leaves . . .

She closed her eyes, and looked again.

Dusk had fallen. And the witch was there with his arms crossed over his shoulders as he impatiently paced the clearing area from one point in the general shape of the star to the other. Cursing softly.

Growing impatient. Pacing, pacing, pausing, shaking his head.

He pulled off the hat. His nose fell off. And he stood in the center of the clearing, and even as dusk fell more fully, the rise of the moon in the heavens cast down a glow upon the earth in the clearing.

And Skye saw exactly why Detective Vince Cason had been among the missing.

Vince was standing there, irate and impatient, holding the hat, the wild mop of orange hair, and the prosthetic nose he'd dislodged when he'd wrenched at the hat.

Vince, not Gavin.

Their instincts had been right, thank God. Because she knew she and Zach wanted to be good at law enforcement, at catching the bad guys; they did not want to be just strangely talented magicians. Their abilities needed to enhance their work, not be the sole basis for it.

She pulled out her phone, hitting Zach's number on her speed dial.

She had lost service out here, and she swore softly. She smiled to herself as a common sentiment pertinent to the twenty-first century popped into her mind.

Technology! Incredible . . . when it worked!

She started moving again, thinking she needed to get back closer to the road where their phones had worked just fine earlier.

As she headed out of the deep woods, she suddenly heard a muffled sobbing, then a soft voice, as if one person was trying to reassure another.

She drew her weapon, listening, trying to find her way through the twists and turns in the almost-trails that wound around closer to the road.

She stopped and stared in disbelief and confusion.

Gavin's cousin, Officer Ben Chambers, was seated on the forest floor, bound to the base of a huge old oak.

He wasn't alone. Next to him, tightly tied as well, was a boy, a young boy, with tears streaming down his face. And the voice she heard was Ben's as he tried to tell the little boy that some-one would come, and they'd be all right.

"Ben!" Skye slammed her gun into her holster and reached to her ankle for her knife, anxious to release the two.

"See, Jeremy! See! Special Agent McMahon has come to help us. I knew that they would find the truth."

As she raced to the pair, confusion swept her mind. How had Ben called Zach from a house down the road if he was here, tied to a tree? Had he been here all the while, and . . .

She paused, ready to pull her weapon again. There was only one answer.

One answer with two twists!

Vince Cason had forced Ben to make a call, threatening to kill the boy if he didn't do so.

Or worse . . .

Ben was involved in murder, kidnapping, and perhaps at-tempted terrorism.

The boy—she was going to untie the boy.

Running to the tree and falling to her knees, she slipped her knife from the little sheath strapped around her ankle and went to work quickly on the heavy ropes that bound him.

Next to Jeremy, Ben seemed to release something like a sob.

"Thank God, thank God, thank God! My cousin told me that you and Zach were amazing, that . . ."

He broke off, staring past her.

She had managed to slit the last strands of the heavy rope holding Jeremy. She looked at the child, aware that they were in trouble. She didn't need to turn around to see that Vince Cason had been waiting in the woods, just waiting . . .

She looked Jeremy in the eyes. The little boy stared back at her. He was just five years old! Would he understand? Could he understand?

"Run! Run and hide! Near the road, a police car will come eventually!" As she whispered, she slipped her knife back into the little sheath. It would have been clearly evident if she'd gone for her gun at the holster around her waist.

She didn't try to draw her gun; she couldn't risk the child's life.

And thankfully, the terrified little boy was a smart one. He seemed to understand the situation and what she wanted him to do.

Either that, or anywhere was better than being where he was.

She used her body to shield the child as he made a swift disappearance into the trees and brush behind them.

Then she turned and faced Cason. And, of course, he was back in costume, a wig with long, yarnlike red hair on his head, along with the pointed hat, skin painted green, prosthetic nose, and encompassing black cape.

"Well, well, the devil really is in the woods," she said.

"The devil you know!" he told her. "But then you don't, do you?"

She smiled sweetly. "Oh, please! Seriously? Detective Vince Cason. Of course, I know." She shrugged. "So does everyone!"

"You're so wrong! They are scared to death for me!" Cason told her. "And when it's all over, they'll find me, injured, desperate, on the side of the road. They'll never know who is pulling the strings that control just about everything!"

She was still next to Ben. If only she could be sure of the truth about the man!

"Oh, Vince!" she said. "You did tell us to call you by your given name," she reminded him pleasantly. "It's just not going to be that easy—"

"It is that easy. All you need to do is steal someone's eyeball and their finger, but you guys don't understand tech that far, so—"

"Facial recognition. You need a face for that," Skye reminded him.

He laughed. "And you think I can't take a face? Have you forgotten, my lovely Fed, that I'm a master of disguise?"

"And I think you've forgotten the power of those who may have needed a little time, but eventually always stop the devil in the woods!" she declared.

The man grimaced at her. "Ah, but you don't understand! I have a number of people completely convinced that *you* and *your kind* are the devils in the woods. And I'm great at segueing when necessary. I didn't think it a good idea to get the both of you at once, but you're a nice start. Of course, Mr. Oh-So-Special-Agent Zach Erickson will come flying to the rescue! And then, I will have you both!" he announced. "For now, toss your Glock over here. Right now!"

"Why would I do that?" Skye asked him.

"Because I'll shoot Ben right in the heart if you don't."

She looked at Ben, and she prayed that her instincts were right . . .

And that her Oh-So-Special-Agent partner would know how to play it when he did rush to the scene.

Zach walked slowly and carefully through the woods.

He'd made some major-league mistakes so far that morning, and he knew he couldn't afford another one.

Maybe not mistakes that were . . . that were . . . Well, his only real mistake was worrying about a child, about believing Ben Chambers when he called so frantically. At the house down the road, there had been no answer.

Protocol or not—he could have always thought of a viable excuse—he had broken down the door.

That had turned out to be a good decision. He found the homeowner bound and gagged in his closet.

Of course, the man had given him a panicked story about a wicked witch who had come at him with a gun and forced him there. And no, it hadn't been that recently; it had been a few hours before Zach had found him.

It had been a mistake to leave Skye. A mistake to assume that anyone associated with Gavin had to be a good person. It had even been a mistake, perhaps, to completely disavow the possibility that Gavin was involved.

With that thought, Zach had called Jackson with his latest discovery. He'd quickly explained he thought the best way to move forward was carefully. He wanted agents from the closest local office to come and see to Mr. Benchley, the homeowner, and he wanted agents out on the road across from the café. He didn't want anyone bursting wildly into the forest, or any local involvement; he needed to find the witch in the woods himself.

And it was morning.

This kind of canopy of trees always afforded a certain darkness. Deep in the trees, it was easy to feel as if the world only existed here in a surreal atmosphere of deep green. The smell of the earth was so redolent, the rustle of leaves could whisper of danger at every turn.

Thankfully, he'd always liked the woods.

There was only one thing that he didn't know now.

But, of course, it was an all-important *thing*.

Was Ben Chambers in on what was going on? Or had he been forced to make the call to Zach? The shrewd witch had known from the beginning that most people would be instantly concerned about the welfare of a child. That a person, especially one in law enforcement, would respond when the welfare of a child was at stake.

Especially when the child might hold the answers they needed.

Zach stood still for a minute, feeling the air and listening.

He came first to the place where he had left Skye. He knew she wouldn't be there, and knew there would have been another lure for her.

But which way, and . . .

He frowned as he stared at the brush. There was something that caught just a bit of a glint of the sun beneath a heavy pile of brush by one of the huge old oaks.

He walked over and picked it up.

Officer Ben Chambers's phone!

He held it. Closed his eyes.

And he knew.

And he could only pray that Skye's instincts would kick in and she would know the truth as well.

"Where the hell is the kid?" Vince demanded, frowning as he realized that little Jeremy was gone.

"Well, I guess I got most of the rope sawed through before you stopped me," Skye said. She had thrown her Glock to him as he'd ordered. She could still be wrong, of course, but she had seen the fear in Ben's eyes when the witch had aimed his weapon at him—automatic fire at that distance and the tree might die as well.

Fear? Or all part of an act?

She needed to see! But under her circumstances . . .

"All right," Vince said, holding his AK-47 on them both, "there's more rope to the right side of the tree there. Tie yourself up—not to the tree. I know your kind! You'd get behind it and try to disappear. I'd just as soon *not* shoot the two of you—not yet!"

"What do you want me to do?" Skye demanded.

"Tie yourself to Ben. And do it right and do it tightly. I'm watching!"

"You go ahead and watch. I will do it tightly. And I will do it right. But you really need to listen to me. I may not be the most brilliant tech person on earth, but I work with a few people who are just about geniuses when it comes to the world of computers and artificial intelligence, keys, controls, and so on and so on. They know what you're planning. And you'll never get away with it."

"I will—unless they want to kill about twenty women and kids, along with a couple of pathetic drug addicts who believe this whole thing, that we are saved only by getting rid of the people—such as yourself—who are truly the ones in league with the devil! You and your boy toy, all this time—so cool, so professional, and so special! Well, sorry, but . . ."

"I'm tying myself, I'm tying myself! I was just trying to warn you!" Skye said quickly. She worked as he had ordered her.

With just a bit of an exception. Down on the ground the way that she was, she could do some twisting and turning and . . .

She closed her eyes for a minute. And she held on to Ben Chambers's shoulder.

"Come on! Finish up!" Vince ordered.

"I am! I am!" Skye cried.

She prayed that her plan would work. And when she finished, she was seated on the forest floor, tied to Ben Chambers, with their backs to the giant oak.

Vince walked a few steps closer to them and smiled.

"Well, well, well." Vince laughed. "So, so sad! You see, poor Officer Chambers was such a caring guy, so happy when he thought he'd found me—the missing detective who was wounded in the woods! Then, of course, he learned the truth. Good guy, of course. He would do anything when I promised to put a bullet between Jeremy's eyes if he didn't!"

"You really think you're incredibly clever," Skye said. "What if Zach realizes that Ben didn't call him from whatever house you invaded? What if he has an army coming out here for you?"

Vince laughed. "No problem. I shoot the two of you, and the good old wicked witch disappears. You see, witches know how to do that out here! Time to watch Mr. Superhero come for you!" he proclaimed.

Then a voice broke out of the woods.

"Mr. Superhero, eh? I'm deeply complimented, thank you," Zach announced. "Drop it, Cason! I'm a damned good shot. I could try to disarm you, or . . . well, your head is in perfect range for me!"

Vince turned, instantly spraying the woods with gunfire, seeking to take out the man who had spoken.

But to Skye's incredible relief, she had been right in her faith in the man at her side.

She had slipped her knife into Officer Ben Chambers's hands as she had tied herself. He was free, and he had freed her, and together they fell flat to the ground as bullets spewed into the forest and . . .

And Zach proved his words.

A single shot took Vince Cason directly in his right shoulder. He screamed in agony, fell to the ground, and his weapon went dead silent as it flew into the brush near his side.

"Oh, thank God, thank God!" Ben breathed to Skye. "Thank you! Thank you for believing in me!"

They helped one another to their feet as Zach appeared, stepping out from behind the trees and walking over to the man on the ground.

Vince was howling worse than any five-year-old. But Skye could see why he was doing so. His shoulder and arm were destroyed, bloodied with bits of bone sticking out here and there.

"He'll live," Zach said, looking at Skye and Ben. "I'm sorry if my method was unnerving for the two of you; but I knew if I challenged him, he'd try to take me out first. And I did avoid his head; we need him to tell us where he's keeping the kids, the people."

"Help!" Vince screamed from the ground. "I need medical attention! Now!"

Zach hunkered down by him. "You do. You definitely do. If you don't get help soon, you'll lose that arm and shoulder. Or worse"—he shrugged—"you could bleed to death."

"You're a Fed! I'll see your ass fired if you don't act like a professional—"

"A Fed and a nice guy, usually," Zach said. "But where are the kids? Sorry, I'd rather see you die than them."

"Call someone!" Vince thundered. "It will take time!"

"So you need to be quick. Hm. For me, living in prison for life without an arm and a shoulder? I might choose death," Zach said thoughtfully.

"They're in the tunnels beneath the abandoned store off the main road, right off there, not even a mile from the café. Now—"

He didn't need to finish. Zach already had his phone out; his call went through immediately. They were in the woods, but apparently close enough to the road.

And Skye quickly realized he'd had people at the ready.

He hunkered by Vince, staring at him, shaking his head. "Help will be here in seconds. So we have seconds, just seconds. And you've got us. Want to give this all a big flourish? Then talk! Tell us! Why? Figured you, but . . . the why. That's what I can't figure out in my head, with any kind of reason!"

Vince laughed, then choked in agony at the pain his laughter had caused him. "*Why?* The better question, *why not?* And it's entertaining. The human mind is as messed up as it's ever been. Blame others, find evil when the world isn't going your way, and then it's just . . . Ah, man! The power. The power of manipulating your fellow humans and knowing that, through your own control, you yourself will be where and how you want to be, as long as you shall live!"

"Got it," Zach said dryly. "Simple greed and selfishness. No great ideal, no attempt to fix the world around you—"

"No one can fix any part of the world!" Vince snapped.

Zach stepped away.

They heard a massive rustling; then agents and EMTs came running into the clearing within minutes.

Zach looked at Skye and Ben.

"Well, it's down to the paperwork for us. And . . . sorry! A moment's license here if I may . . ."

He gave Ben a quick hug.

Then he pulled Skye into his arms, and for a long moment, he held her tightly.

EPILOGUE

Skye clapped enthusiastically at the performance.

It might have seemed a bit bizarre to someone else, but—once the children and the missing adults had been found; the innocents returned to their families; the addicts and mentally challenged were referred to the proper treatment centers, before a few who had fallen completely under Vince Cason's control might face charges—Skye and Zach had wanted to enjoy Salem.

And so they had come to Derby Street to watch an excellent performance of *Cry Innocent*. That afternoon, they'd spent time at the Peabody Essex Museum, the Witch Museum, and the New England Pirate Museum.

The day before, they'd headed to the House of the Seven Gables, the Salem Maritime National Historic Site, the Rebecca Nurse Homestead, and a slew of shops and places they loved, on and near Essex Street: Crow Haven Corner, Count Orlok's Nightmare Gallery, and more.

They'd found the *Bewitched* statue of Elizabeth Montgomery and stood out on Revere Beach.

Leaving the performance, Zach grinned at Skye.

"You do know, some people might have opted for a few days in the Bahamas or some such break. Maybe Bermuda."

She laughed softly. They were holding hands, swinging their arms as they walked down the street.

"Yeah. That would have been nice, too. But I have always loved this city—"

"Me too. And we got to see all the things we love so much. Maybe next time, the Bahamas!" Zach said.

She smiled. She was certain they would both like a "next time."

But at that moment . . .

"Back to our quarters," Zach said.

And she smiled. "Oh, yes, back to our quarters," she agreed.

Because this was their night.

"Tomorrow we're due at a different kind of 'quarters,'" Zach said.

And they were. They were due at Krewe headquarters in the DC area—the plane was being sent for them at noon.

And the night . . .

The nights were beautiful.

They'd spent time doing things . . .

And time just being together.

And back in their rooms, they spent the time that they had. They learned to talk, really talk, lying together, sharing all the good things, the bad things, and the strange things from their pasts.

Skye had never been so happy. Sex was amazing, but just lying next to him, feeling his heat, his touch upon her . . .

She had never imagined she might have such a complete relationship, loving everything about someone, being able to talk with absolute honesty to that someone, and to share thoughts so completely.

Yes . . . The night was truly a magnificent kind of . . . magic!

In the morning, they weren't awakened by an alarm. Rather a phone call.

Zach answered the ring, and after a greeting, he listened, and slowly arched his brow in surprise.

"Sure. Great. No problem!" he said, hanging up.

He looked at Skye, bemused.

"Well?"

"Looks like Lieutenant Gavin Bruns is going to be coming with us. He isn't going to be Lieutenant Bruns anymore. He's going to enter the academy."

"Ah! A candidate for . . ."

"For whatever we are," Zach said. "I heard a rumor that they're starting to call us The Crows, because it was Jackson Crow who brought us all together. And it's good, because . . ."

"Because there will always be another devil in the woods?" she asked softly.

He nodded, then drew her into his arms.

More deadly situations would arise, and they would work them. They would always do anything they could to save innocent lives from the "witches" and the "devils" who lurked in human form around the world.

But for now . . .

They had a few hours before the plane was due to leave.

And the *beautiful* hours could be precious indeed.